WICKED

by Jana DeLeon

CHAPTER ONE

Sunday, October 18, 2015

Amber Olivier awakened in a cold sweat, the bitter taste of blood in her mouth and her head throbbing. The nightmare that had launched her into consciousness turned quickly to fear when she opened her eyes to pitch black. She reached to the right to turn on the lamp on her nightstand, but her hand bumped into something solid just inches from her body. She pushed herself up, but her head struck something above her and she winced and dropped back to a lying position.

She reached to her left and above her, but everywhere, her hands touched a solid structure covered with satin. Her heart pounded so hard that it echoed in her head, almost drowning out the sounds of her rapid breathing. She kicked her feet up and out, but they met with the same resistance as her hands.

Where was she? How did she get here?

Forcing the panic back a tiny bit, she focused her frantic mind to recall the last thing it had recorded, but everything was a blur. She remembered putting on her favorite blue blouse…the party! She was going to a party at the university. Bits of the event rolled through her mind. A big green vase. Crab dip. Dancing with someone. She couldn't see his face.

The punch!

She'd asked for the one with no alcohol but the last thing she remembered was downing the rest of her plastic cup and throwing it in the trash can near the hedges.

Were her sorority sisters playing a joke on her? Had they locked her in a closet? No, that couldn't be. She was lying down. So something else. Were they standing around, waiting to see how long she'd last before yelling? Well, they were going to be really happy because she had no intention of staying quietly in whatever structure this was.

She banged on the top of the enclosure she was in, but the cushioned fabric only created a dull thud. Striking the sides of the structure with her hands and the bottom with her feet didn't increase the noise level. So she screamed. Screamed so loudly that her throat burned and she started to gag. Screamed until she didn't have a breath of air left in her.

When she stopped, she drew in a breath so quickly that it made her chest hurt. And she listened. She listened for any sign that her sorority sisters were standing outside this box, waiting to let her out and laugh at her, even though she didn't want to believe they could be that mean.

And that's when it hit her…the rectangular box, the satin padded sides.

It was a coffin.

She started screaming again.

JANA DELEON

CHAPTER TWO

Tuesday, October 27, 2015
Garden District, New Orleans, Louisiana

Shaye Archer tossed her backpack on the bed and looked around the room that she'd spent the second half of her life in. The better half. Her adoptive mother, Corrine, hadn't relocated so much as a comb since Shaye had moved out of the Garden District estate and into her own apartment in the French Quarter, still holding out hope that Shaye would change her mind and move back home.

Corrine had gotten her wish, but the price had been far too high.

It had been two months since they'd fled the country, trying to get away from the media that hounded them, hoping they could find a time and a place to heal.

Hoping healing was even possible.

Shaye's third case as a private investigator had been her biggest, the most explosive, and the most devastating. The memories that she'd kept locked inside her mind for almost ten years had flooded back in like a tidal wave. Every moment of abuse, every tear shed, every cry for help…all of them rushing through her mind as if on instant replay.

It was so bad it physically crippled her, but that wasn't the worst of it.

Her grandfather's suicide was the worst part.

Pierce Archer had been a victim in a blackmail scheme that had traced back to his plantation-owning ancestors. He'd recognized the pentagram brand on Shaye's back as belonging to his blackmailer, but since he had no way to identify the man, he'd chosen to go the silent route, hiding his family's shameful past. In the end, he saw a future of ridicule for Corrine and Shaye and opted out of life in order to give them a clean slate.

But that slate wasn't so clean.

Corrine had inherited her father's empire and had to make decisions about corporate business that she had no interest in and never had. She'd claimed she would sell it all, but even liquidating was a long road with a lot of work along the way. And all of it would be conducted under the watchful eye of the media, who were frantic to best one another and get an inside scoop on the shame that had befallen the Archer family.

Corrine's best friend, Eleonore, had informed them that camera crews had camped outside Corrine's house for over a month, waiting for them to return, so Corrine had delayed their return to New Orleans, determined to wait until the media had given up. But that didn't mean they'd completely gone away. All it meant was that when they returned, they could drive through the front gate without having microphones and cameras shoved in their faces. At least once.

Shaye wasn't looking forward to the media storm that would follow their return. Given her sensational past, she was already used to being under scrutiny by most everyone whose path she crossed, but things were much bigger now. Reporters would hound her, trying to get her story. All Shaye wanted was to return to her work, but that would be difficult if she was being followed. She'd considered doing an interview just to get it over with, but she knew it wouldn't work. One interview would lead to a request for another and another until her life was nothing more than one of those reality shows she saw on television. She had no idea how long it would take for people to stop caring.

The other alternative was to move. Shaye's trust fund was already more money than she'd ever need in a lifetime. Money was not and never would be a concern, and that was a huge blessing, but where would she go? Shaye had been to a lot of different places, but none like New Orleans. She loved the culture, the architecture, the people, and the food. More importantly, it felt like where she belonged.

"At least it's quiet." Corrine's voice sounded from her bedroom door.

Shaye turned around. "You *did* have us land at two a.m."

"Well, it worked."

Corrine hadn't wanted the first thing they encountered to be a three-ring circus, so she'd forgone use of her father's Learjet, now hers, and instead chartered a private jet to fly them back to the US. In a second bid for momentary privacy, she'd chosen to land in the middle of the night, the hope being that they could at least get inside Corrine's house without disruption.

Shaye knew all of this dancing around was simply stalling the inevitable, but if her mother wanted to have a few hours of peace in her own home before facing the never-ending questions and whispering that were coming, Shaye wasn't about to complain.

"Eleonore is on her way over," Corrine said.

"Now?"

"I don't think she believes we're really here."

Eleonore Blanchet was Corrine's oldest and dearest friend and a renowned psychiatrist. She'd played a huge part in Shaye's therapy and had helped her adjust to and accept a normal life, or as normal as one's life could be given Shaye's previously unknown past. Shaye had no doubt that Eleonore would be first in line to volunteer to help her deal with her returning memory.

If Shaye was being honest, she was looking forward to talking to Eleonore. Shaye loved her mother like no one else, but because of that, she would never tell her everything she'd remembered about her past. The kindhearted Corrine was also tough, but Shaye didn't think she was strong enough to handle more than she already had on her plate. It spoke loads that Corrine hadn't pressed Shaye to talk about her memory returning. For the first time since she'd known her, Shaye had seen Corrine at her limit.

"I guess I better put off undressing and climbing into

bed," Shaye said, even though that's exactly what she'd been planning to do. She'd even forgone a shower in her mind, deciding to let everything slide until she got some decent sleep. No matter how hard she tried, she'd never been able to sleep on a plane, even a luxurious, quiet private jet.

"At this point," Corrine said, "I don't think Eleonore would care if we were both naked, but I'd rather we all hug clothed. I'm going downstairs to fix some decaffeinated coffee."

Shaye nodded and Corrine left the room. She lifted the blinds on her window and peered out into the beautifully landscaped backyard. Every hedge was perfect. The patio furniture was all aligned with not a single leaf or stitch of grass upon it. It was as if they'd never left. All the people paid to keep up the property had done their jobs whether Corrine had been here to oversee them or not.

Life had gone on.

And that was the crux of it. Life would be different now—that went without saying—but it could still be great. There would always be that dark place in her mind where she carried the memories of her so-called childhood, and the grief and sadness she felt over the loss of her grandfather, but she still had her mother, Eleonore, and her work.

And maybe someone else.

She went into the bathroom and washed her face with cold water, trying not to notice the dark circles under her eyes. She was too young to look so old, but then, if experience counted, she was far older than her twenty-four years. Short of putting on makeup, which she rarely did, nothing could be done about it tonight, but eventually, she'd get back into a routine. She'd sleep normally and without the nightmares that plagued her. She'd smile again and mean it, and her skin would return to that of a twentysomething.

Eventually.

She blew out a breath and headed downstairs.

Eleonore was in the kitchen with Corrine when she walked in. Shaye paused for a moment, somewhat shocked at the older woman's appearance. Her slacks and shirt, usually neatly pressed, looked as if she'd spent the last day sleeping in them. Her hair, which was always cut in a neat bob that came to her neck, was pulled back into a ponytail, escaped pieces of silver sticking out in different directions. Her face looked haggard, the lines deeper, the circles under her eyes more pronounced.

Shaye glanced at Corrine and could tell her mother was concerned about Eleonore's appearance as well, but now wasn't the time to ask. Shaye moved across the floor and hugged her friend and therapist. Eleonore clutched her hard and kissed her cheek.

"I can't tell you how happy I am to see you," Eleonore said and released her. "Both of you. It seems like forever."

"How are things here?" Corrine asked and placed a cup of coffee for each of them on the kitchen counter.

They all slid onto barstools and Eleonore poured a packet of sweetener in her coffee.

"Things are...odd," Eleonore said. "That's really the only way I can describe them. Not a day goes by that Pierce's name isn't mentioned on the news. Who will fill his state senate position—which, of course, allows the segue into everything else. I'm afraid it's all still very much the story."

Corrine sighed. "We didn't expect anything else. I kept hoping a bigger scandal would break loose, but I suppose that was too much to ask."

"I don't think it would have mattered," Eleonore said. "The Archer family is practically New Orleans royalty. I'm not certain what kind of scandal would deflect attention from you."

"Nothing," Shaye said. "It's too sensational and there's all that 'human element' with my backstory. It is what it is. They'll go away when they realize they're not going to get anything from us."

Eleonore nodded. "The silent road is definitely the route I recommend taking. Let everyone think whatever they want. They will whether you talk or not."

Shaye clutched her coffee mug, trying to figure out a way to bring up the next topic without sounding desperate or anxious. Finally, she just blurted out the question she'd wanted to ask ever since she set eyes on Eleonore.

"Have you talked to Jackson?" Shaye asked.

Eleonore's expression softened, and she smiled. "Often. We have a standing drink date every other Wednesday evening."

Corrine's eyes widened and Shaye could feel her

mother's anxiety all the way across the counter.

"Not that kind of drink," Eleonore said, cluing in to their worry. "We have fancy coffees at a café in the French Quarter. They give us the same table in a back corner where the press can't hear us when we talk. It drives them crazy." She looked at Shaye. "He always asks about you. It's the first thing out of his mouth every time I see him. He's a good man. I thought so before but I'm certain of it now."

The worry that had been niggling in the back of Shaye's mind for two months started to melt away. She'd worried that Jackson would wash his hands of her. Helping her look into her past had put him in a bad position with the New Orleans Police Department and his partner, Senior Detective Grayson. Even worse, the events uncovered that Chief of Police Bernard had been blackmailed by Shaye's captor and had also hidden things about her past. Unable to live with what he'd done and the fallout that was coming, Bernard had taken the same way out as Shaye's grandfather.

"How is he doing...with the department?" Shaye asked. "Is he having trouble?"

"There's a lot of tension," Eleonore said. "The city got a retired police chief from Baton Rouge to fill in until they can figure out who to replace Bernard with. Jackson says there are several qualified for the position, but they've all been there for decades..."

"And they're being investigated along with everyone else who worked for Bernard for any length of time," Shaye finished. "And I guess Jackson is caught up in that mess."

Eleonore nodded. "They grill him on a regular basis,

but we all know Jackson has already given them everything he had, which wasn't much in the big scheme of things. It's my opinion that Jonal's journals contained the most information we're ever going to see. Everything else is a witch hunt."

Jonal Deremeau was the man who'd started the blackmail of Pierce's grandfather years ago. He was also the man who'd figured out who held Shaye captive and had freed her, trying to make up for the sordid things he'd done in the past, including his guilt over the monster that held Shaye. He'd died shortly after rescuing Shaye, and no one had ever known about his involvement until Shaye had followed the old trail of clues and had been given Jonal's journals by his longtime housekeeper. Those journals had unraveled decades of deceit and lies.

"The police department won't let it go, regardless of whether or not there's more to glean from continuing the investigation," Corrine said. "They feel they have a damaged reputation to repair. Chief Bernard saved them the embarrassment of having to bring one of their own to trial, but he left the rest of his men with a cloud of uncertainty hanging over them."

"In so many ways, it's a no-win situation," Eleonore said. "Jackson says opinion seems to be split down the middle. Half place some blame on him for what happened and the other half are smart enough to know the truth, but they all wish he hadn't been in the thick of it."

Guilt washed over Shaye like a slow drizzle. Everything Jackson was dealing with was her fault. One hundred percent. If she'd never asked for his help, then he wouldn't be facing any of this. Of course, if she hadn't asked for his help, she might not even be here to feel guilty, but that was a thought to ponder on another day. Right now, the only thing that mattered was seeing if she could help alleviate any of the burden she'd brought on the only man she'd ever cared a lot about besides her grandfather.

"I didn't tell him you were coming back," Eleonore said. "I knew you'd want to do that yourself and on your own time. But I wouldn't delay very long or he'll find out another way."

Shaye nodded. The last thing she wanted was for Jackson to hear about her homecoming on the news, and it wasn't the sort of thing she felt she should do by phone, either. First thing tomorrow morning, before the sun was even up, she'd go to his apartment and see him in person. It was the very least she owed him after everything he'd done. And if she was being honest with herself, she wanted to see him.

She just hoped Eleonore was right and Jackson wanted to see her.

CHAPTER THREE

Tuesday, October 27, 2015

Tara Chatry stormed out of the New Orleans Police Department, angry at the so-called detective she'd spoken to but even more angry at herself. It wasn't even nine o'clock in the morning, and she'd already put herself into the red. It had to be some kind of record. Normally it took months of condescension before she lost it, but Detective Vincent had managed to send her straight into the stratosphere in a matter of minutes.

You should have known better.

She blew out a breath and headed into a café across the street from the police department. She was already late for class and she'd get ten points off her next exam because of it. You either produced an emergency room bill or a death certificate, or Dr. Gilbert didn't give you a pass. As far as he was concerned, the sun rose and set over philosophy and there were few excuses for failing to elevate your mind as scheduled by the university. It was just as well. Two angry old men in one day might have had her reaching for her Mace. Worst case, she'd use it on herself just to get a medical pass for a day off.

She tossed her backpack onto a table in the back corner and plopped into a seat. The smell of beignets made her stomach rumble. *Fuck it*, she thought. To hell with the diet and Dr. Gilbert and his boring class and elitist thinking. She was going to sit here, drink coffee until she was about to drown in it, and eat all of her weekly caloric allowance in beignets.

"Can I help you, hon?" the waitress asked.

"God, I hope so. I need a pot of coffee and a huge plate of beignets."

The waitress gave her a sympathetic look. "That bad already, huh?" She glanced at the backpack. "You a student?"

Tara nodded. "Lafitte University."

"I take night classes there. Great school but the professors are a mixed bag."

"Definitely. But right now, it's not school causing my aggravation. It's the police."

The waitress raised one eyebrow. "You don't look like the type who'd have problems with the police."

"Oh, I'm not in trouble. I need help but they won't do anything. I told them my friend was missing, but that butthole detective was all 'you college kids like to disappear sometimes and have some fun.' Then he suggested that if I gave my boyfriend more room, he might tell me when he's going off somewhere."

"Wow. What a douche."

"Ethan's not even my boyfriend," Tara continued her

rant. "He's just a friend, but he would never leave school without telling me where he was going. Besides, his car's still in the parking lot. Am I supposed to believe he hiked off to wherever when he has a perfectly good car just sitting there?"

The waitress frowned. "Maybe he partied a little too hard and is sleeping it off somewhere."

"Ethan hasn't taken a drink in his life. His entire existence is a study in boredom. He's an accounting major, for Christ's sake. He has every minute of his life scheduled, even sleeping."

"Doesn't sound like the type to be lost in a French Quarter alley," the waitress agreed. "What did the detective say?"

"To call Ethan's parents and if they want to file a report they can do it. Then he went on to say they probably still wouldn't look for him until he was missing for a couple of days or there were signs of foul play. Apparently, they're too busy over there to look for missing people."

The waitress flipped her pad over and started writing. She ripped off the ticket and handed it to Tara. "I don't know if she's back in New Orleans, but if she is, you should talk to this woman. I bet she can help you."

Tara looked at the ticket. "Shaye Archer? Isn't that the heiress who's been all over the news? Pierce Archer's granddaughter?"

"That's the one. She comes in here sometimes with a detective friend of hers. I haven't seen her since everything blew up about her grandfather and the police chief, but maybe she's just lying low. I heard she specializes in cases that the police won't take."

"I don't know. I don't have much money. Aren't private investigators expensive?"

"What about your friend's parents?"

"Ethan's parents died in a car wreck a little over a year ago. His grandmother is his only living relative that he has contact with and she's in a nursing home. Dementia. Sometimes she recognizes him. Sometimes she doesn't."

"Did you tell the detective that?"

"Yeah, but he'd already made up his mind."

The waitress tapped the paper. "Find Shaye Archer. If anyone can help, she can."

The waitress headed for the kitchen and Tara traced her finger across Shaye's name on the ticket. Tara knew the name. It was impossible to be a resident of New Orleans and not know Shaye Archer's story. But the news had claimed Shaye and her mother fled the country after Pierce Archer's suicide. No one had reported they were back, but Tara supposed it didn't hurt to check. At this point, all she had to lose was time.

She pulled out her laptop and typed in Shaye's name and "private investigator." A ton of news stories pulled up but she finally located Shaye's website after scrolling through at least ten pages of media blasts. She clicked on the contact and started to send an email but then decided she'd rather go in person. It was supposed to be harder to say no to someone's face. Detective Vincent didn't have a problem with it, but surely someone who'd been through the wringer like Shaye Archer wouldn't dismiss her outright.

First, she'd have her pot of coffee and beignets. Then she'd walk to Shaye's office and chat with her. To hell with classes. Her concentration was already crap and it wasn't going to improve. Not until she knew where Ethan was and that he was okay.

She said a quick prayer that Shaye was back in town and could help her.

Shaye pulled into a parking space next to Jackson's truck and killed her engine. She'd intended to be out of the house before the sun came up, but exhaustion had won out and she'd overslept. With the cover of night no longer available, she'd switched to plan B, which included a long, hot shower and breakfast.

When she'd finally worked up the courage, she'd faked a French accent and called the police station to ask for Jackson, hoping he would have time to meet her somewhere to talk. The dispatcher had informed her Jackson wasn't in today. She'd hoped he was taking a much-needed day off by choice instead of being asked to by the interim chief. Corrine was still asleep when she left and since Shaye knew her mother had been up most of the night, she didn't wake her.

Now she sat staring at his apartment building, trying to work up the courage to go knock on the door. What was she going to say? "Hello, I'm back" seemed a little strange and far too casual. Did she hug him? Shake his hand? What was the protocol for addressing the man who she'd sort-of, almost started a relationship with before fleeing the country and going silent for two months?

Finally, she got out of her SUV and walked up the steps to his apartment. Delaying wasn't going to make the situation any more comfortable or give her the magical answers she was looking for that didn't exist. She simply needed to knock on his door and play it by ear. For a woman who preferred a plan and who didn't allow many people into her personal life, it was a big leap of faith.

She lifted her hand to ring the doorbell and paused. Last chance to change her mind. Drawing in a deep breath, she pushed. The faint sound of the doorbell echoed inside the apartment and she listened anxiously for sounds of movement inside. She hadn't seen Jackson's undercover car in the parking lot. What if he was gone in the car? Or jogging? Or sound asleep and didn't hear the door?

She pressed the doorbell again and heard someone moving inside.

"I thought you said eleven o'clock," Jackson said as he swung the door open.

His eyes widened when he saw her standing there. His hair was all mussed and he had on boxers and a T-shirt. He blinked twice, as if not believing his eyes, and Shaye began to worry that she'd made the wrong call coming here.

Then he smiled. "Oh my God, Shaye. I thought you were the cable guy. Come in."

He moved toward her a bit, like he was going to hug her, but then he took a step back and waved her inside. She was momentarily disappointed, but then reminded herself that Jackson had always been very careful not to cross boundaries with her. He wouldn't touch her unless he knew for certain that she was okay with it. The thought made her heart clench all over again as she recalled one of the many reasons she was so attracted to him, but at the same time, her anxiety level rose because she knew the onus was on her if she wanted their relationship to progress.

She stepped inside the living room and looked around, surprised by what she saw. Most young, single men she knew had a dark leather couch, a huge television, and not much else. Jackson's apartment was tastefully decorated with rich brown couch and chairs, ornate tables, and the expected huge television.

"Can I get you some coffee?" he asked, fidgeting a bit.

"Only if you already have some," she said.

"I don't right this second, but I haven't had any yet, so it's going to get made anyway."

"In that case, I'd love a cup."

"Great. Come into my kitchen," he said, waving his hand at the open room beyond the living area. "It's doesn't have the sitting room that Corrine's has, but I've got a nice two-top and plenty of sunlight."

Shaye followed him into the kitchen and took a seat at a small table in front of a large window that looked out into an attractive courtyard. Jackson put the coffee on to brew and sat across from her.

"When did you get back?" he asked.

"Last night...er, well, technically, this morning. About two a.m. Corrine thought that arrival hour would make it easier."

"Did you have any trouble?"

She shook her head. "No one's noticed yet. It was still quiet when I left the house, but it won't stay that way for long. I'm sure a neighbor or delivery guy or postman or someone else will see me or my mother and the news will spread faster than a cold on an airplane."

His expression shifted from happy to slightly disgusted. "Yeah, you gotta love the media for all the good they do. Like you haven't had enough of them to last a lifetime already."

"That's true enough, but they're not going to give me a pass."

He studied her for a bit, then finally asked, "How are you doing?"

He was one of the only people who could ask her that question and she knew for certain that his concern was real. That he wasn't looking for a round of gossip to run out and share with his friends and coworkers. He was also one of the only people that she trusted with the truth, but right now, the truth was still jumbled and so she couldn't answer with any certainty.

"I'm okay," she said. "I mean, I'm angry, and confused, and still overwhelmed a lot of the time, but I've moved past the severe depression I had right after."

He shook his head. "I can't even imagine...two

months later and I'm still trying to process it."

"I didn't get to thank you," she said. "Everything happened so fast that night, then Corrine and I fled. I'm sorry I didn't contact you. I should have."

"You shouldn't have done anything you didn't feel like doing. You've been through more than any hundred human beings experience over a lifetime. Do you really think I'm so selfish that I expected you to think about me given all you had to consider?" He sighed. "I'm here, Shaye, whenever you're ready to talk or if you just want to sit quietly and stare out the window. All you have to do is ask."

She felt the tears well up and her heart ached with the overwhelming feeling of gratitude. Never in her life had she met a man like Jackson, and she still wondered what she'd done to deserve such good fortune.

"I don't even know what to say," she managed finally, "except that I'm grateful to have you in my life. And thank you for everything you've done for me."

Jackson reached across the table and touched her hand. She felt his strong fingers close over hers, and a feeling of peace and warmth rushed through her.

"You're important to me," he said. "Probably more important than you know. I know what you've got to deal with and can't even fathom how hard it's going to be, but no matter how long it takes or how difficult it is, I'm going to be right there by your side the entire way. If you want me to be."

Shaye nodded as a single tear streamed down her

cheek. "Always."

"Some friend I am," he said. "Your first day back and I make you cry."

She smiled and wiped the tear from her cheek. "I'm okay with happy tears. I've had enough of the other."

He nodded. "I know you have Eleonore and Corrine, but if you ever need to talk—to someone who's not your therapist or mother—I'm always here. I can't even imagine everything you're trying to work through and how overwhelming it all is, so if there's anything I can do to help—anything at all—please let me know."

"There are some things I want to talk through. Things I don't want to share with Eleonore and Corrine yet. But I don't want to talk about them right now. I need to help Corrine with all the business decisions she has to make before I delve into my own issues."

"Is Corrine going to step into the CEO position, or is she looking for someone to run it for her?"

"Actually, she swears she's going to sell it all—the real estate, the manufacturing company, all the smaller interests, everything."

"Wow." He blew out a breath. "I guess I shouldn't really be surprised. Corrine never had any interest in Pierce's businesses, and it's not where her experience and education fit."

"But?"

"I don't know. I guess it will seem strange to see the Archer name disappear from New Orleans. It's been so prominent for so long."

"Yeah, but now it's famous for all the wrong reasons. More than anything, I think my mother just wants her old life back. It was the one she chose for herself and the one she wants."

"Do you think that's even possible?"

"I have to, because I want my life back, too."

His eyes widened. "Are you going to continue investigating?"

"Yes. I thought about it a long time, but the bottom line is there's nothing else I want to do. I am in a unique position where I can help people who've fallen through the cracks, and I don't have to worry about making some boss happy or paying the rent."

"NOLA's answer to Batman?"

"I wish. His car is totally cooler than mine. And I'm not one for ostentatious, but I'd take that house with the secret cave, too."

"We could probably get you a cool car, but I think it might be a problem with the whole surveillance thing."

She laughed. "Not to mention the condition of the streets here pose a problem to anything with low clearance."

He smiled. "Have I told you yet how good it is to talk to you again?"

"I think so too. But enough about me. What's going on with you? Eleonore came to see us as soon as we got home and said there have been some issues in the department. I figure she was underselling it in an attempt to keep from upsetting me, but I imagine you've caught hell over a lot of things."

He held up a finger and got up from his seat. "That is a conversation that requires coffee."

He poured them both a cup and brought them to the table, then retrieved a bowl of sweetener before sitting again and taking a sip of the coffee.

"I'm not going to lie," he said. "It's been a little rough."

"Eleonore said they installed an interim chief."

Jackson nodded. "He's not a bad guy. Got a decent record."

"But?"

"Everything that went down with Bernard left us looking pretty bad, especially with the press yelling corruption. He's got the mayor breathing down his neck to clean up the department, which prompted him to call in the FBI."

"Wow. Eleonore didn't say anything about that."

"They're not here anymore. They spent a month questioning us like I would a murder suspect and finally issued a report stating that they found no evidence that any existing department employee had knowledge of Bernard's involvement or past involvement with the case."

"And that didn't satisfy the mayor?"

"Somewhat, but the press pushed for a long time. The public wants someone to answer for everything that happened and more importantly, to pay. Pierce's and Bernard's suicides took that option away and I think a lot of people are flailing around, trying to figure out where to shove all that anger and need for justice."

"I know how that feels."

"You know better than anyone how it feels, and have the absolute right to complain about it. Everyone else is just being childish. They'll get over it eventually."

"But in the meantime, you're catching hell. How is your relationship with Grayson?"

Jackson sighed. "It was pretty bad at first. He figured out immediately that I suspected him of being the perp. It's not exactly a great bond-building thing if the guy you're supposed to trust with your life thinks you're a serial killer."

"I imagine that puts a strain on things. But he got over it?"

"I wouldn't say that he's completely over it. Once he came off the ceiling and saw all the evidence, I realized he would have thought the same thing. But I don't know if things will ever be the same. I guess I just have to wait it out."

"I'm really sorry about that. I never wanted to cause you trouble. I know how much your job means to you."

"Don't worry about it. In the big scheme of things, a handful of people being pissy with me is a small price to pay for everything we exposed." He looked her straight in the eyes. "For getting you the answers you deserved. I have no regrets."

She nodded, afraid that if she spoke, she'd start to cry.

"So?" he asked. "What's next on the agenda for you?"

She wasn't sure whether he was changing the subject to avoid her discomfort or his own, but it didn't matter.

They could both use a breath from depressing subjects.

"I don't know. You'd think after all that time to consider it all, I'd have a better idea, right?" She shrugged. "I guess the first thing is to check on my apartment and make sure everything is good there and pick up anything I need."

"You're staying at Corrine's?"

"For now. She's not ready to be alone. She'd never admit it, but I know her. Being back here will prompt her into action, though. My mother has never been the type to sit idly by while life is happening. Once she gets started with whatever she decides to tackle first, it will occupy her time and get her mind focused on other things."

"I'm glad. Corrine's place affords you a lot more privacy than you could get at your own place."

"Definitely." Given that the press had the right to stand on the sidewalk quite literally outside her front door, Corrine's estate was practically an island escape. As soon as she stepped outside the gates, they would be on her, but at least she wouldn't be inside the house knowing they were standing inches from her exterior walls.

"So I guess if I want to visit you," Jackson said, "it will be with parental supervision?"

Shaye laughed. "I would tell you I can make her go away, but I'm not about to toss that lie out there. We might be able to step outside for a private conversation, though. Mind you, I'm not making promises."

"That's okay. I'll take you however I can get you. I'm just happy you're back."

A blush crept up her neck and onto her face, and Jackson smiled.

"I'm happy I'm back, too." She rose from her chair. "But I should get out of here. You have things to do and I have to get my bearings and make a plan."

He followed her to the front door and when she turned to look at him before opening it, he moved closer to her and wrapped his arms around her, hugging her tightly.

She'd worried how she'd feel if he touched her. Concerned that her body would unintentionally move away from him. But it had been wasted worry. As his arms tightened around her and she felt the heat from his body radiating against her own, so many emotions swept through her. Comfort, safety, trust, and a couple that she wasn't quite ready to reveal.

Soon, she thought, and that one word made her infinitely happy.

Ethan Campbell awakened, confused and feeling ill. Slowly, he pushed himself up and looked around the dim room, trying to figure out where he was, but nothing looked familiar. The ten-by-ten room had splintered gray wood like what you'd see on a storage shed, but Ethan wasn't friends with anyone who had a lawn, much less a shed. He glanced around and groaned, then clutched his head with his hands. His head pounded and even the slightest movement sent shock waves through his entire body.

He blinked several times, then very slowly turned his head, studying the room for a clue as to how he'd gotten here and why. But the empty shelves and broken broom in the corner didn't tell him anything. Afraid to stand, he shifted onto his knees and inched toward the door across the room. When he reached it, he put his fingers under the splintered wood and tugged, but it remained in place. He clutched the shelves and pulled himself into a standing position, then grabbed the door handle and pulled again.

It didn't budge.

There was a crack between the door and the wall, and he leaned forward to peer out of it. His heart fell when he saw the chain and padlock on the outside. Starting to panic, he pulled on the door over and over again until his head hurt so much he stumbled backward into the wall. He fell down onto his knees and retched, but there wasn't much in his stomach.

What in the world was going on?

Then he remembered the text. Was this about the text? He'd ignored it because Tara had insisted someone was messing with him. Since that happened more than he liked to admit, he'd been reluctant to argue with her. He'd finally decided that she was right and that the message had been intended for someone else. But maybe they'd both been wrong. Maybe it *had* been meant for him and because he hadn't followed the instructions, he was here now.

What if they were going to kill him? Like they did the other girl?

He'd seen her picture on television. Tara didn't think the text picture and the girl on television were the same person, but Ethan hadn't been as certain. People, especially girls, could look a lot different when they changed their hair and makeup. Besides, if this wasn't about the text, what else could it be about? Plenty of people wished he'd mess up on an exam and lower the curve in class, but he couldn't think of anyone who would go to the extreme of kidnapping him just to make sure he missed a test.

He felt his pockets but his phone was gone. His wallet, however, was still in his back pocket. He pulled it out and looked inside, surprised to see the forty dollars he'd gotten out of the ATM still inside. What kind of criminal kidnapped someone and didn't take their money?

Maybe the kind that's planning on killing you and can get the money later?

He took a deep breath in and slowly blew it out.

Think. You're smart.

Unfortunately, he was afraid smart wasn't going to get him what he needed this time. For the millionth time in his life, he wished he were big and strong, not the skinny, nerdy weakling who couldn't fight his way out of a wet paper bag. Someone strong could probably knock down that door or even go through a wall. He couldn't even move without wanting to hurl. The odds of him tearing down a door were so slim they weren't even worth considering.

He looked down and studied the floor. It was dirt, but it was compacted so hard it felt like cement. If he had something to dig with...the broom! The broken broom handle had a jagged edge. Maybe it was enough to dig with. If the hard layer was only a top coat, it shouldn't take more than a couple hours to dig a hole big enough for him to squeeze through.

He started crawling toward the broom, praying that he had a couple hours before whoever had taken him returned.

CHAPTER FOUR

Shaye unlocked the front door to her apartment and stepped inside, rushing to turn off the alarm. As soon as she finished the disarming, she hurried to lock the front door and pull the dead bolt behind her. All of the blinds were drawn, making the room so dim she could barely make out the shape of the office furniture.

She flipped on the overhead lights and walked through the front room, which served as her office, and into the combined kitchen and living area. It looked as it had when she'd left. Eleonore would have emptied the refrigerator and pantry of anything that would spoil while they were gone, but everything else was just as it had been the last time Shaye had walked out the front door.

A layer of dust covered every surface, making the granite countertops and dark wood coffee table look dull. Even the hardwood floors looked faded, as if they'd sat out in the sunlight for a year. It was nothing a mop and a dust rag couldn't handle…if she felt like breaking out a mop and a dust rag. She dwelled on it for a couple seconds but ultimately decided that cleaning could wait until she was living here again. Why dust twice when once would do? It was an efficiency thing.

She went to her refrigerator and was happy to find a case of bottled water chilling inside. She took one and inspected the bedrooms and baths, happy to find everything in order and nothing leaking. Just more dust and some laundry that had needed a wash for so long she probably should throw it away and start over.

If only the rest of life were as easy as dust and dirty laundry. Somebody needed perking up—run a damp rag over them and make them all shiny and new. Somebody worn past the state of usefulness or repair—toss out the bad parts and order some energy, attitude, and a better mental state from Amazon and have it shipped to your door for free with a Prime membership.

She blew out a breath and shook her head.

It was time to leave before someone caught sight of her and the media descended. They could easily block her SUV in and it would take a lot of time and resources that the New Orleans police didn't have to get her freed. And right now, Shaye doubted her popularity with the police department. Granted, nothing that had happened was her fault, but that didn't often matter when people were upset and looking for someone to blame.

She paused at the front door to set the alarm, but as she reached up to press the buttons, someone knocked on the door. Crap. They'd found her already. She lifted a slat on the blinds a tiny bit to peer outside but instead of the camera crew she expected to see, a young woman with short blond hair and a Lafitte University T-shirt stood outside. A quick scan of the street didn't reveal a white van potentially hiding a camera crew. In fact, the only car on the street was her own.

You don't have to answer. Just stay quiet until she goes away.

Shaye dropped the slat and took one step back. It would be easier to stay hidden, but the way the girl chewed on her fingernail and shifted every second or two bothered Shaye. The girl needed help.

You're in no position to help anyone.

That was true enough, but it wouldn't hurt to see what the girl needed. Then Shaye could figure out who could help her. Sending the girl to someone else was something Shaye could live with. Ignoring her completely wasn't.

She reached over, unlocked the door, and pulled it open. The girl, who'd been looking down the street, gave a start.

"Oh!" the girl said. "I didn't think anyone was there."

"Can I help you?" Shaye asked.

"Are you Shaye Archer?"

Shaye nodded.

"Of course you are. I've seen you on television, but that's not why I'm here. Well, maybe it is…anyway, I have this friend, and I went to the police but some douche detective dismissed me like I was six-year-old making up bedtime stories."

The girl's story sounded very familiar. "Does this douche bag detective have a name?" Shaye asked.

The girl frowned. "Vincent."

Shaye sighed. "Come inside, please. I'm trying to keep

a low profile."

The girl stepped inside and stood in the middle of the office, glancing around.

Shaye pulled a dust cloth out of her desk drawer and gave the two leather chairs in front of her desk a swipe to remove the worst of the dust. "Have a seat," Shaye said.

The girl sat down, then Shaye turned the chair next to her a bit so that she could look straight at her while talking. The girl was clearly nervous, and Shaye figured sitting behind the desk would feel more formal and put the girl on edge even more than she already was.

"What's your name?" Shaye asked.

"Tara Chatry," she said, looking miserable. "I'm sorry to bother you. This waitress at the café across from the police station said you could help. I saw the stories on the news about how you saved those kids from that awful man. I know you're in the middle of a shit-storm I can't begin to imagine, so if you tell me to go away, I'll totally understand. If I were you, I'd be hiding under the covers, refusing to get out of bed."

Tara sighed. "I'm rambling."

"It's okay," Shaye said. "My life is a little hard right now, but I *will* listen to you and I *will* take you seriously. If necessary, I'll help you find someone who can take on your case."

Tara's shoulders drooped a bit and some of the tension left her face. "That's great. Seriously. I don't care who helps, but I need someone."

"Of course. You said this was about a friend?"

Tara nodded. "Ethan Campbell. He's a student at the university. Really smart guy, but the nerdy type, you know?"

"I've known a few of them."

"Then you know nerds aren't the kind of people who disappear without a word to anyone, and that's exactly what Ethan did. I haven't heard from him since Sunday night. We have calculus together first thing Monday morning, and I knew something was wrong when he didn't show up. We had a big test. He helped me study for it all weekend."

"Does he live on campus?"

"Yeah. I called right before class started but his phone went straight to voice mail. I sent a text, but he never answered. As soon as I finished the test, I went to his dorm room. The idiot he rooms with said he hadn't seen Ethan since he went to the store for a soda the night before. I checked with the school nurse, with all of his teachers, and searched every corner of the campus and his dorm. No one has seen him."

"Could there have been a family emergency?" Shaye asked. "Some reason he needed to leave quickly and didn't take the time to let people know?"

"I don't see how. Ethan's parents died a little over a year ago in a car wreck. He doesn't have anyone else but his grandma, and she's in a nursing home. Dementia. I called the home to make sure he wasn't there, but they haven't seen him in over a week."

"Any close friends? Someone he might have gone off to help?"

Tears formed in Tara's eyes and she shook her head.

"Ethan didn't have any real friends but me."

Tara pulled out her cell phone and turned it around to show Shaye a picture. Tara and a young man, who Shaye presumed was Ethan, were standing in Jackson Square. Tara was laughing. Ethan wore a shy smile and wasn't looking directly at the camera. He had short dark hair and glasses and looked like he needed to gain a good ten pounds.

"No one hated him," Tara said. "They just didn't notice him, you know?"

Shaye had zero experience with going unnoticed but she understood what Tara was saying. "So if something happened, he would have called you."

"He didn't have anyone else. That detective said Ethan was probably in an alley somewhere sleeping off a drunk, but there's no way that's what happened. Ethan's as straight as they come. One of the older students brings beer to the parties but Ethan won't drink it. Not even a sip. Neither will I, but for different reasons."

"Do you mind telling me that reason?" Shaye asked, wanting to form a solid opinion on the girl and her intelligence and emotional strength. Assessing the client was the first part of her job. In order to properly do the job, she had to have a clear and correct delivery of the facts. Overly emotional people tended to get dramatic, which often led to embellishment.

"I look normal, right?" Tara said. "But I have a congenital heart defect, so I stay away from alcohol, cigarettes, and too much fast food. I still eat some because who doesn't love a pizza, but I can't be like the other students. I'm not supposed to do stuff that's really strenuous, either. I do thirty minutes of low-impact aerobics every day, but anything more involved and I send my heart rate into the stratosphere, so no cool pranks or ski vacations with college buddies...that sort of thing."

"I'm very sorry," Shaye said. "That must be hard to manage."

Tara shrugged. "I've been doing it for so long, I don't even think about the management part of things anymore. But being different isn't all that great a thing when you're in college, you know?"

Shaye nodded. "I know it very well."

"I bet you do. I keep trying to make it work and I wanted Ethan to as well. Heck, if it wasn't for me dragging him out of his room, he wouldn't ever go to a party. He only does it now because I tell him I don't want to go alone and he feels guilty. That isn't true, exactly—I don't have a problem talking to people. Not like Ethan. But I don't think it's good for him to spend all his time hiding in his dorm."

"Probably not," Shaye said, although she'd been guilty of doing the same thing herself, except in Corrine's house rather than the dorm.

Tara let out a single choked laugh. "I always tell him he's got the rest of his life to hide out in some dark, stuffy office."

"You're a good friend," Shaye said. "Ethan's lucky to have you."

Tara sniffed. "Thanks. I don't feel like a very good friend, though. I feel like I ought to be doing something and I can't seem to."

"You're doing the best you can."

Tara nodded but she didn't look remotely convinced. Shaye understood exactly how she felt. It was hard to have so much desire to fix something and be completely helpless to do so.

Shaye paused for a second, knowing that her next question was going to hit Tara hard, but she had to ask. "Have you called the hospitals?"

Tara's eyes widened. "No. I didn't even think...oh my God, I'm so stupid."

"No, you're not. You're just worried and this is not a situation you normally deal with. Can you give me a couple minutes to check on that?"

"Sure. Of course. Maybe he got hit by a drunk or something on his way to get a soda. Maybe he's sitting in the hospital with a broken ankle or something."

"Maybe," Shaye said, but she didn't believe that for a minute. If Ethan were in a hospital with minor injuries, he would have called Tara and told her. The girl hadn't put that together yet, but she would. Shaye knew that if Ethan was in a hospital, he was either unconscious or dead.

"Can I use your bathroom?" Tara asked.

"Down the hall on the right."

Shaye waited until Tara had left the room before pulling out her phone and dialing the hospital closest to the university. She claimed to be looking for her missing cousin

40

and gave Ethan's name and description, but the nurse had no record of Ethan or a John Doe. Shaye repeated the process for the other hospitals in New Orleans, then put her cell phone on her desk.

"He's not there, is he?" Tara's voice sounded behind her.

"I'm afraid not," Shaye said.

"What do I do now? The police don't believe me and I don't have any money to pay for someone like you, even if you were available." She grabbed her backpack off the floor. "I really appreciate you talking to me. I won't waste any more of your time."

Shaye jumped up from the chair and grabbed Tara's arm. "Wait. I'll help you."

She hadn't intended to say the words, but they'd come out anyway. She'd intended to call in a favor with another investigator and pay for it herself, but something about the girl pulled on her so hard, she couldn't let her walk out that door thinking she had no one. Shaye could find someone else to handle the job, but she couldn't think of a single person who would handle it the way she would.

Tara stared at her, her expression saying that she wanted to believe Shaye but was afraid to. "I can't pay you," Tara said, and sniffed. "I mean, I have like sixty dollars, but nothing like what you probably charge."

"Let's worry about all of that later. Right now, just concentrate on finding Ethan." Shaye waved her hand at the chair.

Tara rubbed her nose with the back of her hand and

sat down again, dropping her backpack beside the chair. Shaye's laptop was at Corrine's house, so she grabbed a pad of paper and a pen.

"I need to get as much information as I can from you about Ethan, okay?" Shaye asked.

Tara nodded and Shaye launched into a series of questions about Ethan's physical address, his deceased parents' names, his dorm mate, his class schedule, his acquaintances, and anything else she thought would help her form a mental picture of the missing young man.

"Did he work?" Shaye asked.

"No. He said he would try to get an internship at an accounting firm junior year, but he wasn't planning on working until then."

"How did he pay for school, dorm fees, food?"

"His parents had a bit of insurance. Not much, but he said it would pay his living expenses through college if he got a part-time later on."

"And his tuition?"

"Full scholarship. Ethan is really, really smart. Scary smart."

"His roommate said he went for a soda...what time was that and where would he normally go for that kind of thing?"

"I was there all afternoon and evening. Brett, his roommate, said he went out about nine that night. There's a convenience store behind the dorm."

"So he wouldn't have driven."

Tara shook her head. "It would take just as long to get

out of the parking lot and go around the one-ways as it would to go out of the dorm the back way and cut across the vacant lot to the store."

Shaye had been by the university dorms several times and was pretty sure she knew the area Tara was describing. But she couldn't think of a single reason that a shy, nerdy boy with only one friend would disappear. If he'd been mugged, then he'd be in the hospital, either in a bed or in the morgue. But since he wasn't in either, that meant only one of two things—either Ethan Campbell had intentionally vanished or someone had taken him.

"Is there anyone who would want to hurt Ethan?" Shaye asked.

"Why? He wouldn't harm a fly."

"Emotionally disturbed people aren't always logical. Maybe Ethan made someone angry by breaking the curve in class." Shaye didn't really think that was enough of a reason to make a classmate disappear, but given her own past, she refused to ignore any possibility, even the fantastic.

Tara frowned and looked down at the floor. Shaye knew that look. She'd seen it time and time again during her fraud investigations at her previous job. There was something Tara wasn't telling her. Chances were it didn't mean anything. Maybe it was silly or embarrassing, but whatever it was, Shaye needed to know. Sometimes the things that seemed the least important were the most important.

"Tell me," Shaye said quietly.

"You'll think it's stupid."

"I won't. I promise."

"Ethan got this text a couple weeks ago. There was some sort of strange code thing, then the message said that he had forty-eight hours to decipher the code and save the girl or he'd be next. There was also a picture of a girl. She looked like she was sleeping or passed out maybe. I don't know."

"Did you or Ethan recognize the girl?"

"No, but then last week, everyone was talking about that dead girl who was found in a funeral home casket. You saw it on the news, right?"

Shaye shook her head. "I've been out of the country for a couple months. I just got back last night."

"They said some sorority girl got drunk and crawled into a coffin at the funeral home. Probably a prank or dare or some other nonsense they're all about, but apparently, it closed and she couldn't get out so she suffocated."

"That's horrible, but what does that have to do with the text?"

"Ethan was convinced the girl in the text was the girl in the coffin."

Shaye frowned. "What did you think?"

"I don't know…I mean they were both young and had brown hair with highlights, but the girl in the text didn't have on makeup and the picture on the news did. They didn't look much alike to me but I could have been wrong."

"And neither you nor Ethan knew the girl in the

coffin?"

"It's a big school and we didn't exactly run in the same circles."

Tara looked down at the floor as she delivered that sentence, and Shaye immediately understood what she was saying. The sorority girl wasn't the kind who would hang out with Tara and Ethan.

"I don't suppose Ethan forwarded the text to you?" Shaye asked.

Tara shook her head. "You don't think there's something to it, do you? I mean, I figured the whole text thing was some sort of prank and they got the wrong number. Oh God! What if Ethan was right? What if someone put that girl in a coffin because Ethan didn't go looking for her? I told him it was a joke. What if he could have saved her? What if the same people have him now?"

"Let's not jump to conclusions," Shaye said, trying to calm the girl down. "We don't know that it's the same girl, and we don't know that the text was meant for Ethan or that it was serious. I think your original assumption that it was a prank is far more likely."

"Really?"

"Yeah."

She wasn't lying, exactly. It *was* far more likely that the text was a misdirected prank, but Shaye couldn't ignore the niggling at the back of her mind or the unsettling of her stomach. She hoped that it turned out to be nothing.

But she wouldn't bet on it.

CHAPTER FIVE

Shaye locked her apartment and headed to her car. So far, she'd managed to escape observation, but she knew that wouldn't last forever. Before the media caught wind that she was back, she wanted to talk to Ethan's roommate and locate whoever was working at the convenience store Sunday night. Tara said Ethan's roommate, Brett, often skipped class in favor of sleeping, so she figured she'd try the dorms first in case Brett was still in residence.

Ethan's room was located on the back side of the building on the first floor. Shaye heard music playing inside and knocked on the door. After several seconds, she knocked again. She heard movement and finally the door opened and a half-asleep linebacker-looking guy opened the door and peered out at her through half-slit eyes.

"Brett Frazier?" she asked.

"Yeah."

Shaye held up her identification. "I'm a private investigator. I'd like to ask you some questions about Ethan Campbell."

Her words seemed to jolt him out of the twilight zone. His eyes widened and he stepped back, allowing her to enter.

"You're a PI? For real?" he asked.

"Very real." She scanned the small room, easily discerning Brett's space from Ethan's. One side held a neatly made bed and a desk with a laptop and a bookshelf full of books. The other side probably held a bed, but it was hidden under piles of dirty laundry, blankets, and pizza boxes. The desk contained empty sports drink cans and a stack of DVDs.

"When was the last time you saw Ethan?" Shaye asked.

"Sunday. He said he was going for a soda."

"And you haven't seen or heard from him since?"

Brett shook his head. "Are you telling me he's really missing? That girl wasn't just being all drama?"

"As far as I know, you are the last person to see Ethan. He isn't in local hospitals, hasn't contacted anyone, and has no family or friends he could be staying with. I'd say that constitutes missing."

"Damn." Brett flopped onto the stack of blankets and scratched the top of his buzz-cut head. "I figured it was bullshit, you know?"

"Did Ethan have a drinking problem or a girlfriend?"

"God no. Neither. Ethan is a total geek."

"Then why would his disappearance be bullshit? He doesn't sound like the kind of guy who'd leave without telling anyone unless you think he's pulling a prank."

"On who? Dude didn't have any friends except that drama chick." He stared at her for a bit, looking puzzled. "Oh! I get it. You're thinking there's no reason for him to disappear, so it couldn't be bullshit."

"Probably not. Does Ethan have any enemies?"

"Not that I know of, but we don't exactly have the same interests."

"I imagine not. Has Ethan mentioned anyone bothering him recently?"

Brett shook his head. "This ain't high school. I mean, it was cool to pick on geeky kids then, but you gotta grow up sometime."

Shaye cast another glance around the room. "Of course. Would you mind if I look through Ethan's things?"

"I don't care. Hey, do you think something happened to him?"

"Well, if he has no reason to be missing, but he is, then I think that's a good bet."

Brett blew out a breath. "That's heavy."

"Definitely." Shaye pulled a business card out of her purse and handed it to Brett. "If you think of anything or hear anything around campus, let me know."

"Yeah, sure." He looked at the card, then looked her up and down. "Hey, are you doing anything this Friday, because there's this party and it would be totally cool if I brought you."

Shaye wasn't sure whether to be flattered or amused, and finally settled on both. "I'm afraid that won't work for me."

"Boyfriend, huh? All the hot girls already have boyfriends."

"Something like that. Thanks for your help."

"Yeah, no problem. I guess I should get something to eat and maybe go to class. Hey, what day is this?"

"Tuesday."

"Crap. Tuesday is history. Maybe I'll just do the eating part." He dug his wallet out from under a stack of candy wrappers. "I hope you find Ethan. He's a pretty decent guy, I mean, considering."

He gave Shaye a half wave and left the dorm room. Shaye went straight to Ethan's desk and opened his laptop. The password box came up and she drummed her fingers on the desk for a bit. Maybe she should call Tara. She might know Ethan's password. Then a thought occurred to her and she typed in "Tara." Just because Tara wasn't into Ethan didn't mean Ethan wasn't into Tara.

The screen flashed and then opened to the desktop. Shaye checked his Internet search history and email, then moved into his stored files and located the ones accessed in the past two weeks.

Calculus homework, Biology homework, English homework, Astronomy homework, Calc homework.

She stopped and frowned. Why were there two entries for calculus? Two assignments maybe? But the naming system seemed strange. Why not name the files by date assigned or due date? Why abbreviate one and not the other? For someone as organized as Ethan appeared to be, it didn't seem like a logical choice.

She opened the first file and scanned through the Excel spreadsheet of calculations and notations until she reached the end. Her recollection of calculus was vague, but nothing looked out of the ordinary. She opened the second file and frowned. It was a Word document. Why would Ethan do calculus homework in Word and not Excel?

The beginning of the document contained calculus problems that he'd carefully typed the answers for. It was a completely different set of work than that contained in the first document, but it still didn't look like anything other than a typical homework assignment. She scrolled through several pages and was about to close the file when she glanced down into the left corner and saw the page count.

Three hundred pages.

No one had three hundred pages of homework.

She went to the scroll bar and dragged it halfway through the document. The calculations were long gone and were replaced by nothing but text. Dated text. With very detailed descriptions of Ethan's day and his thoughts.

Ethan kept a journal.

Struggling to control her excitement, she scrolled to the bottom of the document and saw that the last entry was the Sunday Ethan had disappeared. She leaned closer and started to read.

I helped Tara study for our calculus exam most of the weekend. The mental block she has when it comes to math is getting better. I keep telling her she's smart and if she'd just trust herself, math would be easy. I still don't think she believes me, but she's getting the concepts easier and making fewer mistakes. I expect her to do well on the exam tomorrow.

As for the other thing, I'm sorry to say there's been no progress at all. Tara still considers me nothing more than a friend. I get it. I'm the school geek and Tara might not be the most popular girl in school, but she manages to fit in the normal scene without calling negative attention to herself.

People seem to like her and those who don't really know her at least appear to be unbothered by her. She doesn't get the angry stares and snide remarks that I get about blowing the curve and being a teachers' pet.

I brought up the girl in the coffin again, but Tara still insists that it's not the same person. That the text I received was a prank meant for someone else. What she's suggesting makes sense. Only a couple of people even have my cell phone number. It's far more likely that someone got the wrong number than that someone went to the trouble to find out mine and send me such a disturbing text, especially about a girl I don't even know.

She does look a lot like the girl in the coffin, though. The makeup was different but the bone structure of her face looks similar and the hair was the same color. Still, there are a lot of girls who look like the girl in the coffin. I see them sitting on the balconies of their sorority houses when I walk past. It could have been any of them, I suppose. I thought about going to the cops, but if Tara doesn't believe it's serious, then the cops will probably think I'm wasting their time. I suppose if I disappear, as the text warns, then I'll know I should have said something.

That's enough thinking for today. I'm going to grab a soda and chips and watch Star Trek *the rest of the night. Brett is getting ready to leave for yet another party so I should have peace and quiet for several hours.*

Shaye finished the paragraph and scrolled down, but that was the last entry, which coincided with the time Ethan went missing. She scrolled back up to the weekend before and starting scanning the entries, hoping Ethan talked in more detail about the text. On the fifteenth, she hit pay dirt.

I got this weird text today that kinda freaked me out. It was a picture of a girl who was asleep or something. It had a weird set of numbers and said if I could decipher the code, I could save the girl. If I didn't decipher the code, the girl would die and I would be next.

I showed it to Tara, but she blew it off, saying it was probably some stupid sorority game and they'd sent the text to the wrong person. That makes more sense than someone asking me to play a game to keep them from killing someone, but the whole thing creeped me out. If it's a game, it's not a funny one.

This was the code:

19935192185

It doesn't make any sense to me, and numbers usually do. Maybe Tara's right and it's a sorority thing. Probably some secret code they use for their parties or whatever.

The rest of the post was about classes and more mooning over Tara, so Shaye scanned it then moved to the next entry, looking for more mentions of the text or the girl. A few days later, there was another one.

I'm freaking out. I saw a girl on the news who looked like the girl in the text and she was dead. The police aren't giving out much information but she was locked in a casket at a funeral home and suffocated. They're not saying what day it happened so I don't know if it's the same time as the text. She could be in a casket in the text. The background is blurred but looks kinda dark. They didn't show the casket on the news so I don't know what color it was.

I called Tara but she said it was probably an initiation thing for a sorority that went wrong. I know people die from fraternity and sorority hazing but it's usually from drinking too much or taking weird drugs. If it was an initiation thing, why didn't someone from the sorority let her out of the casket? Tara said maybe she had some sort of medical problem that people didn't know about and I guess she could be right. If you look at Tara, you'd never know she had heart problems so maybe this girl had some problem and suffocated quicker than a regular person would have. Maybe her sorority sisters freaked and left her there instead of calling for help.

I just wish I could be sure.

Shaye scrolled through the remaining days until the end but no other entry mentioned the girl or the text. She closed the laptop, wishing Ethan had inserted the image from the text into his journal. The police would have been able to match the image to the girl in the coffin if they were the same person.

Tara's thoughts on the matter were sound, though. Based on Shaye's own college memories, it did sound like an initiation prank, but a rather risky and elaborate one as it involved breaking into a funeral home. Shaye had never been a joiner, so hadn't been in a sorority, but talk of their exploits circulated on campus from time to time. If the girl in the coffin had an underlying medical condition, then it could explain her death and a subsequent reaction of the others to flee rather than face the music.

It all made sense.

Until she got to the part where Ethan was missing.

Maybe they had nothing to do with each other. Given the way things turned out for the girl in the coffin, Shaye hoped that was the case. But either way, an extremely predictable and reliable young man had disappeared. No matter what had happened, Shaye was certain it wasn't good.

Jackson walked into the police department and headed for his desk. The buzz in the open office dropped a notch as he passed through, and he held in a sigh. The department was so fragmented. Chief Bernard's suicide had hit all of them hard, and not everyone had taken it the same way. Some were angry at Bernard's involvement with a cover-up and thought he should have faced the music instead of taking the coward's way out. Some didn't want to believe the truth about the man they'd followed and respected for so many years and looked for others to blame. That's where the Archers' name came in, but since no legitimate blame could be placed on Corrine or Shaye, that left Jackson to take the heat.

"Look who decided to come in today," Vincent said. "It's the Archer family's very own white knight."

Jackson threw his keys on the desk, ignoring the senior officer. Vincent had a problem with Shaye that went back to her first case and her first run-in with the lazy, sexist detective. At the time, Jackson had been partnered with Vincent and he'd convinced himself to stay put and keep his mouth shut until Vincent rode his desk chair into retirement, even though he'd doubted his ability to do so every time Vincent opened his mouth.

But then things had heated up and Shaye found herself in the middle of the biggest and most horrific crimes that New Orleans had ever seen. Chief Bernard, recognizing Vincent's bias against Shaye, had put him on desk duty and assigned Jackson to work with Detective Grayson, his current partner and senior officer. Jackson had been instrumental in helping Shaye take down some truly evil people, leading to her recall of her missing past, but the final showdown had left many dead and so many more devastated.

"What?" Vincent continued to prod. "You don't speak to people anymore?"

Jackson looked directly at Vincent. "I don't answer to you, and the jury's still out as to whether or not you're people."

A couple of the other detectives chuckled and Vincent glared at them before whirling around in his chair. Jackson logged in to his computer and pulled up the case file for the missing persons case he'd been assigned three weeks ago. The boy was nineteen years old and a college student. His parents had reported him missing when he failed to return home after a fraternity party. Because they were one of the wealthier families in the city, Jackson had been asked to give them priority.

The reality was, when young adult males didn't come home after a party, there were a lot of reasons for it that had nothing to do with the criminal element. Sleeping off a drunk. A girl. Pranks with friends. He'd seen a hundred cases of so-called missing college students who turned out to be having fun or avoiding their parents. The worst that had ever come of any of them was a trip to the hospital for alcohol poisoning or overdose, or a night in the drunk tank for fighting in public.

Jackson had suspected the missing boy, Ross St. Claire, would fall in the *having too much fun and avoiding his parents* category, but he'd inspected the pool house that the young man lived in and checked with the fraternity to verify Ross's attendance at the party. Everyone remembered him being there, but no one remembered him leaving, and Ross's car was still in the parking lot.

Past a certain point, Jackson was pretty sure no one had remembered their own names, which hadn't helped the investigation any. Jackson had put out a BOLO on Ross and told his parents not to worry. That students did this all the time and he'd probably show up hungover and in desperate need of sleep by that afternoon.

He'd been right. Ross had shown up, but not that afternoon and not hungover or in need of sleep. He was dead.

Four days after he disappeared, a couple of kids hiking

a well-used walking trail near Lake Pontchartrain had been unfortunate enough to find Ross's body. He was naked and wrapped around a tree with packing plastic, his arms and legs rendered useless. A plastic bag covered his head and was secured with duct tape around his neck. Official cause of death was suffocation, but Jackson hadn't needed the ME to tell him that. It had been obvious just looking at the boy's face, and it was something that had stuck in his mind.

Being secured to a tree naked would have fit the profile of a fraternity prank, but only if the tree were in the middle of the quad where everyone could see. Placing the body on a walking path didn't provide the embarrassment factor that the fraternities were looking for, and suffocating someone to death was well beyond their goals. Kids had sometimes died in hazing accidents, but it was usually from overdrinking or doing something dangerous, such as walking on the roof of a school building and falling.

Jackson had talked to the ME about the possibility of autoerotic asphyxiation, but the ME had said there were no signs of sexual activity. The interesting thing was there were no signs of a struggle, either. Ross's fingernails were clean, no scratches or bruises on his body except for those that were likely due to his transport into the swamp. It was a crime without apparent reason with a victim who had no serious enemies.

Ross had been the rich son of a wealthy business owner. He ran with a group of guys in similar circumstances, several of whom he'd known since elementary school. His girlfriend was the niece of a state representative and spent her time hosting charity events with her socialite mother. Other students had admitted they didn't like Ross overly much, but Jackson had yet to find a case of murder over someone being a "douche bag."

"You make any headway on St. Claire?" Grayson's voice sounded behind him.

Jackson turned around in his chair and looked up at his partner and senior officer. "Nothing to speak of. I've gone over the case notes a million times. No one remembers him leaving the party or saw him afterward. Some students were willing to admit that St. Claire was a bit of a bully, but I didn't find anything worth killing over. I'm drawing a complete blank on motive. What about you? Anything come up when you interviewed the family?"

Grayson shook his head. "Nobody knows anything. Everyone loved Ross, and his father has no enemies, even the business kind, if you're going to believe that rot."

"I can't fathom someone who's been in business as long as Malcolm St. Claire hasn't picked up an enemy or two."

"But even if he had, why go after his son? If he wronged someone in a business deal, or whatever, that doesn't even the score. I've met a ton of Malcolm's type before, and he may be broken up now, but that doesn't mean business won't continue as usual."

"Did you ask for the employee records?"

"Yeah. His HR person is going to copy them all and send them over. Twenty-six people fired over a two-year period. With over four hundred employees, that's not really a huge amount. I know we have to go through the motions on this, but I'm not anticipating answers in those files."

"Probably not, but there's nothing else."

Grayson blew out a breath. "We have to find something on this. Rhinehart is all over me and I'm running out of ways to avoid him."

Jackson frowned. Rhinehart was the temporary police chief who had been drafted out of retirement until a replacement for Bernard could be found. Rhinehart was one of the old-school hard-asses who despised anything not specifically aligned with policy and procedure and pretty much thought everyone under the age of fifty was rash and stupid. He had a particular problem with Jackson because being "involved" with a victim was bad policy and didn't look good for the department. Jackson's pointing out that Rhinehart had met his wife while investigating her carjacking hadn't scored him any points.

"Why is he so hung up on this case?" Jackson asked. "There are other murders and I don't see him riding those detectives."

"Yeah, well, he's not friends with the grandfather of the other victims. A fact he shared with me ten minutes ago."

"Crap."

"Exactly."

"I don't know what he expects us to do," Jackson said. "We can't create evidence out of thin air, and if we lean hard on the local socialites to talk bad about Malcolm St. Claire, he'll hear about that too and won't be any happier."

"Agreed. We need to find someone who is on the inside of things, but isn't beholden to St. Claire. Everyone I talked to is related and has dealings with him on some level with their own business. Even if they know something, they're not going to volunteer it."

Jackson glanced around to make sure no one was listening in, then leaned toward Grayson. "Shaye and Corrine returned home last night."

Grayson's eyes widened. "And you know this how?"

"Shaye came by my apartment this morning."

"That's huge. I'm surprised it hasn't been rolling nonstop on every news channel."

"They chartered a private jet and landed in the middle of the night. The crews aren't sitting out in front of Corrine's house 24-7 anymore, so they haven't caught wind yet."

"So they managed to slip in without notice, but I imagine the circus tents will go up soon."

"I'm sure, but since they're here and we're not the media, maybe we could ask Corrine about St. Claire."

Grayson slowly nodded. "They come from the same New Orleans royalty stock, so to speak, and St. Claire definitely had dealings with Archer Manufacturing, but I didn't think Corrine had much to do with Pierce's businesses."

"No, but I would bet Pierce told her plenty whether she wanted to know or not. And if she asked people who worked for Archer Manufacturing to talk, they probably wouldn't tell her no, especially given that all their jobs rest in her hands now."

"And she'd know all the social gossip. Okay, but this isn't something we want to do by phone. So how do we talk to her without the press catching on? Corrine and Shaye are going to have to face that nightmare sooner or later, but I don't want to be the catalyst that brings it on."

"I have an idea."

CHAPTER SIX

Shaye easily located the convenience store behind the dorm building. She exited at the back of the dorm and crossed an empty lot that needed maintenance, then walked around to the front of the store. An older man stood behind the counter and looked up to scrutinize her when she entered. She stepped up and showed him her identification.

His eyes widened. "Archer? I thought you looked familiar. I've seen you on the news."

Shaye held in a sigh and wondered for the millionth time just how much her past was going to affect her ability to do her job. "I imagine most everyone has." She looked around the store, then back at the man. "Have you worked here long?"

"I own the place. Name's George Moss, but everyone calls me Pops. I been here for going on thirty years. Keep saying I'm going to retire. Gets harder every year to keep the thieves out of here. And it's not even the poor ones you got to worry about. The ones with money do it for sport. I got losses the last two years that I didn't have in my first twenty put together. This generation went to hell in a handbasket, I tell you."

"I'm sorry you're having so much trouble. Maybe you should consider better security."

Pops pointed to the cameras in the corners. "I got security. Can't tell you how many times I went down to the police station with video and even names and they didn't do shit. Too busy with serious crimes to worry about stolen candy bars. File it on my insurance, they said. If it was candy bars, I wouldn't care, but they always go for the energy drinks. Thought about locking them up."

"Maybe retirement wouldn't be the worst thing."

"Darn right it wouldn't be. Anyway, I'm sure you didn't come here to help with my problems, so what can I do for you?"

"I'm looking for a student who lives in the dorm behind your store. His roommate said he left Sunday night to come here for a soda, but he hasn't been seen since."

"Probably on a bender. That's their other scam—fake ID for beer. Like they can pull anything I haven't seen before."

"That's probably true a lot of the time, but this student wasn't the partying kind. He was more of a bookworm." She pulled her phone out and showed Pops the picture she'd gotten from Tara.

Pops leaned over the counter and squinted at the screen. "Yeah, I know him. You're right. He's not the drinking type. Kinda shy, always polite. You said he's disappeared?"

"Yes. Were you working Sunday night around nine?"

"I dropped in to pick up some accounting around that time or maybe a bit before, but I didn't see the boy. One of my employees was working that shift." Pops looked out the front window of the store. "There he is now. Name's Thomas Pitre. He's a student. Another one of them nerdy types and a little uppity. I tried calling him Tommy and he practically blanched."

Shaye looked out the window at the young man who was chaining a bicycle to a post on the far side of the parking lot. He was about six feet tall, slim build, with unkempt hair and wire-framed glasses. He slumped as he walked, looking down, and didn't make eye contact with either Shaye or Pops when he entered the store.

"Thomas," Pops said as the young man approached the counter. "This lady needs to talk to you."

He raised his head and looked at Pops, then Shaye, and his expression shifted from slightly startled to confused.

"What about?" he asked quietly.

"She's looking for some kid who went missing Sunday night on his way to the store. She wants to know if you saw him."

Thomas's eyes widened. "Someone's missing? Who?"

"Ethan Campbell," Shaye said. "Do you know him?"

Thomas shook his head. "I don't think so, but then most students pay cash and we have a credit card machine, so it's not like I see names on cards."

"And they don't bother introducing themselves," Shaye said, giving Thomas an encouraging smile.

"No, ma'am," Thomas said.

65

Shaye pulled up the image of Ethan and showed it to Thomas. "This is Ethan Campbell. Do you recognize him?"

Thomas stared at the phone for a second, then nodded. "He comes in here a couple times a week. Usually to buy sodas and chips."

"Did you see him Sunday night?" Shaye asked.

Thomas frowned. "I don't think so, but I don't know that I'd remember. I go to school full time and usually work nights, so days kinda run together."

"I understand," Shaye said. "Is there anything you can tell me about Ethan? Did he ever come in here with other people? Did you see him talking to anyone? Did he ever talk to you?"

"I saw him with that girl in the picture," Thomas said. "Never anyone else that I can remember. He wasn't much of a talker and neither am I. The girl was talking about math one time and I got the impression he was helping her with a class. I figure he's probably smart."

"He is," Shaye said, and handed a business card to Thomas. "If you think of anything or hear anything around campus, please let me know."

Thomas stared at the card a couple seconds, then put it in his back pocket. "You don't think anything happened to him, do you? I mean, I work alone at night..."

"I don't know what happened," Shaye said, "but I have no reason to believe this area of town is any more dangerous than it ever was. I'm sure Ethan's disappearance has nothing to do with this store."

"Okay," Thomas said, looking a bit relieved. "I'll start

stocking the sodas." He headed through a door on the back wall.

Shaye turned to face Pops. "I don't suppose you keep your security footage?"

Pops nodded. "I usually delete it after a month because it takes up so much space on my computer, and I'm not paying for one of those damned cloud things. Technology is going to send us all into bankruptcy."

"Or an asylum," Shaye said and smiled.

"Got that right. The security company keeps trying to get me to update. What for, I ask? What I got works fine and I know how to use it. Who has weeks to learn something new? Follow me."

Pops waved her behind the counter and pointed to a door behind him. "Thomas!" he yelled. "Come watch the register for a couple minutes."

Shaye followed Pops into the tiny office behind the counter and waited as he accessed the security footage, cursing every time he clicked the mouse. "Here it is," he said finally. "This piece starts at eight p.m. and goes for four hours. If that kid came in here, he'll be on there."

Pops got out of the chair. "You go ahead and watch as long as you'd like. If I don't get back to the counter, I'll be stocking those sodas myself tomorrow and my back's not what it used to be."

Shaye slid into the chair as Pops left the room and turned her attention to the monitor. It was a feed split into four different views of the store. Shaye focused on the one that showed the front door and carefully studied everyone who entered. Thomas was right that the store did a healthy business at night. So healthy, in fact, that she was a little surprised Pops didn't have two people working, but then she guessed the losses on theft weren't as high as the pay for another clerk.

Thomas rang up a steady stream of college kids and the occasional adult, and around nine, things started to slow down. A young woman came inside waving at the gas pumps and Thomas went outside with her, then returned a couple minutes later. After cleaning his hands with antibacterial soap, he went to the door and locked it and headed through the door at the back of the store that Shaye had seen him walk through earlier. He came out about ten minutes later, pulling a dolly with several boxes on it.

He placed the dolly in front of the soda machine and then opened the front door, letting in a couple of guys who were waiting outside. While the guys were making their selections, Thomas started replacing cartridges in the soda machine and checking each offering to make sure it had the proper blend of carbonation and flavoring. After he rang up the guys, he continued stocking straws and napkins.

No one entered the store for another ten minutes, then a guy wearing a black jacket walked inside. Under different circumstances, it might not have stood out, but it was a particularly warm fall night in New Orleans. Most of the students who'd come into the store had been wearing shorts and T-shirts. Shaye leaned forward and watched as the guy went to the coolers and pulled out an energy drink.

She kept watching as he approached the counter,

hoping that the camera focused on that area offered a decent view of his face. He put the can on the counter, then reached into his back pocket for his wallet. At that moment, he looked up and Shaye got a good look at his face. She clicked on the video to pause it and stepped out of the office.

"Would you mind if I made a copy of some of this?" Shaye asked Pops.

"Of course not. Did you find something?" Pops asked.

"Nothing concrete, but I'd like to show the video to a friend of Ethan's and see if she recognizes anyone. One of them might have seen Ethan that night."

Pops nodded. "That's a good idea. You're one smart cookie, Ms. Archer. You're welcome to whatever you need, but I'm afraid I can't help you with the copy-making stuff. Turning it all on is the best I can manage."

Shaye smiled. "I think I've got that covered."

She sat back down, rewound the tape to a bit to before Ethan left the dorm, put in a USB that was always in her pocket, and clicked the Record button, selecting a recording range of an hour. Once she got home, she'd edit the video and pull out the images of people so she could show them to Tara. While the video was recording, she popped back out of the office.

"You don't have cameras outside?" she asked.

"Used to," Pops said, "but they went on the blink about two weeks ago. The feed was always crap. I called that useless security company. They came out and claimed they fixed them, but they're still on the fritz. They keep telling me I need to upgrade the equipment. Everything is a sales pitch these days."

"So you don't have any of the outside video saved?"

"Didn't see no reason for it. Most of it was static and when the cameras did come on, everything was so dark that you couldn't have made out your own mother standing there."

"Did you have cameras in the back of the store?"

"No. Only up front at the pumps. We make cash pay customers come inside before we turn them on, but we've caught people using the hose from another car while the driver was inside the store. There were some complaints and my attorney said it was cheaper to put in a security system than deal with potential lawsuits. I should send him the bill for all these upgrades."

"It couldn't hurt." Shaye stepped back into the office and grabbed her USB from the computer. "Thanks again for letting me do this."

"No problem. I hope you find that boy. We need more of him around and less of the other kind."

Shaye handed him a business card. "If you think of anything else or hear something, please give me a call."

Pops nodded. "Good luck, Ms. Archer."

"Thanks," Shaye said and exited the store. She hoped the luck Pops wished on her was going to be enough, because this case was going nowhere fast. No witnesses. No enemies. No reason at all for an introverted, highly intelligent college student to disappear from the face of the earth.

Except for the text message.

She'd been hoping to find any other reason but a potential game of murder, but as more doors closed, that option was quickly becoming the only one on the table. Which meant the first thing she needed to find out was if the girl in the coffin had been murdered or if it really was a hazing incident gone bad.

No way would the police give her information on an open case, and Shaye wouldn't ask Jackson to risk his job for her. He'd already put himself on the line too many times as it was, and even though he'd whitewashed over how things were at the department, Shaye was certain the amount of scrutiny he was currently under was probably overwhelming.

But there was one person who might be able to get her the information.

He watched as she drove away in her SUV. He recognized her from television, but she looked better in person. He could only assume Ethan's nosy girlfriend had been the one to get the Archer woman on the case. He should have known she wouldn't let it go. The girl was constantly on Ethan about something—go to a party, teach me math—typical. Listening to her unending whining had almost made him wish he hadn't bugged Ethan's room.

He hadn't been able to monitor the other ones before he'd taken them. They lived at home or in fraternity and sorority houses where people were always milling about during the day and were armed with excellent security when everyone was asleep. But monitoring Ethan had made it easy to know his schedule. Easy to know when he'd be alone.

He didn't know if the police had connected the two other murders yet, but he was going to bet they hadn't. If the police suspected that the murders of two college students were connected and another student was now missing, they would have been the ones asking questions, not a PI.

Still, Shaye Archer, Champion of the Unrepresented and Queen of Victims, was a problem. He'd followed her story on the news and filled in some of the blanks that the reports hadn't covered. What he'd decided was that Shaye Archer was smart and brave and had unlimited money to buy whatever she needed to close any gaps missing in her own ability. It was a dangerous combination.

All this additional complication was the fault of the nosy one. The overwhelming desire to take her out coursed through him and he knew he would be forced to act. The girl hadn't been on his original list, but she'd messed up, bringing in a private detective. Now she would have to go too, along with her best buddy Ethan.

She should have thought twice about poking her nose into things that didn't really concern her.

He'd wanted to take his time—roughly one killing every week or so—but with Shaye Archer poking around and forcing him to add one more person to his list, he was going to have to speed things up. He pulled out Ethan's phone and sent a text to the next victim. She had forty-eight hours to find Ethan or he died. So far, no one had even made a move to attempt to find those missing. Probably they all thought the text was a prank.

It was the last foolish assumption they'd ever make.

CHAPTER SEVEN

Clara Mandeville opened her front door and her eyes widened as they locked onto Shaye. A second later, she launched forward and threw her arms around Shaye, squeezing her like she hadn't seen her in years. When she finally released her, Clara stepped back and motioned Shaye into the house, wiping the tears from her eyes as she closed the door.

Shaye smiled at the woman, feeling her eyes mist up. For so many years, Shaye had been unable to face Clara. The nurse had cared for her at the absolute worst time of her life. She knew all the intimate details of the abuse Shaye had been subjected to because those details were spelled out on her broken body. Clara had held Shaye's hand when she awakened screaming in the middle of the night and had sat with her until she fell asleep again.

Clara knew the worst of her. The things she'd tried to put in the past. The nightmares that she never wanted to remember. So once her body was sound again, Shaye left the hospital and she never returned. Until recently. Clara had sent Shaye her first client, a nurse who worked with Clara and was being stalked. Shaye had succeeded in uncovering the identity of the stalker, who had been killed. The nurse had left town to start a new life in a new state.

Later, when Shaye turned her investigative skills toward uncovering her own missing past, her captor and abuser had attempted to eliminate everyone who could help her, including Clara. The nurse had fought back and narrowly escaped with her life. Shaye still felt an enormous amount of guilt for everything that had happened to the people surrounding her, especially Clara, even though she knew Clara didn't blame her.

"It's so good to see you," Shaye said. "How are you?"

"Follow me to the kitchen," Clara said, "and I'll show you just how good I am. I've been baking."

Shaye groaned and followed Clara down the hallway and into the kitchen. Between Clara and Corrine, all of Shaye's ideas about dropping a couple of pounds were quickly fading away.

"Do you know how long it's been since I got in a regular workout?" Shaye asked as she slid onto a stool at the counter.

Clara uncovered a plate of pastries and pushed it in front of Shaye. "That's my famous peach pies. You can just double your workout when you get around to it again. But you'll be wanting to have one of those. My neighbors fight over them if they smell them baking."

Shaye reached for one of the pies and took a bite. "Oh my God, that's delicious," she said, and reached for a napkin to catch the juice before it dripped onto the countertop. "If you sold these, you'd be a millionaire."

Clara smiled. "It's my retirement plan."

"So…are you going to tell me how you are?"

"I'm doing fine. This body is stronger than people think."

"The doctors said you were banged up pretty bad."

"Please. We both know doctors don't know anything."

Shaye smiled. "Well, I'm glad you're doing so well."

"Me too, and now that I've fed you and indulged you with my medical condition, you can go ahead and tell me why you're here."

"I can't be here just to see how you are?"

"Yes. And I'm sure you would have been eventually, but since the news hasn't even broadcast your return yet, I'm figuring it was recent. And while I'm sure you're concerned about me, I also know you wouldn't have come here unless it was important. You could have checked in on me with a phone call and not risked running into the reporters who spend a couple days a week parked outside."

Shaye sighed. "The reporters are still coming here?"

"You didn't really think they'd just give up and go away, did you?"

Shaye knew the reporters wouldn't let go until they had their pound of flesh, but if they were still haunting Clara's block, then that meant they were still hanging around Jackson's apartment and Eleonore's house and office as well. Jackson hadn't mentioned anything about reporters when she'd seen him earlier, but that was just like him. He wouldn't want her to feel guilty or to worry.

"I knew they wouldn't leave me alone," Shaye said,

"but I was hoping they'd eventually give up on others. I'm sorry you're having to put up with it."

Clara waved a hand in dismissal. "I'm not putting up with anything. I park in the garage and they aren't allowed to block my drive, so it's no inconvenience to me at all. Jeremy is playing valet for me at the hospital, so they can't accost me in the parking lot either."

Jeremy was a retired cop and a security guard at the hospital where Clara worked. He'd interrupted Clara's attack, and that was probably the only reason she was still baking peach pies.

"He feels guilty," Clara said. "Poor man. We both know it's not his fault. The only people to blame for evil are those committing it." She narrowed her eyes at Shaye. "You know that, right?"

"I know," Shaye said. "And I remind myself every time I start to feel guilty about all the people who were hurt. I know it wasn't about me, but it's hard sometimes to not feel that way."

"Of course it is. You're a good person with a big heart. I'd be more worried if you didn't have some misplaced sense of responsibility. But as long as you know that none of what happened is on you, then you can move forward."

"I'm working on that."

Clara sat on the stool next to her. "Did you remember?"

Shaye nodded. "The memories came back in a rush when…in the crypt. At least, most of them. It crippled me to the point of collapse. I'm still trying to get a grasp on it.

I've spent hours journaling it, but some days, I don't even want to get out of bed."

"Then don't. If anyone's earned some downtime it's you. Most people wouldn't be alive after what you went through, much less sitting here eating peach pies and talking to me like a sane person."

"Ha. I question the 'sane' a lot. About once a week, another memory comes back to me. Small things mostly, but sometimes it's something bigger. Something that takes me down to my knees all over again."

"Maybe your mind is holding some stuff back to protect you," Clara said. "Feeding you a bit at a time as you can handle it. Our bodies can do amazing things."

"I guess. The problem is, I keep thinking it's everything, you know? Then there's something else."

Clara put her hand on Shaye's and squeezed. "I can't even begin to imagine what you're going through. I know you've got your mother and Dr. Blanchet, but if you ever need someone to talk to, you're welcome to sit down at my counter anytime."

"Will you have peach pies?"

"If you let me know you're coming, I think that can be arranged."

"Thank you, Clara. You've always been a great support to me." Shaye took a deep breath and blew it out. "I'm sorry I didn't visit you all those years."

"Don't you go piling more guilt on yourself. You needed space and time to get right in your own mind. Do you really think I didn't know that?"

"No. You're probably one of the few people who knew just how much I needed it."

"Good. Now that all the guilt trips and apologies are over, why don't you tell me why you're here. Don't even bother to change the subject now. You've got that look about you—like you're tracking something down and you think I might be able to help."

"I sorta took on a case this morning."

Clara's eyes widened. "I can't imagine your mother is going to be happy about that. Are you sure you're ready to jump back in?"

"I'm not sure at all, and I'm certain my mother will have a stroke or two, but I couldn't say no. The girl needs help and a young man's life could be on the line."

"Tell me."

Shaye told Clara about Ethan, filling her in on everything Tara had said and what she'd learned from the roommate and at the convenience store. Clara listened, frowning the entire time, and when Shaye finished, she shook her head.

"It sounds like something out of one of those thriller movies I used to watch. Darn things kept me up at night, so I had to switch to HGTV. The people on there annoy me but they don't give me nightmares."

"Not even granite and hardwood floor nightmares?"

Clara smiled. "Not yet. So do you think Ethan was right about the girl in the text and the girl in the coffin being one and the same?"

"I don't know, but without another reason for Ethan

to have disappeared, I have to pursue this line of investigation."

"And?"

"And something doesn't feel right."

Clara nodded. "That's what I thought. You've got good intuition. Let that guide you and you'll find a lot of answers and stay safe at the same time."

"I'm batting high on the answers thing. Not so much on the safe, but I'm working on it."

"You better be. You're an important person doing a thing that no one else does better. We need you here in New Orleans. There's a lot of people with no other options."

"That's why I can't give it up. Deep down, my mother gets it, even though she doesn't like it. She can't really cry foul given her job. Maybe it's not as dangerous, but she's not exactly running charity events or scheduling museum openings."

"Corrine is a blessing to the social services system, that's for certain." Clara leaned back in her stool. "So I assume you want to know how that girl in the coffin died."

"Yes. I know the police won't tell me, but if it will cause you problems, I don't want you involved either."

"Please. I have the most tenure at that hospital and got attacked in their parking lot to boot. The hospital attorney is so scared of me right now, I could probably set up a knitting business in the middle of the emergency room lobby and no one would utter a word. Besides, I've always been a nosy nurse. If someone's situation interests me, I read their files. Won't no one think a thing about it."

Clara's words offered Shaye an enormous amount of relief. The last thing she wanted to do was cause problems for this woman, who had given her so much.

"The police don't know you're looking for Ethan, do they?" Clara asked.

"No. And I'm not offering up that information just yet. I don't think my name is all that popular with the police department at the moment."

Clara scowled. "Bunch of damned fools is what they are. I get that they're shocked and a lot of them hurt. And those who aren't shocked or hurt are angry and embarrassed and looking for a scapegoat, but you didn't cause any of this."

"I know that. But I'm a handy person to blame. And the last thing I want to do is cause Jackson more problems."

"Are they giving him trouble?"

"Eleonore said as much. I saw him earlier and he didn't really have a lot to say about it, but then he wouldn't to me."

Clara nodded. "Because he wouldn't want you to feel responsible. He's a good man. I hope you plan on keeping him around."

Shaye felt a blush start on her neck and rise up her face. "If he wants to be around, I'm okay with it."

Clara raised one eyebrow. "You look a little more than okay, and you don't know how happy that makes me. I know you're a cautious one and you've got a lot of things to work out in your head before you can add more serious things to the mix, but he's a keeper. And based on what I've seen, that man isn't going anywhere unless you make him."

"I hope you're right. I'm not quite ready…for everything, you know? But I'd like to be."

"And you will."

Brenda Lewis heard her cell phone signal an incoming text and started to reach for her purse.

"Don't even think about it," Brenda's mother said.

Her mother was a tall, thin, and somewhat scary-looking figure, her brown eyes blazing as she glared at Brenda over her desk in the university administration offices. Many students had sat in the seat Brenda sat in now and had received a lecture about their behavior, poor school performance, and a host of other items that her mother's superiors had decided she was the most qualified to handle.

But no one received her mother's wrath like Brenda.

"Explain to me," her mother said, "why I just saw a picture of you funneling beer at a frat party."

Crap. Of all the things her mother might have gotten wind of, the beer funneling was the worst. Her father had been a great attorney, but he couldn't handle the increasing stress of the job, so he'd started drinking. It had gotten so bad that her mother had divorced him last year. Shortly after the divorce, he'd lost his job and Brenda hadn't heard from him in months. Her mother claimed she hadn't either, but Brenda figured she was lying to protect her from knowing what was really going on. Like he was living under a bridge or even worse, with her grandparents.

"You know how I feel about alcohol," her mother continued, "and you're not of legal age."

"It was just that once," Brenda lied. "It won't happen again." At least the part where someone photographed her and showed it to her mother.

"You're right about that. You're grounded. So unless you decide to funnel Scope at home, I'll be quite comfortable in the knowledge that you're not going to ruin your life or worse."

"Grounded? For how long?"

"I haven't decided yet, but way longer than you'll like. I wouldn't make plans for the rest of this semester."

"Are you kidding me? That's months. I can't sit in the house with you for months."

"Unless you want to get a full-time job, move out, and pay your own way, you can and will."

Brenda jumped up from the chair and grabbed her purse.

"I'm not done talking to you," her mother said.

"Well, I'm done listening. I have two months to listen to everything you have to say about how I'm ruining my life. I don't see any reason to get it all in right now."

Brenda ran out of the office and slammed the door behind her. The other office employees looked up from their desks and a couple of them frowned, but Brenda didn't care. As if they didn't know what a bitch her mother was. They worked for her.

She stormed out of the building and into the quad, not stopping until she reached one of the concrete benches. She flopped down on it and let out a long-suffering sigh. Her mother had always been strict, but it had gotten worse ever since the divorce. Brenda found herself lying all the time just to do simple things that other students had no trouble doing. Like attending frat parties. Like underage drinking. Everyone did it. But Brenda couldn't because if she took a drink, her mother was afraid she'd become a big useless asshole like her father.

For months now, Brenda had been thinking about finding a full-time job and moving out. God knows, she wasn't accomplishing anything in school. Her grades were decent but her business administration degree wouldn't get her more than an office job. She could get one of those now. Probably rent a tiny apartment somewhere close to the French Quarter. Maybe get a moped. Okay, so the one and only time she'd been on one hadn't turned out that well for her, the moped, or two parked cars, but she could learn how to ride one. And it would be cheaper and easier to park than a car. Worst-case scenario, she could walk. Walking miles every day was preferable to listening to her mother bitch for even five minutes.

Brenda had been saving her babysitting money for years, shoving it in the back of a stuffed bear and telling her mom she'd spent it on going to the movies and eating out with her friends. Last time she'd checked, she had over fifteen hundred dollars in the bear. That was probably enough for an apartment deposit and to get utilities turned on. All she needed to do was find a job that paid enough for her to cover the basics and then she could sit inside her own place, on the floor, and in complete and utter silence until she decided what she wanted to do with the rest of her life.

Her mother acted like silence was a bad thing, always rushing to fill nice quiet air with a million questions or suggestions for how Brenda should be handling her studies, considering a more relevant major, thinking about her future and retirement. Her mother never managed to exhaust those topics, but sometimes she got bored with the career speech. Then she switched to the food Brenda ate and that fifteen pounds she needed to lose, the hairstyle that she didn't think was flattering, the friends that she had never liked, and a million other things. Since her mother approved of absolutely nothing about Brenda or what she did, it gave her a lot to bitch about.

For the millionth time, Brenda wondered if her dad's stress had really been due to his job or was mostly from being married to her mother.

She fumed for a bit longer, then started to leave when she remembered the text. It was probably her friend Kimmie, sending her the details for the next best party they had to attend. Not that it mattered. Unless her mother died or Brenda sneaked out, she wouldn't be attending anything but classes for a long while.

Or she could seriously pursue that full-time job thing.

She yanked the phone out of her purse and checked the text. Instead of a phone number, it showed a couple of numbers on the display but not enough to be a phone number. She read the text again and frowned. What the hell was this?

Let's play a game, Brenda.
It's called "Save the student."
Use the clue below to find the student pictured here within the next 48 hours and I won't kill him.
If you don't find him, you're next.
19845851652

"What the fuck?" Brenda said. If this was someone's idea of a joke, it wasn't a funny one. And who was that guy? He looked vaguely familiar. Definitely not a frat type. Too nerdy. Not one of the TAs. At least not in any of her classes. But she'd seen him somewhere before.

Oh well, whatever. She tossed the phone into her purse and jumped up from the bench. It was just some bullshit joke or some crazy. She had more important things to worry about than some frat guys getting off on scaring her. Besides, she was hardly the rescuing type. She couldn't even manage to rescue herself.

CHAPTER EIGHT

Corrine sat in an overstuffed couch in her den and watched as Eleonore attempted to fry a steak on the stove.

"Crap!" Eleonore yelled and stuck her fingers in her mouth.

"Put them under cold water," Corrine said. "I wish you'd let me help you. You're not going to have a finger left that's viable before you're done."

"This would have been easier on the grill. I'm not used to doing this in a skillet."

Neither of them had been willing to risk cooking outside, figuring the smell of food grilling would give away the fact that the house was occupied again. So far, Corrine hadn't seen any sign of press vans outside, which was surprising, but also pleasant.

"Well, you can serve up something else that doesn't require a grill," Corrine said.

"There's not anything else. The staff threw out almost everything in here because it had expired and I could only smuggle so much food into my purse. If I went grocery shopping and then came here, that reporter who's been following me probably would have caught on."

"Maybe you should have opted for pita bread and lunch meat."

"Now you tell me. Stop couch-seat driving. I can do this."

Corrine shook her head and picked up the latest local magazine. Neither she nor Shaye was on the cover this issue, which was a good thing. They'd been featured far too prominently for a lot of weeks, but without them in town and with the police keeping a tight lid on everything that they could, news had turned to speculation, which had eventually gotten repetitive and faded out.

Of course, all that would change now that they had returned.

Eleonore cussed again and Corrine smiled. Her friend had insisted on cooking her lunch and refused all offers of help. Corrine was a much better cook than Eleonore and they both knew it, but Corrine also knew that Eleonore needed to do something for her. Needed to attempt to take care of her, even if it was in a small way. Corrine knew that Eleonore felt she'd failed both Corrine and Shaye, but nothing could be further from the truth. Without Eleonore in their lives, neither Shaye nor Corrine would have been strong enough to handle everything that had happened. Eleonore was the backbone that they'd built upon, and even though she hadn't been physically present the last couple months, every word she'd ever shared with them had.

"What do you think Jackson wants?" Corrine asked.

She'd been surprised by the phone call she'd gotten

from Shaye's detective friend, requesting a private chat and followed with promises to maintain secrecy. She'd tried to get information out of him, but Jackson hadn't wanted to conduct the conversation over the phone. Given his involvement with Shaye and Eleonore's description of the current state of unrest at the police department, Corrine figured Jackson didn't want to be overheard, especially talking to her.

"I honestly have no idea," Eleonore said.

"I know Shaye was going to see him when she left this morning."

"She told you that?" Eleonore sounded somewhat surprised.

"Not exactly. I accidentally overheard her on the phone asking for Jackson at the station."

"Accidentally overheard, huh? How does that happen in a ten-thousand-square-foot monolith?"

"Fine. I went to her wing of the monolith and heard her on the phone so I stopped outside her door and snooped. Are you happy?"

"I'd have been happier if you'd have turned around and left," Eleonore said.

"I did that after I heard everything I needed to hear, then I went to my room and climbed back into bed. I didn't even stick around to nag. You should be proud of me for that."

"You're jet-lagged and know that nagging Shaye is practically an invitation for her to do exactly what you don't want. Don't pretend you've reached some elevated consciousness in parenting."

Eleonore stabbed a filet with a fork and plopped it on a plate.

"You don't think it's about Shaye, do you?" Corrine asked.

"Since he's bringing Detective Grayson with him, I'm going to go out on a limb and say no."

"I hate it when you bring logic into a conversation."

"Then you must hate it every time I talk. Get over here. This is ready."

Corrine tossed the magazine on the coffee table and shuffled to the counter, where Eleonore shoved a plate with the filet and a huge serving of mashed potatoes in front of her.

"This is enough for two people," Corrine protested. "How am I supposed to eat all of this?"

"Well, your weight is down to that of half a person, so you'll give it your best effort. Besides, I'm having the same serving and I am not interested in feeling guilty about it."

Corrine put a forkful of mashed potatoes in her mouth and was surprised when her stomach growled. "This is really good."

Eleonore sat a basket of bread and a plate of butter on the counter and sat down on the stool next to her. "You were expecting bad?"

"That's not what I meant. I've been eating your cooking for years. Even your peanut butter and jelly sandwiches are good. I just meant that I'm surprised by how much I'm enjoying it. I haven't really given food much thought since..."

"I disagree."

"With what part?"

"My peanut butter and jelly sandwiches are excellent, not just good."

Corrine smiled. "I certainly thought so when I was twelve."

"You thought so this summer when we ate them out by the pool."

"Ha. True." Corrine took a bite of the slightly charred steak and looked over at Eleonore. "So you and Jackson talked a lot while we were gone?"

Eleonore nodded. "He's a good man. If you still have doubts about him pursuing a relationship with Shaye, don't. Not that he's likely to pursue her. He's afraid to push, so he'll wait."

"If he's waiting on Shaye to make a move, I'll never have a son-in-law."

"She may surprise you."

"She usually does."

The telephone linked to the security gate rang and Eleonore went to the kitchen wall to answer it.

"Dr. Blanchet," the guard said. "I have a John Jones here with another gentleman. Says they're scheduled to do some work in the backyard."

"Yes. That's correct," Eleonore said. "Please let him through."

She hung up the phone and looked over at Corrine. "That was the name Jackson said he'd use at the gate, right?"

Corrine nodded. "I'm anxious to find out what this is about."

"There was a van from the local CBS station parked on the street in front of the gate when I got here," Eleonore said. "I hope Jackson's idea is good enough to fool them."

"Let's throw these plates in the oven and go see."

They hurried out front as a pickup truck with a lawnmower, a ladder, shovels, and other garden tools pulled up and stopped. Jackson got out of the driver's seat and waved. He was wearing jeans, a flannel shirt, a ball cap, and work boots. A sign on the side of his truck read Jones Landscaping.

Corrine smiled as Grayson climbed out of the passenger's side, looking slightly uncomfortable in dress similar to Jackson's. "I have to give you credit," Corrine said. "When you go undercover, you go all the way."

"It's not hard. The truck is mine and I borrow the lawn equipment from a friend when I need to."

"And the sign on the truck?" Corrine asked.

"Magnetic," Jackson said. "It comes right off."

"Genius," Eleonore said. "No one looks twice at contractors."

"Yes, well, you might want to pull around to the side entrance," Corrine said. "They can see the front of the house with binoculars but not the side. I'll meet you out back and let you in that way."

Corrine and Eleonore headed through the house and into the backyard, where Corrine unlocked the gate to let

Jackson and Grayson inside.

"Can I get you anything to drink?" Corrine asked as they entered the kitchen. She wanted to demand they tell her why they were there but even when she was stressed, her manners still won.

They both answered in the negative and Corrine invited them to sit.

"What's this about?" Eleonore asked.

Corrine cast her friend a grateful glance. Leave it to Eleonore to get right to the point.

"It's nothing to do with you or Shaye," Jackson assured her.

Corrine relaxed a little and slowly let out the breath she'd been holding.

"We were hoping you might provide some insight into a person who's come up in one of our investigations," Grayson said. "Someone who moves in your social circles."

"Oh. That sounds easy enough," Corrine said. "Who is it?"

"Malcolm St. Claire," Grayson said.

Corrine frowned. "I know Malcolm and his wife and son, but mostly through charity events. I wouldn't call us friends. More like something beyond acquaintances."

Jackson looked over at Grayson, then back at Corrine. "But you'd know the, er…gossip."

"The police are resorting to gossip now?" Corrine asked.

"We've always resorted to gossip," Grayson said. "We get leads that way. We just don't like to admit it."

Corrine nodded. "And in this case, I'm going to take a wild guess that you won't be putting any leads I provide in your official report."

Jackson looked down at the counter and Grayson's expression shifted from serious to slightly guilty.

"It's not really in our best interest to do so at this time," Grayson said.

Corrine gave him a rueful smile. "Don't worry about offending me, Detective. I understand the politics of this city better than most. I'm happier with my name out of things, although it certainly doesn't appear that way."

"Everyone who knows you knows better," Jackson said. "And anyone who wants to think the worst will, no matter what."

"Listen to the man," Eleonore said. "He's right about that one."

Corrine pursed her lips. "Okay, gossip. I'm not sure what you're looking for exactly, so I'll just dive in. Malcolm has been having an affair with one of his office clerks for the last two years. She got pregnant and we thought shit would hit the fan, but she miscarried. I heard he got a vasectomy shortly after. Not about to roll those dice again."

Jackson and Grayson both stared.

"Does his wife know all this?" Grayson asked.

"Of course," Corrine said. "Who do you think told me?"

"Why doesn't she divorce him?" Jackson asked, clearly dismayed.

"Because she is a shallow individual who enjoys her

lifestyle," Corrine said.

"And the company of the pool boy," Eleonore added.

Grayson opened his mouth, then closed it and shook his head.

"And she told you all of this?" Jackson asked, appearing somewhat confused.

"Not the pool boy part," Corrine said. "We have the same pool boy. He offered me a similar deal."

Both Jackson and Grayson looked slightly horrified and Corrine laughed.

"When you have money and status," Corrine said, "you get all kinds of offers."

Jackson cleared his throat. "I'd just like to make a blanket apology for all men."

"That's sweet," Corrine said, "but not necessary. Anyway, those are the biggies on the personal end of things. On the business front, he's cold, calculating, and pretty much a bastard to deal with. He tried pushing Pierce around a few times, but he couldn't get anywhere. I've heard he treats his vendors and employees harshly, but the pay is good so most of them tolerate it."

"What a nice guy," Grayson said. "No wonder the people doing business with him won't talk."

"I sorta expected this," Jackson said, "but it makes things a lot more complicated."

"I know you can't give me details of the case," Corrine said, "but if you could somehow narrow down the type of thing you're looking for, I might be able to get more information. Lord knows, the Garden District society will be lined up at my door as soon as they hear I'm back."

Jackson looked over at Grayson, who frowned.

"We've managed to keep it out of the news so far," Grayson said, "but Ross St. Claire was murdered."

Corrine's hand flew up over her mouth. "Oh my God. That's awful."

"The longer we can keep it out of the press," Grayson said, "the better chance we have of catching the person who did it. It began as a missing persons case, and we've allowed friends, students, university employees, business associates, and other family members to assume that's still the case."

"I just don't understand," Corrine said. "Ross wasn't an overly likable young man but that's not usually something you get killed for."

"I agree," Grayson said, "which is why we're looking at his father."

Corrine nodded. "Of course. Well, your secret is safe with us." Corrine reached into a drawer and pulled out a pad of paper and pen and started jotting down some names.

"Here are the names of people with Archer Manufacturing that I know had direct dealings with Malcolm," Corrine said, and handed the paper to Jackson. "I doubt they'll have any trouble telling you their opinions."

"Thank you," Grayson said. "For the names and for your time. I'm sorry to bother you so soon after your return."

Corrine thought about everything that was headed her

way as soon as the press discovered she was back in New Orleans.

She looked at Grayson and sighed. "You're not even the storm clouds before the hurricane."

Roots!

Ethan dropped the broken piece of broomstick and flopped backward, his back hitting the wall of the shack.

His prison.

He'd been digging for hours. His shoulders and arms burned so badly it made him cry and now the muscles were so knotted that he couldn't even move them an inch. He had to rest, but he knew he couldn't afford to. Whoever had locked him in here had to have something in mind, and it couldn't be anything good. Ethan had seen enough horror movies to know what happened to people locked in creepy old shacks.

The ground was a mixture of dirt and clay and was hard, sometimes almost like stone. It was such slow going and he needed a hole large enough to fit his head and shoulders through. He was skinny, but his shoulder bones were wide. This was probably the first time in his life he actually wished he were even smaller. Right now, the hole was maybe half as big as it needed to be and the ground had gotten harder the deeper he'd dug.

Now that he'd hit roots, things would go even slower. He didn't have anything to cut them, which meant he'd have to bang on them until he could break them. So far, the roots he'd uncovered were about half an inch in diameter. Not horrible to deal with, but still time-consuming. He hoped there weren't any larger ones beneath.

He leaned over a bit and turned his wrist to check his watch. Three hours since he'd started. The slivers of sunlight that filtered through the cracks in the walls seemed to be coming from overhead and to the right. It was probably midafternoon, which meant it would be dark sooner rather than later. He stretched his hands out and winced at the pain that traveled up his arms.

He could work in the dark. That wasn't the problem.

The problem was not knowing when his captor would return.

Shaye walked into her mother's kitchen and slid onto a stool. Despite her late waking hour, the day felt very long. Probably because she had spent two months sitting and staring at the ocean rather than moving among people and constantly looking over her shoulder for a media van.

Corrine removed a tray of cookies from the oven and sat it on a cooling rack on the counter. "You look exhausted."

"I am." Shaye saw no reason to lie when her mother could clearly see the fallout from her reentry into New Orleans life.

"Did you run into problems?"

"Not press kind of problems, if that's what you mean. So far, we're still under the radar."

"It feels weird, right?"

"It's definitely surprising, but I wouldn't put much hope in another day of this. Once people start talking, it's only a matter of time until someone thinks they can profit from a tip."

Corrine pulled a bottle of water out of the refrigerator and slid it over to Shaye before sitting across from her. "Don't remind me. I'm trying to rebuild my faith in the common man, remember?"

"How's that going?"

"I like Eleonore and you."

"That's efficient, if nothing else."

"So what's bothering you? Is it Jackson? I assume you went to see him this morning."

"I went by his apartment this morning and had coffee."

Corrine studied her for a moment. "And everything's okay?"

"Everything's fine." Shaye knew Corrine was dying to know what her feelings were for Jackson, but Shaye hadn't sorted them out completely herself. She wasn't about to bring her mother and all her opinions into the mix.

"I saw him this afternoon," Corrine said.

"Really? Why?"

Corrine filled in Shaye on the detectives' secret visit. Shaye smiled as Corrine described the clothes and truck full of lawn tools.

"Grayson must have been miserable," Shaye said. "He's always impeccably dressed and groomed."

"He looked more than a little uncomfortable, but it was a great idea. A camera crew from one of the news stations was parked across the street from the gate and they didn't so much as blink."

"Maybe we should try it ourselves."

"It would have to be a hell of a disguise for us to pass unnoticed."

"We could be nuns."

Corrine smiled. "Because nuns parading around my house wouldn't be remotely suspicious."

"You don't date. Maybe people will assume you're pursuing a new career."

"Plenty of people don't date. They don't all become nuns."

"True. Probably better to leave them all assuming you're pursuing Eleonore."

"Shaye Archer!" Corrine threw a dish rag at her. "What a thing to say."

"Admit it. If you and Eleonore were batting for the other team, you'd already be married and arguing about that ugly china."

"It scares me sometimes, how well you know me."

Shaye took a drink of water. Her mother's words were so accurate and yet, strange. Accurate because Corrine was an open book with Shaye and always had been, which made her easy to read. Strange because Shaye had spent so many years knowing Corrine better than she knew herself. Now she was playing catch-up and every returning memory was a new instance of pain to process. She tried to hide it from Corrine, but she was certain her mother could tell when some new horror had come rushing back into her mind.

"So Ross St. Claire is missing?" Shaye asked. "Did they check Malcolm's yacht or their condo in Miami?"

Corrine frowned. "I'm going to go ahead and tell you this, but you have to promise not to mention it to anyone. The police are keeping this part confidential because you know how secrecy is sometimes a good thing for them."

Shaye stiffened. "Is Ross dead?"

Corrine's eyes widened. "Yes. I'm not sure I want to know why you immediately leaped to that."

"Was he murdered?" Shaye asked, her palms starting to sweat.

"Yes. They didn't provide any details and I didn't ask, but they were here asking questions about Malcolm."

"They think someone had a grudge against Malcolm and used Ross as the payback?"

Corrine nodded. "I'm pretty sure that's the case. Like I said, they didn't provide much detail. I don't know if that's because they wanted to make sure the details didn't go any further or because they were afraid it would upset me."

"Probably both."

Corrine leaned across the counter and looked directly at Shaye. "You want to tell me why you're so interested? And how you knew Ross had been murdered? I could see it in your expression."

"I didn't know. I just had a feeling."

"It's a bit of a leap from poor little missing rich boy, which we both know Ross has pulled his share of times, and murdered rich boy."

Shaye sighed. She'd had this idea that maybe she wouldn't have to tell Corrine she'd taken on a case right away, but she'd also known the thought was absolute folly the moment it had entered her head. She was living in her mother's house. There was no way she could conduct an investigation without Corrine knowing. She couldn't conduct a shower without Corrine knowing.

"I sorta took a case today," Shaye said.

"No!" Corrine's dismay was obvious in her tone and her expression. "We just got back. You're not ready and I'm not either."

"All of that might be true, but the girl needs my help now. It can't wait."

"Send her to Jackson."

"She's already been to the police."

Corrine stared at Shaye for several seconds, then sighed. "I assume they didn't take her seriously?"

"No."

"What happened?"

Shaye knew the story would upset her mother, especially after learning about Ross St. Claire's murder, but she didn't see any reason to keep it from her.

"She's a student at Lafitte University. A friend of hers is missing." Shaye told Corrine everything that Tara had told her and what she'd learned about Ethan Campbell. When she was done, Corrine rose from her chair, poured herself a glass of wine, and took a big sip. The color had drained from her face a bit as Shaye explained the situation, and after the drink and a long silence, it started to return.

"You think the three are connected?" Corrine asked. "This Ethan Campbell, Ross, and the girl in the coffin?"

"I don't know for sure, but I find it strange that three students from the same university have gone missing within a week of each other and two of them have been found dead."

"Did anyone receive a text about Ross?"

Shaye shook her head. "I don't know, but if they're all connected, then Amber Olivier, the girl in the coffin, would have received the text about Ross. Unfortunately, I don't know anything about that case except what's been released to the media."

Corrine took another sip of wine. "I'm not even going to ask what kind of person could come up with such a thing—like it's a game. I'll probably never ask that question again as long as I live given what we've seen and experienced. But I will ask why? What could a handful of college students who don't seem to be connected in any way have done to cause this kind of retribution on them?"

"I have no idea. By all accounts, Ethan was a quiet nerdy type who had to be forced to socialize. Aside from breaking the grading curve in classes, it's hard for me to imagine what someone like him could have done. Even his jock roommate didn't have anything bad to say about him."

"What about Amber Olivier?"

"I'm working on a way to find out how she died. If the

police are treating it as a homicide, then I'll pursue that angle and talk to her sorority sisters tomorrow."

"The police have probably already questioned them."

"Yeah, but they might be more willing to talk more openly to a woman who's not a cop."

"And who's close to their own age." Corrine shook her head. "I'm not even going to try to tell you not to do this, because it's insulting to us both, and I've officially given up banging my head against walls. But I will tell you to be extra careful. You of all people know how things can go terribly wrong."

"I plan on doing everything out in the open. No empty-building searches. No trips into the swamp. No venturing into tombs."

"I don't have to remind you that as soon as the media know you're back, you won't be able to take a step without them following."

"I know." It was Shaye's main concern and had been on her mind all afternoon. If the media started hounding her, and she had no doubt about that, she wouldn't be able to effectively do her job. Even worse, if they caught her questioning Amber Olivier's sorority sisters, the New Orleans police would hear about it and have grounds to come after her for interfering in an open investigation. Shaye knew her credit was all used up with the police, at least as far as management went, and the last thing she wanted to do was bring more heat down on Jackson simply because they were in a relationship of sorts.

She stiffened.

A relationship.

She'd actually thought that.

She took in a deep breath and slowly let it out. But what did Jackson think?

CHAPTER NINE

Tara walked toward the back of the library, peeking into the private rooms as she went. So far, she'd been cursed at three times and had received more dirty looks in the past ten minutes than she had in the previous year. In one room, she'd seen more of a girl's body than was appropriate to display in the library, even in a private area. Truthfully, it was probably too much to display on a beach.

When she reached the rows of computers in the big room all the way at the end of the first floor, she flopped into one of the chairs. She didn't know why she felt so disappointed. She hadn't really expected to find Ethan in the library. It wasn't as though he would disappear for days and then just reappear and go study without even returning her calls or texts. And God knows, she'd sent plenty. If anyone but Ethan checked his phone, they'd think he had a stalker.

Even though she knew it was an exercise in futility, she'd checked every single row of bookshelves and the study room on the second floor. She'd shown Ethan's picture at the front desk and asked if anyone had seen him the last two days. No one had. Then she'd pissed off everyone in the private rooms and gotten an eyeful of boobs and still she had absolutely nothing to show for it, except aggravation and a bit of embarrassment.

It had been a big waste of time. She'd known that before she ever left her dorm room, but she couldn't just sit there doing nothing. It was driving her crazy. Shaye had promised to look into Ethan's disappearance, but that didn't mean Tara could just wipe her hands of it all and go back to her life as if nothing was wrong. Because something was definitely wrong. The police might not believe her, but Shaye Archer had. That was something, at least.

She reached into her purse for her cell phone and even though there was nothing on the display, she accessed the text and phone messages anyway. Just in case the phone fritzed and didn't ring or vibrate or display the message on the front screen. All of that.

Nothing.

She dropped the phone back in her purse and headed out of the computer area. Maybe she'd go to Ethan's dorm room and ask everyone she saw if they'd seen Ethan. Maybe she'd get lucky and have something to give Shaye.

The sun was going down as she stepped out of the library and started down the big cement steps. A girl wearing a hoodie approached her as she stepped onto the sidewalk.

"You," the girl said.

"Me?" Tara asked.

"Yeah. What's your name?"

"Tara. Do I know you?"

"I'm Brenda. I saw you at a party a couple weeks ago. The one at Alpha house."

"Oh, right." Brenda looked vaguely familiar, but Tara couldn't remember having spoken to her. "Can I help you with something?"

"You were there with a guy—skinny, nerdy?"

Tara's pulse quickened. "Ethan. Have you seen him?"

Brenda frowned. "I saw him at the party with you."

"I know that. I meant in the last two days."

Brenda narrowed her eyes at Tara. "Why do you ask? You're not one of those crazy, jealous girlfriends, are you?"

"Ethan and I are just friends, but he's missing. Since Sunday night. The police won't take me seriously. They think he's out partying, but they don't know him like I do. Ethan would never take off like this and I had to practically drag him to parties."

"Yeah, he didn't look like the partying type." Brenda pulled her phone out of her pocket. "I got this message earlier. I thought it was someone screwing with me, but then I remembered I'd seen this guy somewhere before, I just couldn't place it. Then I saw you and it clicked."

Brenda turned the phone around and showed Tara the image in her text messages. Tara took one look at Ethan and her knees buckled.

"Oh my God," Tara said. "He looks dead. Is he dead?"

"How the hell should I know? I got this weird-ass message and this picture. I don't know what you guys are involved in, but I don't want any part of it."

"We're not involved in anything. I swear."

"He's missing, isn't he? And I've got some creepy, might-be-dead picture on my phone. That sounds like involved in something to me. I don't need any trouble. I've got enough already without my mom seeing something like this and completely losing her shit. I'm already grounded for the rest of the semester."

Tara tried to follow Brenda's logic but clearly, the girl was mentally processing some battle with her mother and saw the text as something that could cause her more trouble. She either didn't see or didn't want to see any other implication.

"Can you send the text and picture to me?" Tara asked.

"I don't know. I told you, I got trouble already."

Tara clenched her hands and resisted the urge to throttle the silly, self-centered girl. "How much trouble do you think you'll be in if I go tell the police you have a picture of a missing person on your cell phone and didn't report it?"

"You already said the police didn't believe you."

"I hired a private investigator. If anything happens to Ethan and you had information that could have helped us find him, you're going to have to answer for it."

Brenda rolled her eyes. "Whatever. You don't have to be a bitch about it. What's your number? You can have the text. Just don't tell anyone where you got it."

"Fine," Tara said, and gave Brenda her cell number.

Brenda stabbed her finger at the phone, then stuck it back in her pocket, whirled around and stomped off without another word. Tara stared at her a couple seconds, then accessed her texts and read the message. She sucked in a breath and her fingers tightened on the phone until her knuckles turned white.

It was a message just like the one Ethan had gotten.

A wave of nausea washed over her. Ethan had been right. Amber Olivier had been the girl in the text he'd received. Which meant whoever had taken her now had Ethan and put Brenda next on the list.

The surly girl thought she had trouble now. She didn't know the half of it.

He watched them from across the courtyard, Brenda and the nosy one. He knew Brenda wouldn't attempt to find Ethan. Even if the girl had been certain it wasn't a prank and that Ethan would be killed, she still wouldn't have been bothered. Brenda had a single-track mind and it was always focused on herself.

But he hadn't expected her to talk to the nosy one. Hadn't even been aware they knew each other or that Brenda knew Ethan. They weren't anything alike and based on watching her for a couple weeks, Brenda tended to run with those who could provide her with free passage to the things she couldn't afford on her allowance, mostly booze. Still, it was a college campus, not a city. It was possible for students of opposite temperaments and interests to run across each other.

Unfortunately, it presented a problem.

He had no doubt Brenda had shown the nosy one the text. Now the nosy one had proof to take to the police. They might not have believed her before, but if she produced the text, they might give her more credence than they did before. And regardless of what the police thought, Shaye Archer would definitely pursue it.

The question was, could she crack the code?

He didn't think so, but he supposed if she did and she managed to free Ethan before he returned to finish him off, he'd be a sport about it and let Ethan live. After all, he wasn't the one who had broken the rules of the game. But Brenda and the nosy one would have to pay for circumventing the rules. They would have to pay for Ethan's potential freedom.

Everything had a price.

Some people didn't think so.

They were about to find out just how wrong they'd been.

Tara punched in Shaye's number as she hurried across campus. She cursed when it went to voice mail, then left a message asking Shaye to call her as soon as possible and it didn't matter how late it was. She was as likely to sleep as she was to sprout wings and take flight across the courtyard. She shoved the phone into her purse and picked up her pace.

The sun had dropped behind the library and the last glimmers of sunlight faded with each step she took. Tall lampposts were scattered down the sidewalks, but the huge magnolia trees and heavy shrubbery blocked their light completely in many places, leaving dark stretches to traverse before reaching a patch of light again.

She pulled a can of Mace out of her purse, clenching it as she increased her pace until she was almost jogging. Tara had always been cautious, but she'd never been scared to walk across campus alone. Now she imagined a bogeyman behind every bush. In every tree. She needed to get to the dorm where she would be surrounded by walls and other people and doors with locks.

A stick snapped somewhere behind her and she sucked in a breath as she looked back. The only students she could see were at least fifty yards away. Whatever or whomever she'd heard was much closer.

It could be a stray dog.

She'd never actually seen a stray dog on campus but that didn't mean it couldn't happen. Or maybe a squirrel had broken a branch in the tree. It might not have been someone stepping on it. Someone hiding in the shadows, making sure she couldn't see them. Because why would anyone do that? Why would anyone want to stay hidden?

All the reasons why rushed into her mind and she let out a cry as she took off running. At first, she couldn't hear anything but her own breathing and the sound of her heart pounding in her ears, but then she heard it—someone was running behind her. Keeping pace with her. Completely panicked, she glanced around, looking for other people or just one other person, but all she saw in front of her was empty sidewalk.

Her dorm was at least a hundred yards away from the courtyard. No way could she keep up her current pace for that long. Given her heart condition, running wasn't exactly her strong suit, and running while scared to death was probably doing a real number on her.

She turned to look behind her and her feet got tangled up. Desperately, she tried to regain her balance, but it was too late. She crashed down onto the sidewalk, dropping the Mace, the skins on her palms tearing as they slid across the concrete. Her right knee banged onto the ground and she cried out as pain shot up and down her leg. She scrambled to get up and stumbled forward, her arms flailing about as she struggled to pick up speed and maintain her balance.

The footsteps were louder. He was getting closer.

She veered off to the right and ran toward Ethan's dorm. It was the closet building to her and she knew the door code to get in. Tears pooled in her eyes, causing her vision to blur, but she didn't slow her pace. Her hands and knee throbbed and she could feel a trickle of blood running down her shin.

By the time she reached the dorm entry, she felt like her chest was going to explode. She punched in the entry code, yanked the door open, then bolted inside, pulling the door shut behind her. As soon as she heard the lock click into place, she pressed her face to the glass and looked outside, scanning the courtyard.

Empty.

She started at the right, scanning slower this time, looking for any sign of movement, and then she saw it, a shadow peeking around a bush. She squinted, trying to make out a shape in the shadows, and then it moved, separated from the shrubs.

It was a guy. Or person. She couldn't be sure what sex from this distance. They were average height and build, but that was all she could make out. The silhouette began to fade as they hurried away, then it disappeared into the darkness and she couldn't see it at all.

She turned around and leaned against the door, expelling the breath she didn't realize she'd been holding. She wasn't crazy. Someone had been following her. And it couldn't be for any good reason because if so, they would have followed her all the way to the dorm and knocked. First Amber, then Ethan, the text to Brenda, and now someone chasing her. What the hell was going on?

She checked her fitness watch and a second wave of fear passed over her when she saw her heart rate was well into danger territory. She took a deep breath and slowly blew it out, trying to slow her racing heart.

"Are you all right?" A voice sounded in front of her and she lifted her head up and saw a guy who lived across the hall from Ethan staring at her.

"Yeah. I was jogging and I'm in worse shape than I thought."

He raised his eyebrows. "That's a stupid outfit to jog in. You should really get some running shoes before you do it again. Then you might not trip and skin yourself up."

Her knee. Her hands.

She looked down and saw the tear in the knee of her jeans and the dark bloodstains on the denim. Both her hands were scratched and one still had blood oozing from one of the deeper tears.

"You're right," she said. "I guess I should clean this up. Thanks."

He shook his head as she hurried past him and continued down the hall to the girls' showers. She rinsed her hands off first and was happy to see that the scratches weren't as bad as they'd seemed. They stung something awful and were throbbing, but only one scratch was still bleeding and it was only a tiny bit. She wrapped a paper towel around it and bent over to assess her knee.

The jeans were history. A tear stretched from the top of her knee and a good three inches down the leg. It was also torn on the sides, so it flapped around like a denim door to her kneecap. She grabbed another paper towel and dampened it, then cleaned off her knee. There was a pretty decent-sized gash right in the center that was going to need a bandage, and she needed to clean all of it with peroxide to prevent infection. She had a small medical kit in her dorm room, but her fear of going back outside was much larger than her fear of infection.

Maybe Ethan had something in his room. He wouldn't care if she used something. Besides, she needed to sit and control her breathing until her pulse was down to a safe level. She headed out of the bathroom and down the hall to

Ethan's room, then knocked on the door. She heard banging inside, then the door swung open and Brett stared at her, blinking. He must have finally regained focus because he nodded and stood back to allow her inside.

"Sorry, Tara," he said. "I must have dozed off. I was trying to study for a history exam." He grinned. "That explains the dozing off part. Are you here about Ethan?"

"Sort of. I guess you haven't heard anything."

The grin disappeared. "No. I'm sorry for being a douche the other day when you said he was missing. I mean, college dudes sometimes need to take a break from stuff, you know? Sometimes a break with some beer and a hottie, but then I guess that's not really Ethan."

"No. It's not."

"I hope he's okay. We're nothing alike but he's a good guy." He looked at her hand and noticed the paper towel. "Did you hurt yourself?"

"I...uh, fell, on my way over here and skinned up my hands and knee. I was hoping Ethan had some peroxide and a bandage I could use."

"I don't know what he has but I'm sure he wouldn't care if you looked through his stuff. If you can't find anything, the nurse has everything. Between football and doing stupid shit when I'm drunk, I'm sort of a regular over there."

"Thanks."

He looked outside and frowned, then grabbed his phone from his rumpled bed and checked the display. "Shit. I've got to run. If you can sit still until the bleeding stops on your knee, you're better off. It's impossible to keep from bending it when you walk. I've tried."

"You don't mind if I stay here for a while?"

He shrugged. "I don't care. There's a few sodas left in the refrigerator. Without Ethan here, I had to make a store run myself." He opened the door, then turned around and looked at her. "Let me know if you hear anything, okay?"

She nodded and he closed the door. Seconds later, she could hear his footsteps as he ran down the hall. Instantly, her back and neck tensed as she recalled every frightening second of her run across the courtyard. It was the footsteps that reminded her, right? She looked over at Brett's side of the room and frowned. A black hoodie, inside out, was tossed on his desk chair, about to slip onto the floor.

She reached over and picked up the hoodie and turned it right side out. When she pulled the fabric straight, pieces of leaves fell out of the hoodie and onto the floor. She picked up one of the leaves. It was just like the ones from the shrubs in the courtyard.

Stop!

Before she got all hysterical, she needed to think. Plenty of people had black hoodies and while most of them probably didn't go running through shrubs, she definitely wouldn't put it past Brett. Besides, he was in the room sleeping when she knocked. Wasn't he?

But then, he could have slipped into the building while she was in the bathroom and pretended to be asleep.

You're talking about Brett here. He's not that smart.

But was she sure about that? If Brett was some genius

killer but didn't want people to catch on, wouldn't playing the dumb college jock be the perfect disguise? She turned the hoodie inside out again and put it back on the chair, trying to remember exactly how it was lying when she'd found it. Then she pulled open Ethan's closet and located a first aid kit.

She knew a guy on the second floor who worked part time for campus security. He usually had one of their golf carts at the building. She would doctor up her hands and knees and ask him to give her a ride to her dorm. She'd limp if she had to in order to convince him. Originally, she'd thought about staying in Ethan's room in case whoever had chased her knew where she lived. But now, nowhere seemed safe. At least in her own room, she had another can of Mace.

And first thing tomorrow, she was going to buy more.

Shaye stepped out of the shower and wrapped her long hair in a towel. It had been a long and trying day, and she knew she needed to rest, but part of her was excited about taking on a new investigation. She'd worried that she wouldn't be able to commit to it again. That the service she'd wanted so badly to offer would become part of a big nightmare constantly recycling in her mind and leaving her unable to perform well enough to do the job.

But as she'd listened to Tara's story, everything that she'd known from before came filtering back in. Her assessment of the client and the story, even that tickle in her gut. It was all there. Now she just needed to make sure she stayed sharp and watched her back as she'd never watched it before.

Corrine was right. As soon as the press latched onto her, it would make things harder, and the last thing she wanted was for the New Orleans police to find out she was investigating a case that they'd declined to look into. It was typical Vincent, but at what point did the department learn from past mistakes? Vincent had turned her away the first time she'd gone to the police on behalf of a client. That hadn't work out so well for him or the victims.

She dried off and walked into her room and pulled a wrinkled pair of shorts and tee from the travel bag she still hadn't unpacked and probably wouldn't. Unpacking meant she was staying a while, but that wasn't what Shaye wanted. As soon as she felt Corrine was stable and occupied enough to manage everything, Shaye would return to her apartment in the French Quarter and continue her efforts to move on with her life.

She didn't have a choice in becoming a victim, but she definitely had a choice in remaining one.

Shaye wasn't about to give the people who had abused her the satisfaction, just in case they could see her from the grave. If all her years talking with Eleonore had taught her anything it was that a person should be judged by what they do, not what was done to them. She was determined to help people get through the worst times in their lives so that they could regroup and move on to better things. And she truly believed better things were always out there for the taking.

She checked her phone and saw she'd missed three calls from Tara. Crap. She'd left her phone upstairs while she was talking to Corrine and hadn't checked it before getting into the shower. The first call was thirty minutes ago, then two more within ten minutes of each other, the latest one just minutes before.

She put the phone on speaker and listened to the first message while she dressed. Tara sounded excited and scared but hadn't given any details. The second message was different. Again, Tara asked her to call as soon as possible, but her voice had taken on a tone that was all fright and no excitement. On the third call, she'd disintegrated into frantic.

Shaye reached for the phone and dialed Tara. The girl answered on the first ring and started talking so fast that Shaye had to interrupt her and ask her to repeat what she'd just said.

"This girl, Brenda, got a text with one of those messages like Ethan got," Tara said. "It had a picture of Ethan with it." Her voice broke as she delivered the last sentence.

"You're certain it's Ethan?"

"Positive. He has this mole on his left cheek. He looked...looks dead. Oh my God, what if he's dead?"

"Don't panic. Until we are certain of anything different, we have to operate on the assumption that Ethan is still alive."

"Yeah. Okay. I can do that."

"I know this is scary," Shaye said, "and it's a lot to deal with, but we'll get through it."

"Someone was following me."

Shaye's hand clenched the phone. "When?"

"After Brenda left, I started across campus for my dorm. I heard someone behind me but I couldn't see anyone. He must have been in the bushes, which just freaked me out even more. I mean, why would someone hide in the bushes unless they were, you know…so I started running and he came after me."

"Did you see him?"

"No. I could hear him behind me and he was getting closer. I tried to look back, and I tripped and fell. I didn't even think about looking then. Just got up as fast as I could and ran straight for Ethan's dorm because it was the closest."

Shaye's heart clenched as the girl described her experience. She's been in the same position before and it was terrifying. "Did you hurt yourself when you fell?"

"I skinned up my hands and knee and they're probably going to hurt like heck tomorrow, but I was more worried about having a heart attack. My pulse rate still hasn't dropped to normal."

Shaye's grip tightened even more on the phone. She'd forgotten about Tara's heart condition. "Do you need me to take you to the hospital?"

"I don't think so. I've been monitoring my pulse and it's coming down, just not as quickly as my doctor says is acceptable, but I'm sure fear is keeping it from moving any faster."

"I'm sure it's making things harder, but if it doesn't continue to drop, you have to go to the hospital."

"I will. But why was he chasing me? What if he knows where I live? The dorms have pass codes, but people leave windows open and buzz anyone in without even checking."

"You have a lock on your room, right?"

"Yeah, but they're cheap. I forgot my key last week and opened it with my driver's license."

"What about your family? Can you go home until we figure this out?"

"My parents are missionaries in South Africa and the rest of my family is out of state."

"Do you have a roommate?"

"Darla, but she had her tonsils out this week and won't be back until next week at the earliest." Tara sucked in a breath. "What if he gets me, too? It could be days before anyone found me. Ethan's roommate is around a lot and someone still managed to get Ethan. I have to go to class. I have to stay in the dorm."

Tara picked up pace with every word she said and Shaye could tell she was starting to hyperventilate.

"Okay, I need you to calm down," Shaye said. "Take a deep breath in and blow it out slowly."

Shaye heard Tara take in a breath and then release the air.

"That's better," Shaye said. "Where are you now?"

"I'm in my dorm room. I had a guy who works

security give me a ride here from Ethan's building."

"Give me your address. I'll be there in about thirty minutes. In the meantime, can you find someone to talk to so that you're not alone?"

"There's a couple of people watching television in the rec room. I can go there."

"Good. I'll call when I'm there so you can let me in. Get yourself a bottle of cold water if you have it and remember to take long deep breaths and keep an eye on your pulse."

"Thirty minutes? Swear?"

The fear in Tara's voice broke Shaye's heart. "I promise."

Shaye tossed her phone on the bed and yanked a pair of sweatpants and bra out of her bag. They were just as wrinkled as the shorts and tee, but she was fairly certain Tara wouldn't care. The girl was freaked out and Shaye didn't blame her in the least. The situation was frightening and it appeared to be escalating.

"Do you want me to heat up some steak?" Corrine poked her head into Shaye's room and frowned. "Are you going out again? I thought you were in for the night."

"Change of plans," Shaye said, and gave Corrine a brief rundown on Tara. "I need to make sure she's okay. Her family all live out of state and her parents are missionaries in South Africa. She doesn't have another adult around to help her."

"That poor girl. Is there anything I can do?"

Shaye headed to the door and kissed Corrine on her

cheek. "Don't wait up, and don't worry."

"I can handle the first. You can forget about the second."

"I figured as much."

Shaye headed out to the garage and hopped into her SUV. So far she'd gotten lucky and no news van had been out front when she'd left that morning or returned that night, but she knew that wouldn't last long. She inched up to the gate without turning her headlights on and checked the street.

Clear.

She pressed the remote to open the gate and turned out onto the street. She just needed to make a quick stop for hardware and then she'd head straight to Tara's dorm. She hoped the people Tara mentioned were still watching television. Shaye didn't want to imagine the girl scared and alone in her dorm room. She was safer with other people around.

CHAPTER TEN

Brenda crept down the hall and stopped before she reached the living room. The television was on, playing the news. She could see the top of her mother's head over the couch. She crept closer and heard a faint snore. She smiled. The brownies always worked. Her mother couldn't resist them and the overdose of sugar put her out like a light. Or maybe it was the cold medicine Brenda had slipped into her mother's milk. Regardless, she could count on a good two hours of her mother snoring on the couch before she headed down the hall for bed.

She'd check on Brenda before she went to bed, but that could be managed as well.

Brenda went down the hall and into her bedroom, then stuck her body pillow in her bed and retrieved the mannequin head from the back of her closet where she kept it hidden in a boot box. She put the head on the pillow, slipped a wig and a set of headphones on it, then she pulled the covers up so that only the hair and the headphones were visible. She turned her stereo on so that the lights were on and turned the volume to zero.

When everything was set, she put on her tennis shoes

and pushed open her bedroom window. Her mother had an alarm installed on the house the previous year, but Brenda had quickly figured out how to disable the connections on her window. With the alarm armed and the figure of Brenda in the bed sleeping, her mother would go straight to bed without another thought, and Brenda would have an entire night to herself.

She'd done it enough times to know.

She swung one leg over the windowsill and stepped into the flower bed. She reached back to close the window, then set out down the sidewalk. It was a two-mile walk to the French Quarter but she'd done it a million times. The fall air was a little chilly, and she was glad she'd worn her sweatshirt. She pulled her cell phone out of her pocket and sent a text to Zack, telling him to meet her at Club 21. Her fake ID wasn't great, but they never looked closely there.

A few seconds later, Zach texted back okay, and she smiled. Her mother could try all she wanted to keep Brenda down, but one day she'd understand it was a losing battle. You couldn't lock up a free spirit. It simply didn't work.

At the end of the block, she turned the corner and headed toward the French Quarter. Another thirty minutes and she'd be sipping a beer and putting the moves on the sexiest guy on the swim team. She'd been admiring his body from a distance for months now. It was time to take that admiration up close and very personal.

She never knew he was behind her until something cold and hard struck the back of her head. Then everything went black.

Tara sat in the rec room with three other girls, staring at the television but not seeing or hearing a single thing. In fact, if someone had asked her what they were watching, she wouldn't be able to answer. Every time the volume ticked up she had to force herself to keep from jumping and screaming. Then she reminded herself to breathe, and she calmed down enough to check her phone and see that all of two minutes had passed since the last time she'd almost freaked out. She sighed. At least her pulse rate had continued to drop. It still wasn't back to normal, but then she couldn't expect her pulse to be normal when her stress level was still through the roof.

She'd left her dorm room right after she hung up with Shaye and had been in the rec room for twenty-five minutes now. Shaye should be here any minute. Assuming she actually made it in thirty minutes. Her apartment wasn't far away from the campus, but from the layers of dust on the furniture and the floor, Tara had gotten the impression Shaye hadn't stayed there in a while. Which meant she was probably at her mother's place in the Garden District.

Everyone knew where Corrine Archer lived. Her house had been featured in every home-and-garden magazine in the city. Corrine's house wasn't too far away, either, but there was always construction or a stoplight that was out or drunks blocking the street. Anything could put her a little behind. It was way too soon to panic. If forty minutes passed and Shaye hadn't turned up, then Tara would call her.

Fifteen more minutes.

She had to sit here and pretend she was normal for at least fifteen minutes. She checked her phone again. One more minute passed. This was never going to work. She got up from the couch and walked down the hall but didn't round the corner to the front door. With the double doors to the rec room open, the girls in there could see her in the hallway. No one would bother her if there were witnesses. At least, that's what she hoped.

At the end of the hall, she turned around and walked back toward the rec room. When she reached the doorway, one of the girls looked up at her.

"Are you all right?" the girl asked.

"Leg cramp," Tara said. "I jogged earlier. Probably should have started slower."

The girl nodded. "I did that when I first started. Take some potassium. It will help with the cramps."

"Thanks." She turned around and paced the length of the hall again. She hadn't been lying when she'd complained of cramps. Her calves had knotted into two stones inside her skin, but she wasn't about to go in search of potassium. Besides, it would probably take a truckload of the stuff to fix her.

She was on her fifth pass down the hall when she got a text message. Shaye was there. Tara hurried to the front door, peering out one of the glass panes, waiting for Shaye to arrive. When she saw the PI appear from between two parked cars, relief coursed through her. She waited until

Shaye was right at the door before unlocking it and pulling it open.

Shaye hurried inside and Tara quickly closed the door behind her.

"Are you all right?" Shaye asked, looking at her bandaged hand.

"It's fine," Tara said. "My knee got the worst of it. I should be able to take this off tomorrow."

"Good. Can you show me your room? I stopped for reinforcements." Shaye held up a bag that read Murphy's Hardware.

"Sure. It's on the second floor. I usually take the stairs but if you don't mind, I'd rather take the elevator. It's slow as Christmas but my calves are killing me."

Shaye nodded and followed her into the elevator. "Your muscles knotted up from the sprinting."

"Big time. When this is over, I'm going to slowly introduce some running into my routine—with my doctor's permission, of course. You don't realize how hard it is until you need to do it."

"That's true," Shaye said. "My goal is five miles three times a week. Sometimes things interfere, but when I go too long without getting the five in, I feel it."

Tara shook her head. "And you really need to be in shape, with your job and all. I don't know how you do this every day…chasing bad guys. The entire time I was running, all I could think about was how he would kill me if he caught me. When I fell, I almost passed out from fear alone. I've been in the rec room forcing myself to sit still, and every time the volume on the television changed, I almost came out of my skin."

"I'd love to tell you that you get to a point where you feel indestructible, but I'd be lying. However, you can build up your confidence in your ability to defend yourself or flee a dangerous situation. You should take a self-defense course, at the very least. You might even find that you enjoy it and continue with a martial arts class."

Tara nodded as they exited the elevator and walked down the hall to her dorm room. "They offer self-defense courses free at the university. I keep meaning to sign up and never do. I bet I'll be first in line when they start up again."

Tara pulled out her key and unlocked the door to her room. She pushed it open and stepped inside. "Please excuse the mess. I've been studying a lot and it's gotten kinda bad."

Shaye smiled as she stepped inside, then closed and locked the door behind them. "I was in Ethan's room, remember? Brett's side gives a whole new meaning to the word 'pigsty.'"

Tara forced a smile. "That's true. It drives Ethan crazy. Do you want to see the text?"

She'd been dreading this part, somehow afraid that Shaye would look at the text and decide there was no hope. That Tara's memories of Ethan were all she had from this point forward. She knew it was crazy thinking but no matter how hard she tried, she couldn't seem to force her mind back to rational.

"Not yet." Shaye put her hand on Tara's arm and gave it a light squeeze. "First, I want to help you feel safe here. Then you can tell me everything."

"I don't want to keep you. I mean, I do but it's not fair. You have a life and all."

"I'm not going anywhere. You said your roommate won't be back for a week, right?"

Tara nodded.

"Then would you mind if I stayed the night?"

The energy drained out of Tara's body and she flopped down onto the bed as her knees buckled. The tears she'd been holding in spilled out, and she swiped at them with her hand. The relief of having someone she trusted stay the night with her—the kindness of a woman who was essentially a stranger—had completely done her in.

"Thank you," Tara managed to get out between sobs.

Shaye sat on the bed next to her and put her arm around Tara's shoulders. "It's good to let it out. Holding in the tears doesn't make pain or fear go away."

Tara sniffed and rubbed her nose with her fingers. "What does?"

"Facing it head-on."

Tara knew Shaye was right. Jesus, the woman was the poster girl for survival and recovery. If Shaye could go through everything she had and still come out sane, then Tara should be able to deal. She owed it to Ethan and to herself.

"I want to do that," Tara said. "I just don't know where to start."

"Let me be clear. You don't have to remain here to face your fear. If you can leave school until this is over, no one is going to fault you for that."

Tara bit her lip. The thought of running off to her aunt's house in Idaho had crossed her mind a million times while she was waiting on Shaye, but no matter how tempting it was, she didn't consider it a viable option.

"I can't," Tara said finally. "I have midterms coming up and if I miss them, I'll fail my classes and lose my scholarship. That's why Ethan was tutoring me in calculus. I have to keep my grades up."

"Okay. Then you'll stay here and I'll help you figure out how to deal."

"Thanks," Tara said, grateful for any advice Shaye could provide. "What's in the bag?"

Shaye pulled out a dead bolt. "I'm sure the university would frown on my changing the locks, but they can't complain about a dead bolt. When you're inside, you make sure this is latched. Unless someone kicks the door down, they're not getting past this."

Some of her fear began to dissipate and Tara felt something she hadn't in days. Hope.

"Do you have any night classes?" Shaye asked.

"Not this semester."

"Good. During the day, make sure you're around other people. No shortcuts through alleys or in between buildings. Even if it means your sore calves and pitiful knee have to walk twice as far to get where you need to go. Main pathways with people on them only. At night, you lock yourself up in here."

Tara nodded. She could do this. It would be easy enough to make sure people were around during the day and at night, she could hole up in her room, and that dead bolt meant she'd be able to get the sleep she needed to keep going.

"Just give me a couple minutes to get this installed," Shaye said and headed to the door with the dead bolt and a screwdriver. "Then you can tell me everything that happened. Do you have something to drink? Have you taken an aspirin or something for the pain?"

"I took a Tylenol earlier, and I have some water in the fridge. Would you like one?"

"Thanks, but not right now."

"Okay, then I think I'll go to the bathroom and rewrap my knee. The bandage is loosening some."

"Would you like for me to come with you?"

"No. It's just down the hall and I can scream pretty loud." Tara gathered up her first aid kit and a washcloth and headed down the hall to the bathroom. Just having Shaye there and knowing she'd stay the night had already relieved so much of her stress. At least the part associated with being killed while she slept. The dead bolt would help her sleep after Shaye was gone.

She removed the old bandage from her knee and gave it a once-over. The bleeding had stopped, so she cleaned it again, reapplied antibacterial cream, and bandaged it up. Her knee was already slightly swollen, and Tara expected she'd be walking a little stiff the next day. But she was still in far better shape than she could have been.

Don't think about it.

She shook her head. It did no good to imagine what that psycho might have done to her. She needed to focus on helping Shaye find Ethan. He was the one in real danger. She packed up her supplies and headed back to her room, surprised to see that Shaye had finished with the install.

"That was fast," Tara said.

"I've had some experience."

"Right. Sorry, I keep forgetting about all of that, uh, stuff. You're so together and I can't imagine being that way if those things had happened to me."

"You'd be surprised what a hard head and a great psychiatrist can do for you."

Tara smiled. "I love that you're serious but still have a sense of humor. When I'm an adult, I want to be like that."

"Then I'm sure you will be. Are you ready to tell me what happened?"

"Yeah." Tara put her bathroom supplies in the closet and sat cross-legged on her bed. Shaye kicked off her tennis shoes and mimicked her position on her roommate's bed. Tara started her recount with bumping into Brenda, pausing only long enough to pass Shaye her phone with the forwarded text message, and continued all the way until her mad dash into Ethan's dorm. Shaye listened in absolute silence.

When Tara finished, Shaye shook her head. "That's really scary. I'm sorry you had to experience it."

"Me too."

Shaye looked at the phone. "This definitely looks like Ethan, and it fits with the strange message Ethan received and the subsequent death."

"So you think the text was about Amber?"

"Seeing this, it's difficult to find a reason why it wouldn't have been. Tell me about Brenda. How well did Ethan know her?"

"I don't think he knew her at all. Neither did I. I saw her at a party recently but that's it. Until this evening, we've never even spoken."

Shaye frowned. "No apparent connection between Ethan and either girl, but there has to be something because the same person has targeted them all. Do you know anything about Brenda?"

"Nothing at all. I don't even know her last name. God, that was stupid! Why didn't I ask?"

"Don't worry about that. I can trace her cell phone number and get a name."

"And then what?"

"I need to find out everything I can about Amber and Brenda. There is a connection to Ethan. We just don't know what it is."

"How does finding that out help?"

"Because my guess is, whoever is targeting them is the only connection they share."

"Oh, so if you find out what they have in common, you know who took Ethan."

"That's the idea." Shaye looked down at the phone. "I

also need to figure out this code."

"Do you think it will really lead to Ethan?"

"Maybe. Or it could send someone walking into a trap. But it's still important that I figure it out. It could help me identify the killer."

Tara pulled her legs up and wrapped her arms around them, a sudden chill passing through her.

"That's what he is, right?" Tara asked quietly. "He killed Amber."

"I don't know that for sure yet, but I'm leaning strongly toward yes."

Tara looked down at the floor, then back at Shaye. "Do you think he's planning to do the same thing to me? Is that why he chased me?"

Shaye shook her head. "I don't know."

CHAPTER ELEVEN

Wednesday, October 28, 2015

Jackson rolled out of bed at 6:00 a.m. and trudged into the kitchen for coffee. He'd remembered to set the automatic timer the night before, so the fragrant scent already permeated the room, giving him a lift with just the smell. He grabbed a cup and filled it up before reaching for his cell phone. He frowned when he saw a text from Shaye.

Call me as soon as you can.

Five a.m. There was being a morning person and there was alert and working at 5:00 a.m. He assumed she'd sent the message so early because she wanted to speak to him before he got to work. Was it personal or was she working a new case? He shook his head. She'd just gotten back a day ago. Even if she'd wanted to start back to work, she had to have a client. And since only a handful of people knew she was back in town, that seemed rather a long shot.

But what else could it be? Shaye was hardly the type to text him at that hour if it wasn't important. Maybe the media had found out about their return. Maybe it was a zoo over at Corrine's home and they needed help. He sat down at his kitchen table and dialed her number, slightly surprised when she answered on the first ring.

"Are you all right?" he asked. Her voice sounded normal. Maybe a tiny bit strained, but nothing screamed "I'm in the middle of a breakdown" to him.

"I'm fine, but I need to talk to you. Can I swing by before you go to work?"

"Yeah. I leave here at seven thirty. Come by any time before then."

"Great. I'll be there in ten minutes."

She disconnected the call and he stared at the phone in dismay. Ten minutes? Corrine's house was a good twenty minutes away with traffic, and even if Shaye was at her apartment, she'd be pressed to make the drive in that amount of time.

Where the hell was she? And why was she already out this early in the morning?

He took another sip of the coffee, then headed into the bedroom to throw on some clothes. The one thing he was certain of was that Shaye would never waste his time. Whatever was going on was big, and the only thing he could think of that she'd come to him for at this hour was police help. He pulled on a pair of jeans and blew out a breath.

The acting chief had made it crystal clear that he didn't want Jackson spending time with Shaye. Granted, the man had admitted that he couldn't force Jackson to end any personal relationship, but he could hold his feet to the fire if he felt Jackson was sharing confidential information with her about ongoing investigations, or if he felt Shaye had accessed information through Jackson in order to solve a case for a client.

The long and short of it was that people were watching, and Jackson's relationship with Shaye had to be 100 percent aboveboard because his job was on the line. That didn't mean he wouldn't help Shaye if she needed it and he was able, but it meant he had to be extremely careful about the manner and method of any help he gave.

Shaye was a reasonable person. She would understand.

At least, he hoped she'd understand.

He managed to finish a full cup of coffee and start on another before the doorbell rang. He opened it to let Shaye in and took a couple seconds to take in her appearance. It was clear that she hadn't slept much. Her eyes had dark circles underneath them and the lightness in her step was missing as she moved into the kitchen and reached for the extra coffee mug he'd placed on the counter.

Her clothes were an odd choice as well. Shaye was not one of those women who refused to leave the house unless she was fully made up, every hair in place, and garbed in designer wear, but wrinkled sweatpants and a T-shirt were more of an exercise thing than a work thing. Nothing about her expression or demeanor led him to believe she'd been out jogging and suddenly needed to speak to him, so he was anxious to hear what was going on.

She took a sip of the coffee and closed her eyes for a couple seconds, then took another sip. "I almost feel human again," she said.

He waved her to the table and she sat down, clutching the mug with both hands. He waited for her to talk, but she took another drink of the coffee and sat in silence.

"Are you sure you're all right?" he asked. "You look a little...uh, ruffled."

"Ha. That's a polite way to put it. I look like something the cat dragged in."

"Did something happen to Corrine?"

"She's fine. She's not overly happy with recent decisions of mine and I expect an earful when I get home, but that's to be expected. It's been a long time since she could yell at me for staying out all night."

"What were you doing?"

"I was sitting guard in a dorm room on the Lafitte University campus."

Jackson frowned. If anything she'd just said was supposed to make sense, then he might need another cup of coffee himself. "I'm sorry, but I'm completely lost."

"I know. I want to explain, but I'm trying to figure out the best place to start. I guess I'll start with my client."

"Client? You're working a case? How can that be? You just got back here."

"And the client just happened to show up at my apartment when I was there yesterday. She told me a story I couldn't refuse."

Shaye began to tell Jackson about her case, starting with Tara's story and ending with the reason Shaye had spent a sleepless night in a college dorm room. When she finished, he leaned back in his chair and shook his head.

"Just when you think you've heard everything," he said, "now we have pre-obituaries being dealt out by text."

"When I got home last night Corrine told me about your visit as a landscaping professional. I would have paid money to see Grayson dressed down, by the way."

Jackson smiled. "He was less than enthusiastic about the wardrobe requirements."

"She also told me why you were there. I hope that doesn't get her a black mark."

"I'm not worried about you repeating what you were told."

"I won't, but I can't push it out of my mind either. When Corrine was telling me about the case, I got a bad feeling. That kind that makes you itchy?"

Jackson frowned. "You think your missing boy and Ross St. Claire are somehow related?"

Shaye nodded. "And the girl in the coffin, Amber Olivier."

"What are you basing the connection on?"

"Nothing concrete, and that's the problem. They're all college students, but none of them were friends that I'm aware of. I'm going to look into that more today. I know Amber's death is an open investigation, and I know she died horribly of suffocation fighting to get out of that coffin."

"And you know that how?"

Shaye smiled. "I have my sources."

"Clara Mandeville."

"I can neither confirm nor deny. Can you tell me if

Amber's death has been declared a homicide?"

Jackson knew he shouldn't tell her anything at all, but that was the politics talking. Shaye was hardly going to walk out of his apartment and sell the information to the highest-bidding news channel. The reason the police played things close to the vest was to make it easier to catch perpetrators. As soon as details of a case surfaced, it gave people an exact idea of which tracks to cover.

"It's a suspicious death given the circumstances," he said, "but it hasn't been ruled a homicide yet."

"They think it might be a sorority prank gone wrong," Shaye said. "She had Rohypnol in her system."

He nodded. "Unfortunately, not exactly uncommon among the college-age crowd."

"I have to ask—how did Ross St. Claire die? If you can't tell me, I understand."

He knew he shouldn't tell her. If the acting chief found out, Jackson would be kissing his detective career good-bye, but then he thought about the possibility that Shaye presented—that one person had targeted three kids—and he thought "to hell with it."

"He was tied to a tree and a plastic bag was duct-taped over his head," Jackson said.

"He suffocated."

"Yeah. I didn't make the connection on cause of death to the Olivier case," he said, feeling frustrated.

"No one did because the police are still assuming Amber's death could have been an accident. And since the fabulous and always consistent Vincent blew off my client, no one knew that yet another college student was missing and he might have had information about Amber's death. Where was Ross's body found?"

"A hiking trail."

"Doesn't sound like an easy task—carting an unconscious man down a hiking trail."

"It was near the beginning and fairly flat. Our guess is he used a cart of some sort, maybe a wheelbarrow, but it rained that night, so any tracks were long gone by the time we got there."

Shaye pulled out her cell phone and showed him the text that Brenda had received. "That's Ethan Campbell, the boy who received the text with what he believed was Amber's picture. He had no idea who she was, but now he's missing. Brenda, the girl who received this text about Ethan, has never even spoken to him before."

"So if we knew why they were targeted—"

"We'd know who was targeting them. That's what I believe, anyway. I need Tara to report this to the police. I'll keep working things from my end, but there's too much I don't have access to. You need to officially have all the information I have so you can connect these cases and work them as one."

He blew out a breath. Nothing about Shaye's theory could be proven but damn it if he didn't believe she was onto something. "Bring Tara in. I'll have Grayson talk to her."

"What will Chief Rhinehart say?"

"Not a damned thing. You're bringing a frightened girl

to the station to report a crime. Her friend is missing and she was stalked. If anything, he should be apologizing for Vincent, but there's nothing he can fault you for just for bringing her in."

"Okay," she said, and rose from the table. "As far as I'm concerned, we never had this conversation. If Chief Rhinehart asks, tell him I asked you to set up an interview between my client and Grayson. You need to make the connections after the interview if Grayson doesn't."

He nodded. "I don't have to tell you to be careful."

"No. But it's nice to hear."

Silas checked up and down the block before he slipped behind the hedges and headed to the back of the abandoned house. All the windows had been boarded up but he'd removed the plywood from one on the back—the one that none of the neighbors could see from upstairs in their own homes. At a glance, it looked like the plywood was still in place, but all he had to do was lift it up a bit and it slid right off the nails that were propping it up.

He couldn't remember exactly how long he'd been homeless. Living on the streets tended to blur one's focus on time. Everything moved slowly when you had no job or money, unless you had a fix. Then days could be lost in a drug-induced haze. It might be three years. That sounded about right but he'd have to know the date to be sure.

Anyway, the last couple months had been different

from the rest. He'd finally kicked the drug habit, which is what had put him on the street to begin with. Family and friends had tried to help, but attempting to get in between a dedicated junkie and drugs was a waste of everyone's time and eventually, people wised up and cut their losses. Then he'd found the girl behind the Dumpster.

She'd been young, maybe fifteen or sixteen, most likely a runaway. The needle was still sticking out of her arm. Her final pose on this earth. But the girl wasn't what disturbed him. He'd seen plenty of overdoses. It wasn't exactly uncommon with people in his situation. No, what had sent him straight for a priest and NA was the dead baby on her chest.

Probably, the baby had been born addicted and the poor thing never stood a chance, but something about that tiny pale infant, who would never cry again, pierced Silas straight to the core. He'd been clean for fifty-eight days now and employed for two weeks. It was a night shift at the docks, loading and unloading, with low pay and no benefits, but it was the first legitimate work he'd had in years.

Another couple months of squatting and he'd have enough saved to get his own place. It would be small and rundown, but the apartments he had in mind were close to the dock. Once he got an address and some clean clothes, he might be able to find something that paid better. Or he might be able to pick up something part time to make some more.

But until then, this abandoned property was what he called home.

He slid the plywood off the nails and leaned it against the wall, then climbed in the window. He reached back and picked the plywood up, pulling it back into place using the two screws he'd attached to the back of it. With the window covered, the house was pitch black, but one of Silas's first purchases had been a flashlight. He didn't use it much because he didn't want to run down the batteries, but he kept it next to the window to help get him to the room he was using as a bedroom.

He reached down and felt around, trying to locate the flashlight, which was usually against the wall and just to the right of the window ledge. But his hand passed through open air, not connecting with anything. Frowning, he bent down and used both hands this time, wondering if the flashlight had tipped over, maybe even rolled. The floors weren't level, so it was a possibility. When his extended search yielded nothing, he rose back up and removed the plywood from the window, allowing the moonlight inside. If the flashlight had rolled somewhere, he'd never find it in the dark.

He turned around to scan the room that used to be a kitchen and realized something large and covered with a blanket was in the corner. Something that wasn't there before today.

Someone had found his hideaway.

He reached into his pocket and pulled out his hunting knife. They may not have real homes, but the homeless were highly protective of the spot they'd chosen to stay. Invaders were often violent and needed persuading to move on.

He crept toward the corner, silently cursing every time the floorboards let out a shriek, but the lump in the corner never stirred, not even a tiny bit. Probably stoned. He hoped that meant it was one of the milder drugs. He'd made the mistake once of taking on a girl on PCP and despite the fact that he had a good fifty pounds and four inches on her, it had taken three men to get her off of him. After that, he'd learned the signs of a PCP high and had avoided those people like the plague. You never knew what might set them off.

When he reached the lump, he paused, not sure how to handle it. Finally, he decided an attack was the best way to scare the intruder into finding a different place to squat. He clutched the knife in his right hand, ready to jab if the intruder jumped up to fight, and reached out with his left hand and pinched the top of the blanket. He blew out a breath and started counting.

One. Two. Three.

He yanked the blanket off in a single tug and threw it behind him, jumping back at the same time in case the intruder charged.

It only took a second to determine the girl under the blanket couldn't attack anyone.

She was propped up in the corner, slumped against the wall, her legs and arms bound together and then tied to each other. Duct tape covered her mouth and nose and wrapped around the back of her head over and over again. He took a step closer and saw plastic peeking out of the top of the duct tape.

Her eyes were wide open with fright, probably struggling to free herself before she suffocated, but with her hands and feet bound together and to each other, she'd had no way of ripping the tape from her face. Silas's stomach rolled and for the first time in his life, he was glad he didn't have a lot of money for food. This was worse than just death. This was evil.

A piece of paper with writing on it was pinned to her shirt and he leaned over to make out the single word in the dim light.

Cheater.

Silas headed back for the window. He'd already seen more than he wanted to see.

CHAPTER TWELVE

Shaye drove straight to her apartment after she left Jackson's place. She'd already texted Corrine that she was fine but wouldn't be back until later. Right now, she wanted a shower and a change of clothes, but she wanted them both in peace. If she went back to her mother's house, Corrine would have a million questions that Shaye didn't have the energy or desire to answer.

She parked one block over and walked to the corner, scanning the street before she crossed it and let herself into her apartment. None of the cars parked on the street looked like they belonged to a news crew, but then it was early. Things could change once people got up and headed out for the job.

In her bedroom, she paused next to the bed and gave it a wistful look. Between the horribly uncomfortable dorm bed and Tara waking up every hour and tossing and turning in between, Shaye probably hadn't gotten a single stretch of sleep more than thirty minutes long. Around 4:00 a.m., she'd finally given up and started making notes on her laptop, then sent Jackson the text an hour later. By the time 6:00 a.m. rolled around, Tara had finally fallen into a deep sleep.

It would be light outside soon and Shaye had figured the girl was calm enough to handle the rest of the early morning by herself. She'd left Tara a note on her desk and made sure the door was locked behind her before she'd slipped out. As she was climbing into her SUV, Jackson had called and she'd driven straight to his house, not even stopping for a cup of much-needed coffee. Thank goodness he'd had a pot ready when she got there.

Forcing herself back into reality, she ignored the bed and headed into the bathroom and turned on the shower. While she usually preferred to stand under a hot stream of water until her skin turned pink, today called for cold to help her wake up. And wake her up, it did. She yelped when she stepped into the cold blast of water and turned around in circles, allowing it to run over her entire body, giving every inch of her the message that it was time to get moving.

Five minutes of turning and jiggling was all she could manage before she hopped out and grabbed a towel. She dried off and pulled on jeans, T-shirt, and tennis shoes and headed to the front door. A quick check of the street revealed no new cars parked since she had arrived, so she hurried to her SUV and directed it toward the campus. With any luck, Amber's sorority sisters would be up and moving around. Shaye wanted to talk to them before she took Tara to the police station.

Once Grayson heard Tara's story, and assuming he bought into the theory that it could all be the work of one perpetrator, the first thing they'd do would be to try and figure out the connection between Ethan, Amber, Ross, and Brenda. Which meant questioning all of the sorority sisters. Shaye had every right to talk to the girls herself, although she couldn't compel them to talk to her, but if other cops found out she was talking to potential witnesses on an open case, it could make trouble for her, Jackson, and Grayson. So her plan was to talk to as many of the sorority sisters as she could find before the police started doing the same thing.

Twenty minutes later, she knocked on the front door of the sorority house. It opened quickly and a young woman with long brown hair, full makeup, and a smile on her face answered the door. Behind her, Shaye saw several young women milling around, chatting, and preparing to start their day.

"Hi," Shaye said. "My name is Shaye Archer and I'm a private investigator."

The girl's eyes widened. "Oh my God. You're the lady from the news. You're famous." The girl clutched her arm. "I am so sorry for what happened to you. At first I thought it was all a really bad joke because who wants to believe there are people like that right here in New Orleans, but when I realized it wasn't a joke, I ate a whole chocolate pie and cried. We all did. I mean, you went to school here. You're practically one of us."

"Thank you," Shaye said, not sure what response was appropriate. She'd hoped her status as a younger woman might get the sisters to open up more than they might with a cop, especially a male one, but she hadn't counted on her horrific past getting her an honorary membership status. Not that she was complaining. If the sisters were that upset about what had happened to her, then they should be dying to talk about what happened to Amber.

"I'm Marybeth," the girl continued. "Do you want to come in? We have coffee and herbal tea. Some of the girls won't drink caffeine. I think that's crazy talk, but then I'm pretty sure my mom was giving me coffee in my bottle."

Shaye followed the girl inside and into the kitchen, where more girls were busy making breakfast and doing last-minute studying.

"Sisters," Marybeth announced. "I am so excited to introduce Shaye Archer. Can you believe she's in our house?"

All the sisters stopped what they were doing and looked at Shaye, most of them wide-eyed and staring. Finally one of them started clapping and the rest followed suit.

"Thank you," Shaye repeated, still completely lost as to what protocol was in this situation.

"Okay," Marybeth said, "I'm sure you didn't just stop by out of the blue to visit, so how can we help you?"

"I wanted to ask some questions about Amber Olivier. I'm sorry. I know it's got to be really hard for you right now, but I wouldn't be here unless it was important."

Everyone sobered at once and Shaye heard a few sniffles.

"They're blaming us, you know," Marybeth said

quietly. "The cops said it was a sorority prank, but it wasn't. We would never do a prank like that, especially to Amber."

"Why not?" Shaye asked. The specificity of the statement struck her as important.

"Amber was claustrophobic," Marybeth replied.

Shaye's stomach clenched as she imagined what the girl must have gone through when she realized she was trapped inside a coffin. "That's awful," Shaye said. "I didn't know."

"Most people didn't," Marybeth said. "Just her family and us. We told the police, but they just figured that gave us even more reason to put her in that horrible place. You know, as a test."

"I know it doesn't mean much," Shaye said, "but I don't think you had anything to do with Amber's death."

"Really?" Marybeth perked up a bit. "I was afraid maybe her parents sent you or something. I'm sure her mother believed us but Amber's father just looked angry."

Another girl stepped closer. "If you don't believe we did it, then what do you think happened? There's no way Amber climbed in that coffin willingly."

Shaye saw no reason to lie. The truth didn't require all of her reasoning or details of her case. "I believe she was murdered," Shaye said.

There was a collective intake of breath, and the girl who'd asked her the question nodded.

"I think so too," the girl said. "I'm Brittany. I'm a forensic science major. Only a junior, but I read a lot and watch a lot of documentaries. The others thought I was being morbid, but there's really only so many answers.

Either we did it, Amber did it, or someone else did it."

"I'm afraid you're right," Shaye said. "I'm so sorry for your loss."

"So if Amber's parents didn't hire you, then who did?" Marybeth asked.

"A student, who wants to remain anonymous. A friend of hers, also a student, is missing and the circumstances are suspicious. She retained me to find him."

"And you think the two are connected?" Brittany asked.

"That's what I'm trying to find out," Shaye said.

Brittany nodded and looked around the room. "Everyone who doesn't have class or can skip, go to the meeting hall. It will be more efficient for her to talk to all of us at once." She looked over at Shaye. "Is that all right?"

"Perfect." Shaye could barely control her excitement. It couldn't have been better if she'd scripted it herself.

"Can I get you something to drink?" Marybeth asked. "It might take a while."

"Water would be great," Shaye said.

Marybeth passed her a bottled water from the refrigerator, and Shaye followed her down a hallway toward the back of the house. They entered a huge room with the longest banquet table Shaye had ever seen. Twelve girls total, including Marybeth. If they didn't know anything, then there probably wasn't anything for Shaye to find here.

She pulled her laptop out of her shoulder bag and put it on the table. "If you guys don't mind, I'm going to take some notes. I assume you'd prefer not to be recorded."

"Definitely," Marybeth agreed. "My dad's attorney would have a heart attack. He's already halfway there just with the police being idiots."

"My dad *is* an attorney," one of the girls said. "I thought he was going to make me move out and join a convent."

Shaye nodded. "I understand the issues and I promise you, I only want information to try to help my client and her missing friend. I won't involve myself with anything that attempts to make trouble for you."

"Great," Marybeth said. "So where do you want to start?"

"Did Amber receive any strange text messages before she disappeared?" Shaye asked. "Specifically a text with a picture of another person?"

The girls shook their heads, then one of them frowned.

"There was that text from Ross St. Claire," the girl said. "He's a guy Amber knew from high school."

Shaye's pulse quickened. "And she told you about it?"

"Amber and I were roommates," the girl said. "I'm Katey, by the way. Amber wasn't a huge talker but she wasn't extremely private either. Just about certain things, like the claustrophobia."

"Were Amber and Ross friends? Did Amber tell you what the text said?"

"They definitely weren't friends," Katey said. "Amber thought he was pompous and mean, which is probably why the text made her mad. It had this picture of Ross and looked like he was passed out and said something like she had two days to find him or he would die."

Katey's eyes widened. "Oh my God. He's not dead, is he? I heard some guys talking in history class saying he was missing, but they figured he had skipped out to his parents' beach house."

Shaye hesitated, trying to formulate the right response. No way was she divulging unreleased police information but she also hated lying outright, especially when it was decent people she was lying to.

"I've been in another country until yesterday, so I'm out of the loop on most everything," Shaye replied. It wasn't a lie. More of an avoidance of the facts. "Did Amber hear that Ross was missing?"

Katey nodded. "Yeah, but she didn't think anything of it. He's hit on her before at a Greek mixer so she figured he was drunk texting."

"If she didn't like him, why would Ross have Amber's phone number?" Shaye asked.

Katey shrugged. "He asked around and got it probably."

Shaye believed what Katey said was true enough. College students tended to share and trust more than adults out in the workforce did, especially within their own social scene. But something told her that Ross wasn't the person who'd sought Amber's number, and if she knew who had, she'd have her killer.

"Do any of you know a student named Ethan Campbell?" Shaye asked. She would keep Tara's name out of the questioning, but without bringing Ethan into the conversation, she had no way of figuring out the connection.

All the girls shook their heads, and Shaye pulled up an image of Ethan on her cell phone that she'd cropped Tara out of. "Here's a picture of him," Shaye said. "Does he look familiar to anyone?"

Shaye handed the phone to the girl next to her and she studied it, then passed it down. It was almost back to Shaye when Brittany got hold of it and stared, her eyes widening.

"He's in my English class," Brittany said. "Sits in the back corner. Really quiet and really smart." She looked up at Shaye. "He's missing?"

"Yes," Shaye said. "He was last seen Sunday night, leaving his dorm to go to the convenience store."

Brittany made a face. "We stopped going to that store. The owner is crazy."

"What do you mean?" Shaye asked.

"A couple of us were in there one night when some frat guys came in drunk. They pushed a guy into a display and knocked the whole thing down. The owner's face turned so red I thought he was going to have a heart attack, and he screamed at them to get out or he'd call the police. He followed them all the way to the sidewalk, still yelling like a madman."

"Do you know who the guys were that he yelled at?" Shaye asked.

Brittany shook her head. "I didn't really pay attention to their faces, but one of them was wearing a T-shirt with a

Lafitte logo."

"Do you remember how long ago it happened?" Shaye asked.

"It was Tuesday before last," Brittany said. "I remember because we'd been studying all day for a biology exam and were burned out on coffee, so we went to get sports drinks."

"Great. Thanks," Shaye said, making a note of the date. "Is there anything else you guys can tell me? Was anyone bothering Amber? Was she afraid of anyone? Had her behavior changed in the days leading up to her death?"

The girls all looked at one another and shook their heads.

"Nobody is liked by everyone," Marybeth said, "but I can't think of anyone that Amber had real problems with. Petty jealousy over stuff is common, especially from girls who didn't make it through rush week, but everyone made it in this year."

"Did she have a boyfriend?" Shaye asked.

"No," Katey said. "She kinda liked this guy on the basketball team but she hadn't worked up the nerve to let him know."

"There was a high school boyfriend," Brittany said. "She told me about him once and I got the impression she was still kinda hung up on him. She said her dad made her break it off with him. Something about his family."

"Did she tell you his name?"

Brittany shook her head.

"What was her major?" Shaye asked, wondering if the

connection could somehow be academic.

"She hadn't picked one," Katey said. "She was taking basic requirements and trying to decide. Her dad is a doctor and he was pushing her to go into medicine, but I know she didn't have any interest."

Shaye made a note to get information on Amber's father. A successful physician might move in some of the same social circles as the St. Claires. Maybe that was where one of the connections was. "And her mother?" Shaye asked. "Did she work?"

"No," Katey said. "Amber said she came from a poor family out in the bayous and that her dad's parents were really upset when he married her. I know she volunteers for one of the homeless shelters. Not like *at* the shelter, but she gets people to donate clothes and food and stuff."

"Sounds like a nice woman," Shaye said.

Katey sniffed. "She is and she's falling apart. I went to see her yesterday and it was bad. I hope you find Ethan, and if the same person who took him killed Amber, then I hope you shoot them dead."

"Katey!" Marybeth stared at her sorority sister in dismay.

"I'm not apologizing," Katey said. "And I'm not taking it back. I meant it. Whoever did such a thing doesn't deserve to live. It's wicked."

Brittany put her hand on Katey's arm. "I don't think he deserves to live either."

Tara located the only pair of clean sweatpants she owned and bent over to put them on, but as soon as she lifted her leg, pain shot through her knee and she dropped her foot back onto the floor. She flopped onto the bed and leaned to the side, pulling the sweats over her foot while trying to keep her leg as straight as possible. It wasn't a perfect plan, but it was better than dressing standing.

She managed to wriggle her feet into her tennis shoes without bending the knee, then grabbed a new can of Mace from her desk and dropped it into her purse. The first thing she needed to do was see the school nurse about her hands and knee. She planned on playing up the headache and pain angle so that the woman would give her a medical pass. Most of Tara's instructors didn't care whether students attended class or not, but two were sticklers for attendance and marked off if you missed without a good reason.

The nurse's office was on the opposite end of campus from her dorm. It was a long walk when she was in good shape, but it was going to be painfully long with her banged-up knee. Resolved to a long morning of walking and aspirin, she headed out of the dorm. But when she reached the parking lot, she thought about Ethan's car. It was a much shorter walk to his dorm than to the nurse's office, and Ethan wouldn't mind if she borrowed his car, especially for this. As long as Brett was there, she could get Ethan's keys from his desk drawer.

She wavered for a bit, then finally turned and headed for Ethan's dorm. Worst-case scenario, Brett had decided to go to class today and she had an even longer walk to the nurse's office once she backtracked from Ethan's dorm. Hopefully, Brett was living up to his reputation and had partied all night and would be sleeping half the day.

Her knee did all right for most of the walk, but she did stop once to let it rest for a minute. Sometimes when she took a step, pain shot up and down the knee like a bolt of electricity was firing through her leg. She knew it was nerves but hoped they were just momentarily angry because of the injury and not because the wound was getting infected. She'd been careful about cleaning it, but maybe the nurse would give her an antibiotic just to be sure.

She knocked on Ethan's door and waited for any sign of life inside, then knocked again, this time louder. Another ten seconds or so passed with no sign of Brett and Tara sighed. Unless she just happened across a student she knew with a car who wasn't on their way to class or work, it looked like her knee was going to have to make do with a much longer walk. As she turned around to leave, the door swung open and Brett looked out at her.

One glance at his angry stare and Tara regretted her choice. All of the fears about Brett that she'd dismissed last night as irrational came flooding back in. Brett was a fool, but he was a big, strong guy. He could easily overpower her.

"Why are you banging on the door so early?" he asked. "And so loud. I'm trying to sleep."

"I need to borrow something of Ethan's," she said.

Brett turned around and walked back to his bed, then fell onto it and turned his back to her. She hesitated for a second, then hurried over to the desk and grabbed Ethan's keys from inside before practically jogging out the door and closing it behind her. She was so spooked, she didn't slow down until she was in the parking lot.

She climbed into Ethan's car and locked the doors, feeling overwhelmed and foolish. Her knee had hurt before, but now it was throbbing.

What is wrong with you?

She hadn't been this jumpy since junior high school when her older cousin had made her watch *Halloween*. It hadn't helped that it was October. She'd spent weeks having nightmares and jumping at every shadow. After the third night of being awakened by screaming, her mother had finally gotten the truth out of her, and once shared with her aunt, her cousin had been grounded.

Tara had never watched another horror movie again. To be honest, she wasn't a big fan of the news, either. It was all mostly scary and depressing. Look at what had happened to Shaye and to all those street kids. Tara had always known about the dangers surrounding her. Her mother had made sure of it. But something about the whole story surrounding Shaye had made her think yet again before she did things, and even more especially since Ethan had disappeared.

She started the car and drove to the nurse's office, making sure she overdid her limp as she walked inside. The nurse, an older woman who'd retired from the hospital a couple years before, took one look at her as she entered and shook her head.

"You poor thing," the nurse said. "What's wrong?"

"I banged up my knee pretty good last night," Tara said. "I cleaned it well and put antibiotic cream on it, but it hurts to walk and it's throbbing. I'm afraid it might be getting infected."

The nurse waved her toward the examination room. "Sit on the table and pull up your pants leg so I can take a look."

Tara climbed onto the table and exposed her knee. The nurse removed the bandage and inspected the wound, touched the red area around it with two fingers, then touched her calf in two different places.

"You did a decent job with the bandage," the nurse said. "Knees are a tough one to keep covered unless you have the luxury of not walking. How did it happen?"

"I fell last night on my way from the library to my dorm room."

The nurse raised one eyebrow. "Must have been walking pretty fast to do that kind of damage. It looks like you skidded some, the way the skin tore."

"I was running, actually," Tara said, seeing no reason to lie about part of the event. "It was dark and someone was following me."

The nurse narrowed her eyes at Tara. "Did you get a good look at him?"

Tara shook her head. "He was in the bushes at first and when I started running I could hear him behind me running as well. I fell trying to look back. I didn't try again after that."

"I don't blame you. That must have been frightening."

"It scared the shit out of me. I'm sorry—the crap."

"No apology needed. I imagine it's an accurate description. I had a guy come after me once when I was in my twenties and had just started at the hospital. I was working the night shift and he followed me to the parking lot. Put a gun in my face and took my wallet and my car."

"Oh my God." Tara couldn't imagine what she'd have done if her pursuer had caught her, but she was going to guess it would have involved fainting or simply having a heart attack on the spot.

"I was lucky. He didn't care anything about a young woman. There's plenty out there that do. You be careful. Even campus isn't safe for a woman alone at night. Try to stay with others and if you find yourself alone, call security. They can get out of that shack and walk you to your dorm."

"That's a good idea. Right now, my plan is to never be alone in the dark. Well, unless I'm sleeping."

The nurse smiled. "Good plan." She opened a cabinet behind her and took out bandages and gauze. "I'm going to clean this again and re-bandage it. It looks a little inflamed, which could be the start of an infection or from the bandage rubbing on it. The skin around it feels a little warmer to the touch than uninjured parts of your leg, so I'll play it safe and give you an antibiotic."

"Thank you. The last thing I need is an infection. It's hard enough to walk now."

"It's quite a hike from the dorms. Do you have a car?"

"No, but I borrowed a friend's."

"Smart. The more you can avoid walking, the quicker that wound will close."

"Believe me, I'd love nothing more than to go back to my dorm and sit on the rec room couch with my laptop, but I have a couple of professors who will mark off for no attendance."

The nurse shook her head. "Don't you worry about them. I'll write you a pass and they can't say a thing about it. I imagine after something like that, you wouldn't be much use in a classroom anyway. No sense risking your grade point average because you need a couple days to recover from a big scare. I'll be right back with the rest of the supplies."

Ten minutes later, Tara was back in Ethan's car, a package of antibiotics and a nurse's pass in her hand. Her knee smarted a little from all the activity and the cleaning, but it wasn't as bad as she'd thought it would be. She pulled her cell phone out of her pocket and checked the display. It hadn't made a peep all morning, but she couldn't help looking.

Tara had awakened early, but Shaye was already gone. She'd left Tara a note on her desk that she was going to check on something and would call her later that morning. They'd talked for hours the night before, Tara telling Shaye everything she knew about Ethan, hoping something would help the detective find him. Then Shaye had shown Tara security footage from the convenience store, hoping Tara might recognize some of the students who had entered the store around the time Ethan disappeared. But although a couple of them looked somewhat familiar, Tara didn't know any names.

She wondered what Shaye was checking on and if she'd found out anything useful. Ethan had been missing over two days now, and Brenda had received the text the day before. Time was running out. They needed to find Ethan before what happened to Amber happened to him.

Her cell phone rang and she let out a yelp, then mentally chastised herself for being so jumpy. She saw Shaye's name in the display and hurried to answer.

"How are you doing?" Shaye asked.

"Okay. I just had the nurse check out my knee. I got antibiotics and a two-day pass from classes."

"Good, because I need you to go with me to the police station and file a report."

"Why? They didn't want to listen last time."

"I've arranged for you to speak to Detective Grayson. He'll listen. I promise."

Tara bit her lip. "Does that mean you're quitting the case?"

"No. But I think this is bigger than either one of us realized, and the police need to know what we know. I'll still look for Ethan."

Some of the tension left Tara's shoulders. With Shaye and the police looking for Ethan, surely they could find him before things got really bad.

"Have you eaten breakfast?" Shaye asked.

"What? Uh, no."

"I'll pick you up in thirty minutes. We'll have a nice

breakfast so you can take those antibiotics, then we'll go talk to Detective Grayson."

"Okay." Breakfast sounded nice and she *was* hungry. Plus, it would give her time to prepare to talk to the police again. Maybe she'd flubbed it the first time and that's why they didn't take her seriously. But they had to if she was with Shaye, right?

"See you in thirty," Shaye said and disconnected.

Tara tossed her phone on the passenger seat with the drugs and the pass and started the car. Everything was going to work out. She'd talk to the police and they would find Ethan, and everything would go back to the way it was before all this crazy shit started happening.

She was going to keep repeating that until she believed it.

CHAPTER THIRTEEN

Jackson stared down at the girl in the abandoned house and shook his head. How many more young people were going to die before they figured out what was going on? The girl in front of him had yet to be identified, but her hoodie had the university name on it and she looked the right age to be a student. That made three dead and one missing from the same school.

He looked over at Grayson, who blew out a breath. Grayson's frustrated and somewhat nervous expression let Jackson know that his senior officer had reached the same conclusion Jackson had.

"We've got a real problem here," Grayson said.

Jackson glanced around to make sure no one was standing close enough to overhear. "We've got a serial killer."

"Shit! When is this city going to catch a break?"

Jackson shook his head. "I'm hoping before the boy Shaye told me about this morning winds up like this girl."

Grayson ran his hand through his hair. "You said she's bringing the girl in this morning to file a missing persons report, right?"

"Yeah. I gave her the go-ahead as soon as you agreed to do the interview. I don't want the girl running up against Vincent a second time or she may never talk to police again."

"Good. We have to find that boy before he's another name on a toe tag."

"If he's not already prepped for the position."

"You've got to think positive," Grayson said. "I know it's hard, especially with everything you just went through, and it's even worse because it all centered on someone you care about, but you've got to keep your mind on all the people you save. You can't dwell on the ones you couldn't or you'll be looking for another career."

"I know." Jackson had been telling himself for months that the work he'd done with Shaye had saved lives. A serial killer, stalker, and a human trafficker had been eliminated from the population, and there was no telling how many lives that saved over the next decades. But it was hard to absorb the ones already lost and even harder to absorb the damage that those still living had to cope with every day.

Grayson glanced around, then looked at Jackson. "You and I need to talk. We've maintained a working relationship, but we're not in sync like we were before and we're never going to be again until the air is cleared."

Jackson nodded. It wasn't a conversation he was looking forward to, but it was one that was long overdue. Grayson was right. Neither of them was clicking on all cylinders. Grayson was still pissed that Jackson had suspected him of being the man who'd kidnapped Shaye and tortured her, and Jackson still felt guilty for suspecting him, even though the evidence had strongly supported the idea. It was time for them to talk it out, get over themselves, and get back to solving crimes and saving lives with their combined ability working at 100 percent.

"Let's finish up here," Jackson said, "and see if we have time for coffee before we head back to the station."

"You want to have this discussion in a coffee shop?"

"I figure you can't shoot me there."

Tara clutched her purse strap as she walked into the police station behind Shaye. The desk sergeant's eyes widened when he saw Shaye and he jumped up from his chair and came around the desk to hug her.

"It's great to see you," he said. "And you look good. How are you? How is your mother?"

"We're both fine," Shaye said. "Considering. How are you doing?"

The desk sergeant's expression changed from happy to immensely sad. "It's been rough. I never would have believed that Bernard could, you know, go that way instead of facing the music. I worked with him for thirty-five years and in a single moment, realized that I never knew him at all."

"I understand," Shaye said.

"Yeah, I suppose you do," the desk sergeant said. "What can I help you ladies with?"

"We have a meeting with Detective Grayson," Shaye said.

The desk sergeant nodded. "He's in interview room three. You know the way."

"Thank you," Shaye said, and motioned Tara toward a door that led into a long hallway with numbered rooms on each side.

One. Two.

Tara counted as they walked and when she saw the big black *3*, she drew up short. Shaye turned around and gave her a sympathetic look.

"I promise it will be fine," Shaye said. "Detective Grayson is a good cop. Just answer his questions as best you can, and that's all anyone can ask of you."

Tara took in a huge breath and slowly blew it out, then she nodded and Shaye knocked on the door, then poked her head in. A second later she motioned for Tara to follow. As Tara stepped inside the room she saw two men standing near the door. One was older and looked very proper. The other was younger and really cute. He and Shaye looked at each other and immediately, Tara saw the chemistry. It perked her up a bit. A happy thing in the middle of all this bad.

"This is Tara Chatry," Shaye said. "Tara, this is Detective Lamotte and Detective Grayson."

Detective Grayson stuck out his hand to Tara and she shook it, still feeling a bit insecure.

"Thank you for coming down," Detective Grayson said. "Can I get you something to drink?"

Tara held up the bottled water she'd gotten at the café where she and Shaye had eaten breakfast. "No, thank you."

"Then let's have a seat and get started," Detective Grayson said. "I'll be recording this interview, if that's okay."

Tara slid into a chair next to Shaye and across from the two detectives and nodded. "Whatever you need to do. I just want you to find my friend."

Detective Grayson nodded. "That's what we want as well."

"Where do you want me to start?" Tara asked, confused about whether her story started with Ethan disappearing or with the weird text.

"Why don't you start with the text Ethan received," Detective Grayson said, "and then we can work forward from there."

Tara took a drink of her water, then started talking. She told the detectives about the text, about Ethan's disappearance, and about her less-than-positive experience with Detective Vincent that led her to hiring Shaye. Detective Grayson looked frustrated when she described how Detective Vincent had dismissed her concerns outright. Detective Lamotte just looked pissed.

When she finished, the detectives asked her some questions to clarify points and then there was a silent pause. Shaye looked over at her.

"Tell the detectives what happened at the library yesterday," Shaye said. "And afterward."

Tara felt her pulse tick up a notch and her palms

started to sweat as she recounted her conversation with Brenda and her flight from the stalker. The detectives listened intently, both of them leaning forward over the table as she talked.

When she was finished, Detective Lamotte asked, "You're sure her name was Brenda?"

Tara nodded.

"Brenda Lewis," Shaye said. "I traced her cell phone number."

The two detectives glanced at each other, and it was clear from their expressions that they weren't happy.

"What is it?" Shaye asked. "Something's happened."

Detective Grayson blew out a breath. "This is confidential information so neither of you can speak of it outside these walls, but since it appears Ms. Chatry is in danger, I think it's only fair that she be aware of the facts."

Tara dropped her hands in her lap and clutched the edges of her T-shirt. "What facts?"

"Brenda Lewis was discovered this morning in an abandoned house," Detective Grayson said. "She was murdered."

Tara's hand flew up involuntarily over her mouth. "Oh my God! But it hadn't been two days. The text said she had two days to find Ethan before he took her."

Detective Grayson cleared his throat. "There was a note on the body. It said *Cheater.*"

The room began to spin as the magnitude of what Detective Grayson said registered completely with Tara. Panic set in and she started to hyperventilate.

"She told me," Tara said, placing her arms on the table to keep from swaying. "She told me so he killed her. And now he's after me. He must have seen her tell me. It *was* him that chased me."

Shaye leaned closer and put her hand on Tara's arm. "I need you to breathe. A long breath in, then slowly out. Just like last night. Go ahead."

Tara stared at a blurry Shaye, her chest burning from the lack of oxygen, and she forced herself to drag in a breath. Slowly, she let the air out and the room stopped moving. Then everything started to come back into focus.

"Another breath," Shaye said, "then drink some water."

Tara focused on her breathing, now completely embarrassed that she'd lost control in front of the detectives. They probably thought she was some weepy, incompetent girl who couldn't handle anything.

"You have every right to be afraid," Detective Lamotte said quietly. "In fact, it's better if you're afraid because then you'll be more aware."

Tara felt some of her shame slip away. The detective was right. If this accomplished nothing else, she'd be questioning everywhere she went, what time she went, who she went with, and who else was there every time she stepped out of her dorm room.

"I..." Tara started, then her voice broke. "I don't know what I'm supposed to do. Am I safe going to class? Do I need to just quit school and go to my aunt's house? Would I be safe there or would I be exposing my family to all of this? Are the other people in my dorm safe if I'm there?"

"Let's work through one thing at a time," Detective Grayson said. "How critical is class attendance right now?"

"It's always critical," Tara said. "I'm barely scraping As in a couple of classes and I need to keep my grades up. I don't have much scholarship money, but without it, I'd have to get loans. My parents struggle to make up the rest because they don't want me to start out in debt. A couple of my professors mark off for no attendance. I guess a note from the police would be excused, but for how long? And how far behind would I be by the time this is over?"

"Okay, don't get upset," Detective Grayson said. "We'd prefer you have as little disruption to your life as possible."

Shaye nodded. "It's better for your mental health to keep your normal routine whenever possible. Trust me, I'm the expert on this."

Tara gave Shaye a grateful look. It really helped having someone on her side who knew exactly what it felt like to be so scared and to not even know who to be scared of.

"How secure is your dorm?" Detective Grayson asked.

"It's got one of those keypad entries," Tara said, "and you have to let people in if they don't have the code, but I don't suppose that's very secure. Everyone gives it to their friends so they don't have to let them in. But Shaye secured my dorm room for me last night."

Shaye told Grayson about the dead bolt.

"That's good," Grayson said. "When you're in

common areas, make sure there is more than one other person around. Don't be alone, even with another girl. Women are not beyond such crimes and even if it was a man who chased you, he could have someone working with him. Same goes for showering. Do it at a time when you're in the room with more than one girl. Do you have a roommate?"

"Yes, but she's at her parents' house right now. She had her tonsils out," Tara said. "You don't think she's in danger, do you?"

"I don't think so," Detective Grayson said, "but if things aren't resolved by the time she's due back, you'll need to inform her of the situation so that she can decide if it's better to stay put."

Detective Lamotte leaned forward. "A couple of things—when you return to the dorm, open the door and leave it open until you can check the closets or anywhere else a person could hide. Once inside, engage the dead bolt immediately. Every single time. If your roommate returns, tell her to do the same."

"Exactly," Detective Grayson said. "He can't get through the dead bolt without breaking down the door, which he won't do with a dorm full of students, so I think you're safe in your room. Do you have any night classes?"

"No." She'd had two night classes the semester before but had been fortunate to get everything that she needed during the day this semester. If she'd had night classes, she probably would have ended up dropping them.

"Good," Detective Grayson said. "It's better if you're

not out at night at all, but especially on campus alone."

"So I should stay in at night?" Tara asked. "I shouldn't even go somewhere there's people?"

"You're better off sticking to the rec room in your dorm," Shaye said, "and only when others are around. Amber disappeared from a party at a frat house. With all the noise and drinking, it's easy for someone to drug a drink and then appear to be helping a drunken girl home. That's probably why no one noticed her leave. And there's also the travel back and forth between your dorm and wherever you go. I know you're borrowing Ethan's car, but you still have to navigate parking lots, and that's the easiest place to wait for someone."

Tara bit her lip. So many things she'd never thought about. Hadn't needed to think about. It wasn't like she'd ever been stupid, but she probably hadn't been as careful as she should have been, and now she had to be more careful than ever.

"Okay," Tara said. "I'll stick to the dorm at night and surrounded by people unless I'm locked in my room. And I won't take food or drinks from anyone or leave mine where someone else has access to them."

"Do you have Mace or pepper spray?" Detective Grayson asked.

"Yes, and I keep my phone charged and on me unless I'm in my room, and then it's still close by."

"If you don't mind," Shaye said, "I'd like to link your phone to my Findiphone app. Someone did that for me, and it made me feel better." She glanced over at Detective

Lamotte.

"Sure," Tara said. "I don't mind at all."

"And any time you get scared or think there's something wrong, you can call me," Shaye said. "Day or night. Doesn't matter."

Detective Grayson pushed two business cards across the table to her. "That is my contact information and Detective Lamotte's. Same goes for us. If you learn something new or feel that something isn't right, call either one of us."

Tara took the cards, her hands shaking as she put them in her purse. "Thank you," she said, tearing up as the words tumbled out.

Finally, she had people who not only believed her but were willing to help find Ethan and protect her while doing so. It was comforting to know that such capable people were there for her, and at the same time, she was scared to death that she needed them to be. The entire thing was so overwhelming, she was certain she was unable to process even one more thing.

The only thing she could think about was what Ethan must be going through.

And that terrified her more than anything else.

He watched as they entered the police station—Shaye Archer and the nosy one, the other cheater. The first cheater had paid the price for attempting to change the rules of the game. Now this one needed to as well.

He didn't know her school schedule, but just as soon as he took care of Ethan, he'd be watching her to find out. Maybe he'd get lucky and she'd have class at night, or maybe she'd be foolish enough to think she was safe outside the dorm and in the company of other people. Even if she stuck to the dorm like glue except for classes, a smart person could always find a way inside.

Tara wasn't stupid, but she wasn't nearly as smart as he was. And she was also something he wasn't.

Afraid.

Archer was a problem. Her reputation as the ultimate victim, championing the underdog, was the kind of thing legends were made of. Clearly, the local media didn't know she was back in town or she wouldn't be able to open a blind without someone there to film it.

He smiled. He'd just figured out the simplest way to get rid of Shaye Archer.

CHAPTER FOURTEEN

When they finished the interview, Tara asked for directions to the restroom and Shaye hung back in the meeting room to speak to Grayson and Jackson. She knew they wouldn't give details about Brenda's death in front of Tara, but maybe now that the girl was out of the room, they'd be willing to give her more information.

"Is there anything else you can tell me about Brenda?" Shaye asked as soon as Tara disappeared into the restroom.

Jackson looked over at Grayson, who nodded.

"A homeless man found her," Jackson said. "He'd been squatting in the house for some time. He didn't expect a visitor, especially a dead one."

"I'm surprised he reported it," Shaye said.

Grayson nodded. "He wasn't a bad sort. Cleaned his act up recently and is working now. Wasn't planning on being in the house much longer."

"He's probably wishing he'd cleaned up a few weeks sooner," Shaye said. "So you don't like him for it?"

"No reason to that I can see," Grayson said, "and my guess is he's going to have an alibi once we have time of death from the ME. He works nights at the docks."

"How was she killed?" Shaye asked. She didn't know why but something told her it mattered.

"He covered her mouth with plastic and duct tape," Grayson said, "then taped her hands and feet together so that she couldn't remove the binding on her face."

Shaye stared at Grayson for a bit. "Oh my God. That's horrible."

"It's definitely one of the less pleasant cases I've seen," Grayson agreed.

Shaye frowned. "They all died by suffocation."

Jackson nodded. "That and the texts are the main reasons to think they were all committed by the same person or persons."

"Suffocation is his method," Grayson said. "If I had to guess, I'd say he likes the fact that they struggle before dying. It's sick, but there's no accounting for crazy. We all know that."

"No doubt," Jackson said. "We should check for similar cases. And not just here. If this is the same guy, there's a reason for his choice in method and his victims. If we can figure out either, we'll have a better chance of nailing this guy."

"Do you have any forensic evidence?" Shaye asked.

"Plenty, but these were college students out partying," Grayson said. "Except for Brenda, who's still being processed, we probably have DNA from fifty different sources per body."

"But only one would be common to all of them," Jackson said, getting excited.

"I'll get the lab to compare the findings from each case and see if we have a match," Grayson said.

"Even if you find a match," Shaye said, "it might not lead to an identification. If he's never been processed for anything, he'll still be an unknown."

"True," Grayson said, "but if we have matches across all the murders, it will be strong evidence for a trial when we catch him."

"What else do you know about Brenda?" Shaye asked. "If you can say."

"She's a student. Her mother works for the university," Grayson said. "Single parent. She collapsed when we told her. She thought Brenda was still in bed when she left for work, but apparently, Brenda had rigged a dummy in her bed to fool her mother and slipped out her bedroom window sometime last night."

"Did you recover her cell phone?" Shaye asked.

Jackson shook his head. "The only thing on her was a fake ID in her pocket. Same name but different birthdate."

"He took the phone," Shaye said. "No one under the age of fifty leaves their house without a cell phone, especially a teen girl. I wonder where she was going."

"Probably to meet friends or a boy," Jackson said. "The dummy in her bed was fairly elaborate, down to the wig that matched her own hair. My guess is she's been using that ploy for a while."

"Overprotective mother. Rebellious teen," Grayson said. "Usually it leads to a bit of trouble, maybe an arrest or two before they outgrow it. I wish that had been the case here."

"She's connected to the rest of them somehow," Shaye said.

"I don't doubt that," Grayson said. "Not with everything laid out the way it is. It's just a matter of finding that connection."

Shaye nodded. "I know how the climate is here right now and I don't have any rights to be in the loop, but if you discover anything that affects Tara's safety, will you please give me enough information to ensure she's secure?"

"Of course," Grayson said. "The last thing we want is another victim. You were smart to install the dead bolt on Tara's dorm. And it was nice of you to stay with her last night. I'm sure she was terrified."

"Probably even more so now," Shaye said. "In the morning light it's all clearer, and then Brenda...I hope Tara can hold it together long enough for you to catch this guy."

"I'll request a patrol unit make sweeps past her dorm," Grayson said. "As long as she keeps to what we told her to do, I believe she'll be okay."

"I hope so," Shaye said. "I'll check in on her regularly, and you should both know, I still consider her my client and will continue looking for Ethan."

"We can't prevent you from doing your job," Grayson said. "We just can't aid you, and if you interfere with our investigation, I'll have no choice but to arrest you." He gave her an apologetic look. "I'm afraid that some of the courtesies extended before are no longer available."

"I understand," Shaye said. "I didn't expect anything

more. If I find anything, I'll let you know."

"And we'll inform you if we feel the risk to Tara has altered or increased in any way," Grayson said. "Thanks for bringing her down. Working all of the deaths and Ethan's disappearance as a single crime changes our focus and will hopefully yield leads sooner than working them individually."

Shaye grabbed her keys and headed down the hallway. Tara was just exiting the restroom. Her face was a little pale and Shaye noticed the girl's hands shaking as she put lip balm back into the side pocket of her purse, but she seemed steady enough.

"Let's get out of here," Shaye said.

"That would be great," Tara said, her anxiety clear in her stiff posture and her voice. "Are we going back to the dorm?"

"Eventually," Shaye said, "but I thought it would be a good idea to stop by a grocery store and get you some supplies first. We don't want you starving, and vending machines aren't the best choice for a decent meal."

Tara's shoulders slumped. "I hadn't even thought about food. I almost always miss lunch because of my class schedule so dinner was my big meal. Walking to the sandwich shop after dark isn't an option anymore."

They headed out of the police department and into the parking lot where Shaye was parked.

"What am I supposed to do?" Tara asked as she slid into the passenger seat. "The more I think about it, the more I just want to go to my aunt's, but then I'll mess up everything for my parents and myself. I know you guys think I'll be safe in the dorm but what if I'm not? I sometimes think that if I had money, I'd get on the first plane out of here and stay gone until the police catch the guy. Then I remember that Ethan is out there somewhere, and we have to find him before he's killed too."

She covered her face with her hands and started sobbing.

"And more than anything," Tara said through the sobs, "I'm disappointed in myself for not being stronger. I swear, I'm not a weak person but right now, I feel like the biggest loser and wimp. What's wrong with me?"

"Nothing is wrong with you," Shaye said, surprised at how stern the words came out.

It must have surprised Tara as well because she stopped sobbing and looked over at Shaye. "How did you handle everything you went through?" Tara asked. "Why didn't it break you?"

"Because I didn't allow it to," Shaye said. "So many times I thought it would be easier to just give up. And I had all that money you talked about. I could have gone anywhere in the world and stayed there forever."

"Why didn't you?"

"Because then I would never have known the truth. And regardless of how awful the truth was, it's still priceless to have it. A lifetime of wondering is a lifetime of living under a dark cloud of oppression."

"Do you think Ethan's still alive?"

"I have to believe so. That's what motivates me the

most."

Shaye started the SUV and pulled out of the parking lot. She wasn't lying, exactly. She hoped Ethan was still alive, and if the killer was living up to his end of the text message bargain, then Ethan would remain alive for another day. But Brenda's murder changed things. Whatever plan the killer had was now off track, and that made him even more dangerous than ever. Which meant Shaye needed to figure things out quickly.

There were two different directions she could go. The first was establishing the connection between the victims in order to identify the killer. The second was cracking the code on the phone in order to find Ethan. Both made large assumptions. The first assumed that the victims were connected in a way that would identify the killer. The second assumed that the clue was actually relevant and provided legitimate information as to Ethan's location.

And then there was Tara. The girl was holding it together, but barely. Shaye considered keeping the girl safe as much her job as finding Ethan. It was a whole lot of things for one person to cover. She had to pick a place to start.

And then something else occurred to her. A horrible, awful thought. She looked over at Tara, trying to gauge her stress level. The girl was still pale and was fingering the hem of her T-shirt as she'd been doing in the interview room at the police station, but her breathing appeared to be more normal than before and she didn't look as fearful as she had when they first got in the car.

"I want to put a theory out there," Shaye said, "but I don't want to upset you any more than you already are."

"I've calmed down some. Besides, this won't get better until it's over, so I need to get used to handling the really bad stuff now."

"The killer could be another student."

Tara's eyes widened and she sucked in a huge breath, then blew it out. "I already thought about that. I mean, he's only killing students, right? And he chased me on campus." Her expression darkened. "When I ran to Ethan's dorm room that night, I found leaves stuck to Brett's hoodie. The same kind of leaves the shrubs on campus have. It kinda freaked me out, but then, there's a lot of reasons the leaves might have been on his clothes. I've gotten them on mine."

Shaye processed Tara's words and recalled her conversation with Brett and any impression she'd gotten about him. He hadn't struck her as a good candidate for a killer. He was too obvious. Not outwardly clever. But then that could all be a ruse. Maybe Brett was a lot smarter than he pretended to be. It was definitely something to look into.

"There are a lot of reasons to have leaves on your clothes," Shaye agreed, "and it's far more likely that Brett is exactly who and what he appears to be. But if it's another student, you have to be extra careful, even in your dorm."

"Oh my God! What if he lives in my dorm?"

"Anything is possible, but as long as you stick to all the things we discussed at the police station, he won't be able to get to you."

"Tonight maybe, but what about when Darla comes back? He could wait for her to go to the bathroom and I'd be in there alone without the dead bolt drawn. If I'm sleeping, I wouldn't even know it before it was too late."

"Don't worry about that right now. I'll come up with something before Darla gets back. You just do everything we talked about."

Tara nodded but she didn't look convinced.

Shaye wasn't convinced, either.

Ethan cried out as the broken broomstick he'd been using to dig the hole snapped in half. It had been growing weaker and finally, it couldn't hold up any longer against the hard clay ground. A piece of the wood splintered as the stick broke and he fell forward, jamming the splinter into his finger. He sat on the ground next to the hole and inspected the damage.

The splinter was a good size and had jammed clean through the side of his finger. If he pulled it out from the bottom, he risked it splintering further and getting a smaller piece lodged under his skin. If he pulled it out through the top, he had to force the larger end through the smaller hole, which would be far more painful.

Another wave of hopelessness passed through him and he struggled to keep from crying. He wasn't made for this. He was the quintessential geek. His survival skills included things like knowing tips and tricks to pass a science exam or the quickest way through level-seven dungeons in MMORPGs. He didn't know anything about escaping locked buildings or performing on-the-fly medical procedures. Those had been the kinds of things his roughhousing neighbors had been into.

Now he wished he would have paid more attention to all their "manly" endeavors. If he had, he might already be out of this building and on his way to the police. Maybe if he'd been stronger, he wouldn't be here at all. He still wasn't sure exactly how it happened, but he'd bet someone big and strong could have gotten away.

He grabbed the splinter on the top of his finger and closed his eyes, counting. When he reached three he pulled as hard as he could, screaming as the piece of wood ripped through his tender flesh and finally popped out. He flung the splinter across the shed and wrapped his T-shirt around the finger, squeezing it to stop the bleeding. He could feel it throbbing, and pain shot through his hand and up his arm like tiny bursts of lightning. He rocked back and forth and recited the lyrics to an old folk song his mother used to sing to him until the shooting pain began to subside. It still hurt and if he didn't get out of here soon, it would likely become infected, which was a bigger worry than the pain.

Another problem was his energy level. He had no idea how long he'd been missing but he knew it was way too long to go without eating. Yesterday, his stomach had rumbled and growled for a while, but it had finally given up. The longer he'd dug, the more tired he'd become until he'd finally fallen asleep while digging. Just slumped over onto the ground and crashed from exhaustion. It had been dark outside when he'd fallen asleep and it was light when he woke up, so he assumed he'd slept for several hours. That scared the heck out of him. What if his abductor had returned while he was asleep? The worst part was he didn't feel like the sleep had done him any good. His entire body ached and his head was foggy, like he felt last year when he'd had a horrible flu.

He studied the hole, wondering if it was wide enough yet. It looked deep enough to fit his body if he turned his head to the side, but he wasn't sure if his shoulders would fit the gap. If it was close, maybe he could put his arms over his head and angle them through a little at a time. It was going to be tight no matter what, and he'd probably be scraped up and down if he managed to get through it, but scrapes would heal. Death wasn't something peroxide and Neosporin could repair.

He decided it would be easier if he lay on his back and scooted out that way than attempting a stomach crawl, so he moved in front of the hole and turned around, then lay down. He stuck his arms through the hole and inched forward until his head was right up to the wall. He lowered his head into the hole, then braced his hands on the side of the shed, pushing himself forward with his hands and feet. The uneven boards cut into his scalp and cheek as he inched under them, and he winced but managed to remain silent. His cry earlier hadn't brought anyone to the shed, but he needed to remain quiet, just in case the killer came back.

His jaw hung a bit on the wood and he closed his eyes, then gave his body one big shove to force it through the opening. He felt the skin on his chin rip, and a warm trickle of blood ran down his face and onto his neck. He turned his head up to see his surroundings and realized he was in the middle of a swamp. The foliage and trees were common in undeveloped areas, and somewhere in the distance, he could hear lapping against a bank.

That meant the killer could access him on foot and probably by boat. Maybe by car. He couldn't see a road from where he lay but it was possible there was one around another side of the shed. He inched forward again, pressing his shoulders against the opening, but it was just a tiny bit too small for them to fit through straight. He twisted his shoulders so that the right arm was higher than the left arm and pushed through at an angle. The splintered wood tore his shirt and he felt the shards pierce the tender skin under his arm, but it was working. His right shoulder popped free of the shed and he wrestled his left shoulder through the opening.

He lay there for several seconds, trying to get his breath. The amount of exertion required was so far beyond what he thought it should have taken, but then his body had started giving out a long time ago, and his muscles were so knotted he wasn't sure what it would take to get them loose again. He would have loved to take more time to recuperate, but the urgency he felt to get away from the shed completely overrode the pain and weariness. There would be plenty of time to rest later. Preferably when he was sitting in a police station surrounded by armed officers.

He took in one last breath and blew it out, then he placed his hands against the shed and pushed while digging his heels into the ground to propel him forward. Inch by inch, he forced the rest of his body through the hole.

When his feet popped out, he heard the car.

He jumped up from the ground and staggered as his weak legs attempted to gain hold, clutching the side of the shed to get his balance. Once he was steady, he crept up to the side of the shed and peered around.

A dirt road led up to the shed. It was covered with weeds, but tire tracks in the mud indicated that a car had recently been there. The sound of the engine nearby was proof that one was close now. He hurried to the other side of the shed and peered around, but all he saw was swamp. He couldn't stay here. As soon as the killer saw he was gone, he'd come after him, maybe with a gun. Ethan wasn't all that great of a runner and he definitely couldn't outrun a bullet. Given his knotted muscles and weakened condition, he probably couldn't outrun a toddler.

He had to do everything possible to stay out of sight.

He half ran, half limped into the swamp on the side of the shed, heading toward the water. If he was lucky, he'd find a boat to use or some fishermen passing by. No matter, it was better than standing here and waiting for the inevitable. He was about twenty yards into the dense brush when he stopped. Maybe he should stay long enough to get a glimpse of his abductor. What good was he to the police if he couldn't even describe the man who took him? If the police couldn't catch the guy, then he'd spend the rest of his life looking over his shoulder…suspecting everyone.

Damn it.

Logic told him one thing and survival instinct told him another.

Praying that he wasn't making the wrong decision, he turned around and headed back toward the shed.

CHAPTER FIFTEEN

Shaye helped Tara carry the bags of groceries up to her dorm room and waited as she placed the cool things in her small refrigerator. Space limitations prevented them from buying a lot, but what she had would easily cover Tara for three days. Perhaps not in the variety arena, but she had plenty of protein and enough calories to sustain her. A bag of chocolates would probably help areas of stress and general boredom.

When Tara finished unloading the groceries, she sank onto her bed. She'd been quiet while they shopped and on the ride back to the dorm. Shaye knew Tara had a lot to process, both with what had already happened and with what could potentially happen.

"Did she suffer?" Tara asked quietly. "Brenda? I figure they told you how she died when I left."

"Yes. She did." Shaye wouldn't lie to Tara but she had zero intention of giving her details.

Tara swallowed. "I think he must want them to, you know? I mean, why lock that girl in a coffin? He could have just shot her or stabbed her or hit her on the head with a shovel and it would have been over quickly. But he doesn't want that, does he?"

"His method does imply something personal."

"So they all knew him? Know him?" Her face twisted in anguish. "I wish we knew if Ethan was alive."

"We have to remain positive and working. Your part is staying safe and watching and listening to the people around you very carefully."

"You do think it was someone they knew."

"Maybe. Or it's someone who chose them because they remind him of the people he seeks revenge against for whatever slight, real or imagined."

Tara frowned. "Wouldn't you be able to see it? Someone walking around with all that hate…wouldn't they look different?"

"I think some people are unable to hide the darkness inside them, and it shows through their disdain for other people and their treatment of those around them. But others are very clever. They move through life appearing as everyone else does, just waiting for their opportunity to strike."

"Like when they have us all fooled and we're sitting ducks."

"In some cases, yes. In this case, it remains to be seen. But even if this person is a stranger to his victims, I'd still ask the same things of you. Your classmates might have seen or heard something that is relevant and probably wouldn't even know it. But I believe if you hear or see something that doesn't fit, you'll realize it right away. And then I want you to contact me."

"I guess that could happen."

"Trust your instincts, Tara. You sensed the danger at the library, even before he made you aware of his presence. Those instincts will not only keep you safe, they might provide the one thing that breaks all of this wide open."

Sitting on the edge of the bed, her shoulders slumped and her hair lying limp against her pale face, Tara didn't look like anyone's savior. But Shaye knew better than anyone what people were capable of when they paid attention to the voices in their head and the feeling in their gut.

"Thank you," Tara said, "for everything. The police wouldn't have believed me without you."

"The right policemen would have. All I did was get you in front of someone smart enough to pay attention."

"They're going to find this guy, right?" Tara asked hopefully.

"They're going to do everything they can to. I promise you that. Detectives Grayson and Lamotte are two of the best New Orleans has. If anyone can catch this guy, they can."

Tara glanced down at the floor, then looked back up at Shaye. "Is he your boyfriend? Detective Lamotte?"

"He's a friend for now."

Tara gave her a shy smile. "And later?"

"I'm not sure. I suppose we'll have to wait and see."

"I think I've already seen. I know everyone thinks we're all still kids and can't possibly know about real love and all, but I saw the way he looked at you. He'd do anything for you."

"He already has."

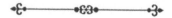

Ethan crept up to the tree line and crouched down behind a group of bushes. He pushed the branches to the side and peered through the foliage at the dirt road that led to the shed. He'd just stay long enough to see who was driving the car, then he'd take off out of here as fast as his legs would carry him. He hoped his decision to get a glimpse of his captor wouldn't be the dumbest thing he'd ever done.

The car emerged from the trees, moving slowly on the narrow, bumpy path. It was an old silver Toyota Camry with rust spots. He had a feeling that he'd seen it before, but couldn't associate it with an individual. As the car swung left toward the shed, Ethan stared at the windshield, but the setting sun created a glare on the glass that prevented him from seeing inside the car. He rose up a bit, wavering between cutting his losses now and running, and waiting for the driver to emerge. Every second he waited was one second more advantage to his captor.

He started to take off but then the car door opened. Another second wasn't going to make a difference at this point, so he remained in place. The figure emerged, facing away from him. All Ethan could gauge was approximate height and build and the color of his hair. But none of those things brought on recognition.

Then he turned around and Ethan sucked in a breath.

How could it be? Why him? And what in the world did he have against Ethan?

He lingered only a second more before hurrying into the swamp. He had to find help. A house or fishermen…someone with a phone. If someone had already received a text about him, then that meant the next victim was already on the hook. He had to get to the police before someone else disappeared.

When he reached the bayou, he drew up short, almost sliding over the edge and into the water as his feet connected with the loose dirt on the embankment. He scanned the area, looking for any sign of life, but the water was devoid of boats and the bank on the other side only contained thick foliage and tall groups of cypress trees. He looked back and listened for any sound that he was being followed, but so far, he appeared to be in the clear. Still, it wouldn't be long. No way was he going to be allowed to just walk away.

He studied the bayou for several seconds, wondering how deep it was. Probably too deep to wade across, and that might present a problem giving how swift the current was. Ethan could swim just fine, when the muscles in his arms and legs weren't in knots and he wasn't completely spent on energy. Still, he wouldn't leave any signs of passage in the water. Maybe he could get in and float, letting the current carry him downstream for a while, then get out on the other side and follow the bayou until it led to someone.

He bent down and grabbed a cypress root to help him down the embankment. It was only a ten-foot drop, but something could be submerged in the murky water, so jumping in wasn't a good idea. A slow lowering was the safest approach. With a good grip on the root, he turned around and began to lower one leg down the embankment, trying to find another root to place his foot on.

The first bullet tore right by his head, grazing his scalp just above his right ear. He released the root to grab his head and immediately lost his balance. He pitched backward into the water, his back slamming onto the moving surface and sending shock waves through his body. He sank immediately and began to swim, clawing his way back up to the surface.

The second bullet hit the water right beside him and he dived back under, swimming as quickly as he could to get away. When he thought his lungs would burst, he surfaced again, gasping for air. He couldn't hear footsteps over the current, but a third bullet striking the bank behind him told him everything he needed to know. He dived again, this time swimming for the opposite bank. There was a spot with a gradual slope that led into the bayou. If he could make it up that slope and into the swamp beyond, then he might have a chance.

He swam at an angle, praying the current wasn't carrying him too far downstream and pushing his arms and legs until he wanted to scream at the pain. His chest burned and he could feel his pulse beating in his throat. When he didn't think he could take another second, he burst onto the surface.

And right in front of an enormous alligator.

He choked back a cry and tried to dodge to the right of the floating beast but it was too late. The gator lunged and grabbed hold of his left arm with its powerful jaws. Ethan screamed as the gator pulled his shoulder from the socket and a second later, he was back underwater, rolling under the surface over and over again.

His last thought before he blacked out was that he wished he would have told Tara how he felt.

Jackson headed into the lab, Grayson right on his heels. The call had come only seconds before and they'd rushed upstairs to see what the scientists had discovered. The lead forensics tech waved them behind the glass wall that separated the work area from the office area, and they headed around to where he stood next to a computer on a table.

The tech nodded to each of them and immediately started talking. "I had my team run a comparison on the DNA obtained from the St. Claire and Olivier cases. We still haven't finished processing all the evidence from the scenes, but once we excluded law enforcement personnel, we found common DNA between the two."

"Did you run it?" Grayson asked.

"Unfortunately, there was no match," the tech said.

"Sex?" Jackson asked.

"Male. We ran the matching DNA for familial results but came up negative there as well."

"It was a long shot that we'd get a match," Grayson said, "but it was definitely worth it."

The tech nodded. "Because of the match in the first two cases and because of the matching method of death used in the Lewis case, I've moved evidence from that case up in priority. We're running each piece as they're prepared rather than waiting to run them all at one time. I'll call you as soon as I know more."

"Thank you," Grayson said. "We appreciate you making this a priority."

"The last thing this city needs is another serial killer on the loose," the tech said.

Jackson and Grayson headed out of the forensics department and down the hall.

"Isn't that the truth?" Grayson muttered. "This summer, this city was rocked by some of the most horrible crimes in the history of the state. The police department was left practically in ruin, everyone pointing fingers at each other or afraid to say anything at all. Things were just starting to settle down a little and now this."

"Right when the Archers return home."

"No one is blaming them," Grayson said. "Besides, Ross St. Claire and Amber Olivier were killed before the Archers set foot back on American soil."

"I know that, but you know it won't matter. When it gets out that we've got another serial killer in New Orleans, and that Shaye is involved on any level, nothing else will matter but that."

Grayson sighed as they stepped onto the elevator. "I would like to say that I wish she'd chosen a different profession, or no profession at all, but the truth is she's really good at it."

Jackson nodded, pleased that Grayson felt that way. Their conversation earlier had really helped clear the air between them, and the tension that had been present before was all but gone now. For the first time in months, Jackson felt he and Grayson could get back into their groove again and make a difference.

"And most of the people she helps have already been turned away by the police," Jackson said, "or would be and know it. Nor do most of them have the ability to pay for the services she's providing, and I'd bet anything she's not taking anything from them."

"Which she can do because she doesn't need the money. A regular superhero."

Jackson grinned. "I called her Batman, but she argued the description because she doesn't have the cool car."

"It might stick out a bit."

"That's what I said."

They stepped off the elevator and headed back to their desks.

"What now?" Jackson asked.

"I was on the phone with St. Claire's office when the lab called. They've got those employment records ready for us. I figured I'd go interview those employees at Archer that Corrine gave us and you could start on the employment records."

"So a long afternoon of paper pushing."

"Who knows? Maybe our match is in those files."

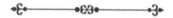

Shaye pulled a ball cap from her glove box, grabbed her laptop from the passenger seat of her vehicle, and headed into the coffee shop. It wasn't her usual hangout, and that was deliberate. Her café of choice near her apartment and the one she frequented when she'd lived with Corrine weren't good options. Everyone knew her at those places and the ball cap probably wouldn't throw them off. But across town in the Marigny, people probably wouldn't take a second look at a young woman wearing jeans, a tee, and a ball cap.

She needed an Internet connection and for whatever reason, she felt that avoiding her apartment and her mother's house was a good call. So far, she hadn't seen any signs that the press had been alerted of her return, and she knew Corrine would notify her at the first sign of a microphone or camera, but the longer she could remain hidden, the more efficiently she could go about her work.

She walked into the café and took a seat at an empty table in the back corner. A sullen-looking woman, around thirty years old, came over and asked for her drink order. Shaye ordered a Diet Coke and the woman shuffled back off to the kitchen with barely a glance at her. Smiling at her bit of good luck, she opened her computer and logged on to the café's Internet. Whatever was bothering the waitress, she was too deep in to pay much attention to Shaye.

The woman returned a couple minutes later and sat the soda on the table. "You want something to eat?"

Shaye hadn't thought she was hungry when she'd walked inside, but now that the waitress had mentioned food, Shaye decided she might as well eat while she worked. She glanced at the chalkboard up front with the specials written on it.

"I'll have the club sandwich special," Shaye said.

"Chips, fries, or a salad?"

A couple seconds of internal argument ensued, but finally, guilt won out and she ordered the salad. The waitress turned around without another word and Shaye went to work.

She pulled up a browser and started with Ethan's seemingly clueless roommate, Brett Frazier. A surprising amount of information loaded but as she scanned it, she realized it was a lot of sports reporting, most of which she could read the short description of and skip. She was about to decide that the only thing Google could produce on Brett was his player stats when she saw an old article and frowned.

Local High School Freshman Wins Chess Championship

And there was Brett's name in the description.

She clicked on the link. It wasn't as if Brett or Frazier was an uncommon name. Perhaps there was another more cerebral Brett Frazier in New Orleans.

But the photo at the top of the article was Ethan's

roommate. The boy in the photo lacked the maturity that the current Brett did. His shoulders hadn't broadened and his jaw was still rounded. But the cheekbones, eyes, nose, and lips were all the same. This was definitely the Brett Frazier that Shaye had met.

As she read the article, she struggled to fit the description of the highly intelligent overachiever in the article with the seemingly clueless jock she'd spoken to in the dorm. If she weren't looking at the article herself, she wouldn't have believed it to be true. Maybe Brett had cruised through lower-level studies but hit a wall at some point. Or maybe his age had caught up with his IQ. That happened a lot. Still, freshman was old enough that one would think his IQ would be rather set.

Was Brett Frazier hiding his intelligence?

Tara had mentioned that he was always skipping class. Shaye had assumed he was blowing off his education, but what if the lower-level courses were simply so easy for Brett that he didn't have to attend class? Or perhaps he'd decided that professional athlete was the direction he intended to go and he didn't feel like spending time on harder pursuits.

Maybe it was just as Shaye had suggested to Tara—that the killer had presented himself as someone else to his victims. Had Brett been pretending all this time? If so, it was an elaborate game and a risky one as well. At any point, someone could have looked harder into his past and found out that the goofy sports star used to be considered a whiz kid. It was hard to hide with the Internet at everyone's fingertips.

The waitress returned with her salad and Shaye pushed the laptop to the side while she consumed the bit of lettuce and shredded carrots. What was her next move? She couldn't depend on leads or information from Jackson unless it directly concerned Tara. She definitely needed to work on deciphering the code, but she could do that tonight when it wasn't as safe to be roaming around alone.

She was pretty sure she'd gotten all she was going to get out of the sorority sisters, and besides, the police would be questioning them again and since Shaye couldn't be certain that Jackson or Grayson would conduct that questioning, it was better for her to stay away. It was one thing to do it before she'd gone down to the police station with Tara. It was completely another to do it now that she had been told it was an open investigation.

The waitress returned once more with her sandwich and she abandoned the less-than-stellar salad and took a bite out of the surprisingly decent club sandwich. She opened a document and made some notes about the interview with Grayson and Jackson and other thoughts from her talk with the sisters that morning. As she reread the notes, she got to the comment about George Moss and wondered about the temper tantrum Brittany had witnessed.

The convenience store owner had been somewhat surly and clearly aggravated with the young people for stealing his merchandise, but Shaye hadn't seen any sign of the level of anger that had been described. Was George hiding a dark side behind his usual complaining outward look? Had the increasing theft been the thing that pushed him over the edge from ranting to something more insidious?

A quick search on the convenience store gave her the basics. The building was owned by George Herbert Moss and the business license was in the same name. She did a search on the business name but didn't get anything except business-related websites and commercial listings. She did another search, this time on George Moss, and hit pay dirt.

George Herbert Moss wasn't a hardened criminal, but he was no stranger to the police. He'd been arrested four times for assault and battery. Twice the charges were dropped. The other two times, he'd gotten away with a fine, probation, and court-authorized attendance in an anger management program. All four incidents had occurred at the store and Moss had claimed they all concerned stolen merchandise.

She frowned. Why risk your business over someone stealing sports drinks and candy bars? All it took was laying hands on the wrong parents' kid and George could lose everything. She checked the dates on the arrests. All were within the last two years. Had the frustration over the increasing losses pushed him over the edge? Had he escalated right past anger and into insanity?

So many unanswered questions.

It was time to take a closer look at the store owner. As soon as she finished her sandwich, she'd head for the store and park across the street to watch for a bit. Maybe get a better idea of how George reacted when it was just him and the kids around. Then she'd do some more checking into Brett Frazier. Both had access to Ethan Sunday night. Both had the size and strength to manage moving his unconscious body.

She'd gone from no suspects to two. At least that was something.

CHAPTER SIXTEEN

Shaye parked her SUV across the street from the convenience store. She'd lucked out and managed to pull into the parking lot just as a car was leaving a front-row spot. That meant she could see everything she needed to see from the comfort of her own car. She pulled her binoculars out of the glove box and sat them on the passenger seat. She wouldn't use them unless she felt it was absolutely necessary, because that might look a bit strange. The last thing she wanted was someone telling George that a lady was spying on him. With the store owner's apparent anger issues, he might come after her.

For about ten minutes, the only thing she saw was the regular traffic of cars getting gas and the occasional student going in and out of the store. Everything appeared to be normal, and then she spotted a familiar figure. Brett Frazier walked around from the back of the store and entered. Through the plate-glass windows, she saw him walk to the rear wall where the coolers were. She saw him reach for a can and then turn around and head for a chip display.

She lost sight of him behind the display and didn't see him again until he walked up to the counter. A young man

Shaye hadn't seen before rang up Brett's items and Brett picked them up and left the store. He walked around the side and started toward the dorm when George pulled into the parking lot. The store owner parked behind the store and came around the side as Brett was about to step into the empty lot. George strode directly for Ethan's roommate, so Shaye picked up her binoculars and zoomed in on the situation. George's face was red and he moved his hand back and forth as he pointed his finger at Brett.

Brett looked taken aback at first but then his expression shifted to one of anger. He began to argue back and George glanced around, then moved closer to the student. Brett continued to shake his head and argue with the irate store owner, but it didn't appear that either was interested in backing down. Finally, Brett whirled around and stalked off across the empty lot toward the dorms. George watched his retreating back for a couple seconds, then headed back for the front of the store.

Thomas wheeled into the parking lot on his bicycle as George walked around the corner of the building. He spotted Thomas and made a beeline for him, accosting the student as he chained his bicycle to the post. Shaye could tell the owner's mood hadn't improved one bit since he'd finished his argument with Brett. George yelled at Thomas, waving his hands and pointing to the trash, then stalked back around the building again. Shaye started up her SUV and pulled across the street and into the convenience store parking lot as George was pulling out onto the street, tires squealing.

She pulled up to the pump and got out. Thomas was putting the lid back on the trash can and looked over as she walked to the pump.

"Oh, hi," Thomas said. "You're the PI, right?"

"That's me. Your boss looked like he was going to blow when I pulled in. Is he always like that?"

Thomas shrugged. "He gets a little crazy over shoplifting and then starts yelling over everything."

"Did he catch someone shoplifting?" Shaye asked as she removed her gas cap and started fueling the SUV.

"Who knows? He sits back there and watches those cameras all the time. I've seen guys pocket a sports drink and snacks, but if I'm working alone, I don't say anything. All that does is invite a fight, and calling the cops is useless. They're not coming down here over a candy bar."

"Probably not. Well, I'm sorry he took his frustration out on you. I had a professor like that when I was in college. It's not much fun."

"It's no big deal. His wife is sick, cancer. He's been stressed ever since she was diagnosed. My mom had breast cancer so I know how hard it can be seeing them so sick."

"I'm sorry to hear that. How is your mother doing?"

"Oh, she's fine now. I know George can seem a little crazy, but I need a job to help pay for school and this one doesn't require me to have a car."

"You live on campus?"

"No. Bywater, but I like working next to campus in case my work schedule runs close to class schedule."

"Bywater? Wow! That's quite a trip."

"It's doesn't take that long, really, and as long as the weather's decent, it's not a bad deal."

Shaye smiled. "And it's good exercise."

"I guess so. Well, I just stopped to pick up my paycheck. Do you need any help with the fuel?"

Shaye looked at the pump. "Nope. Almost done. You have a good evening and enjoy that bike ride home."

Thomas gave her a shy smile. "Yeah. Thanks."

Shaye finished up with the fuel and climbed back into her SUV. If Brett had stolen something before why had George waited until now to come after him? The owner hadn't been inside the store when Brett was there, and given his aversion to technology, Shaye would bet he didn't have the security cameras streaming to his phone. Which meant George had no way of knowing if Brett stole anything unless the other employee had called and told him as much. On the flip side, though, that meant the other clerk would be sticking his neck out telling George about the theft. From what Shaye could see, the other clerk wasn't a big guy. Someone like Brett could probably overpower him with ease. More likely, the clerk kept his mouth shut as Thomas did.

So if the argument wasn't about shoplifting, then what was it about?

And then a thought occurred to her. What if the killer wasn't one man but two?

It would be far easier for two people to have pulled off the abductions than one person. Unconscious people were dead weight and were gangly to cart around. Brenda had been hauled into an abandoned house. Ross St. Claire had been found some distance into the swamp on a hiking trail. A single person could have accomplished both, especially with a cart of some sort, but it would have taken longer, which would have increased the risk of being seen. Two people would allow for an increase in speed and a lookout or even a decoy if needed.

Shaye started her SUV and pulled out of the parking lot. Brett Frazier and George Moss needed more looking into, and Shaye knew just where to start.

He clenched his fists and cursed as he stared across the campus. The drugs he'd given Ethan should have kept him incapacitated for longer. Ethan shouldn't have had time to break out of the shed and he shouldn't have had the strength to dig the hole or run away. He must have made a mistake in his calculations. Either that or Ethan had a strange metabolism and had burned off the drugs more quickly than normal.

He thought he'd hit him with that first pistol shot and had been surprised when he rushed up to the bank and saw Ethan pop up down the bayou. The student had looked straight back at him before he'd gone back under. He'd been standing in overhanging branches of a cypress tree, but there was still a chance Ethan had gotten a look at his face.

He shook his head, wiping that thought from his mind.

He'd reached the opposite bank just in time to see the alligator grab Ethan and pull him under. Then he'd heard a boat approaching and took off before anyone caught sight of him. The gator was huge, at least twelve feet. There was no way Ethan could have survived the attack. And if he'd hit him somewhere with that first shot, then Ethan was good and dead.

It annoyed him that he hadn't gotten to suffocate Ethan as he had the rest.

Any chance at a decent life had been slowly suffocated out of him. It was only fair that the others paid as well.

At least he still had the nosy girl to look forward to.

He pulled out Ethan's cell phone and started a text.

Shaye gripped the steering wheel as she rounded the corner to her mother's home. She could see the spillover from the madhouse a block away. Vans with camera crews lined the side street and reporters rushed to her vehicle as soon as they spotted her. Her windows were heavily tinted so they couldn't get a good shot of her from the side, but the cameras in front of her vehicle would have no trouble getting footage for the evening news. She'd known when Corrine had called her in a panic earlier that the reprieve was over, but she hadn't expected this level of crazy.

When they crowded around the front of her vehicle, she put her foot on the brake and pressed her accelerator down, causing her engine to roar. She immediately began to move forward and the crews scrambled to get out of the way. She could hear shouting but didn't bother to register any of the words. They didn't matter. She wasn't ready to talk to the press. Not today. She wasn't even going to think about it until after the case. A case that she would have a hard time working now that every media source in New Orleans would be hounding her.

She waved to the security guard at the gate and parked up front in the circular drive. She practically ran into the house, careful not to look back so they couldn't get a shot of her face with a telephoto lens. As soon as she entered the house, she headed for the kitchen, willing to bet money that Corrine was baking.

Her mother looked up at her from the kitchen counter, patches of flour on her face and her hands covered in it. "Raspberry Danish," Corrine said when Shaye walked into the kitchen. "Eleonore made an emergency run for the ingredients before her yoga class."

Shaye slid onto a stool with a sigh.

"We knew it couldn't last," Corrine said.

"I know, but that whole day of peace lulled me into believing we might not matter any longer."

"You know better. News hasn't been real in forever. Investigative journalism is dead. They're reporting the most sensational thing they can find to keep ratings."

"Wow. You sound even more cynical than me."

Corrine shrugged. "I just sound honest."

"So what are you going to do about that three-ring circus?"

"I'm not sure what I can do. They can park out on that street as long as they'd like and won't be breaking the law. If we leave, they can follow us to any public place."

"Which makes either of us doing our jobs rather difficult."

"I don't think I'll be returning to my job," Corrine said quietly.

Shaye stared at her mother in surprise. Of all the things Corrine had said since all the horror happened, this was the one thing that she hadn't seen coming.

"But you love your job," Shaye said.

"Yes, but with everything that's happened, I won't be able to do it the way I used to. The people I dealt with before didn't make the connection between Corrine the social worker and Corrine the wealthy socialite. They just thought I was one more government employee trying to tell them how to live. But now? Everything will be a hassle. The reporters, the accusations…I don't want to cause social services problems they don't need. They already have their hands full."

Shaye understood what Corrine was saying, but she didn't necessarily agree. If she agreed with her mother, that meant admitting that her own choice of profession wouldn't work well, either. And maybe it wouldn't. Right now, she needed to be out on the streets hunting down information, but if the news was streaming her every move, then the killer could chart her progress. It would give him a definite edge.

"Besides," Corrine said, "I'm no longer safe doing the

job. I mean, I wasn't completely safe before, but back when people thought I was a public servant, there was no reason…" She sighed.

Shaye knew exactly what Corrine wasn't saying. When people didn't know she was a multimillionaire, there was no reason to kidnap her and demand a ransom. The people Corrine dealt with weren't usually the type to read the social magazines, so they wouldn't have recognized her. But Shaye would probably be hard-pressed to find someone in New Orleans who wouldn't recognize her mother now. She was already experiencing that herself.

Still, even though Corrine had good reasons, Shaye couldn't fathom her mother leaving the work she loved. Corrine had already declared her plans to sell off all of Pierce's business interests and real estate. Her mother wanted nothing to do with the empire Pierce had built, and boardroom meetings had never been her calling.

"What will you do?" Shaye asked. "You and I both know you can't stay locked up in this house and bake. Our waistlines can't afford it. And the last thing you'd ever do is become a full-time socialite. You hate that crap."

And then a thought occurred to Shaye. One that hadn't crossed her mind before.

"You're not thinking of moving, are you?" Shaye asked.

"If only it were that easy," Corrine said. "I doubt I could go anywhere in the States that wouldn't result in a media frenzy. Perhaps not as bad as in New Orleans, but I'm not going to pretend this wasn't national news. The story is too big and too juicy. Friends in Europe have been emailing me that it's even on the major news channels there."

Shaye frowned. "You haven't told me that."

"I didn't want you to feel trapped while we were overseas the same way you'll feel trapped here. We weren't exactly running out shopping, so I figured no one would find us. I wanted you to have some peace and quiet to sort things out."

"So what then? You have to do something."

"I've got something I'm thinking on. It's too loosely formed for me to talk about it, but I promise I won't become the crazy lady who calls her daughter twenty times a day because she can't be bothered to get her own life."

"And I appreciate that. When you get it figured out, let me know what I can do to help."

"Since you're volunteering—"

Shaye held up her hand. "Unless it involves giving up my work. I already have enough problems with that as it is. I don't need more."

Corrine frowned. "As much as I'd like to see you doing something safer, I'm sorry that this happened. I know you want to find that boy and I can't imagine that's going to happen with a media storm tagging along."

"I need to find a way to lose them."

"How? Now that they know we're here, they're not going to give up. Eleonore went by your apartment and there's a line of vans up and down your street. I've already heard from my coworkers at social services and the president of Archer Manufacturing. Both offices are covered up. We can't pull out of the driveway without a procession behind us. And even if we lost them in traffic, they have crews scattered every place we might show up."

Shaye glanced at the backyard and the tall stone fence and remembered the last time Corrine thought someone was safe inside her home. The street teen, Hustle, had gone right over the wall and off to confront a killer. Shaye and Jackson had gotten to him in time to save his life and Jackson had killed the perpetrator. Now Hustle was in an entirely different living situation and he and Shaye had become friends.

The longer she thought about the wall and Hustle, the more an idea began to take shape.

She pulled out her cell phone and called Jackson, who was happy to help but couldn't manage a break for an hour or two. Shaye thanked him and pulled out her laptop. In the meantime, she'd do some more research on George Moss and Brett Frazier. Maybe she could locate a former teacher or two of Brett's who was willing to talk. If she could run down the victims of George Moss's temper, she might find someone else who felt chatty.

She looked up from her laptop and saw Corrine shaking her head.

"Go ahead and say it," Shaye said, knowing that her mother was unhappy with the plans she'd just made.

"There's no use. You're as hardheaded as I am. I sometimes forget we don't share DNA."

"I'll take that as a compliment."

"Somehow, I knew you would."

Tara stared at her laptop without really seeing the show playing on the screen. Hours on end of streaming television and movies had her on the verge of death from boredom. If she'd simply been sick, she would have gladly crawled in bed and watched movies until she slept, thankful for the break. But this was different.

She wasn't resting in her room because she was ill. She was trapped in her room because she was being stalked and the longer she sat there, the more jittery she became. The same as any caged animal. In addition to the huge restriction of freedom, she also had her hands tied as far as finding Ethan went. Logically, she knew she didn't have the talent or experience to contribute anything to an investigation, but she still had the overwhelming feeling that she should be doing something. She just didn't have any idea what.

She'd looked at the code in the text message for an hour or so earlier, trying to make sense of the stretch of numbers, but no revelations had been forthcoming. Not that she'd expected to have an epiphany. After all, Ethan hadn't figured it out and he was a numbers genius. If it didn't make sense to him, then what chance did she have? For that matter, what chance did anyone have? Which was probably exactly what the killer counted on.

Her watch vibrated and she looked down to see a

message telling her it was time to get up and move. Whatever. Her knee was looking better as far as potential infection went, but it was still swollen and walking wasn't all that comfortable. She blew out a breath, wondering if she should go check the rec room again. No one had been around earlier. Probably everyone was in class, studying, working, or having fun somewhere in the French Quarter.

She'd never realized how quiet the dorm was during the day. Occasionally, she heard footsteps in the hall and doors open and close, but the high-pitched chatter that filled the halls at night wasn't present now. She glanced out the window and saw the sun starting to set. In no time, it would be dark. That meant people would be around and she could come out of hiding, at least for a couple hours.

She eased her legs off the bed, giving her injured knee a lift with her hands, then slowly rose, giving her knee plenty of time to adjust as she straightened. She took a couple of slow steps toward the minifridge to loosen things up and grabbed a soda. As she turned toward the door, her cell phone signaled an incoming text. She pulled it out of her pocket and gasped when she saw the display. The text was from Ethan.

I'm in trouble and need your help.

Bring all the cash you have and car keys to my dorm room.

What in the world? Tara stared at the phone, as surprised by the message as she would have been if aliens had dropped through the ceiling and into the room. Had that asshole cop been right? Had Ethan been hiding out all this time? She texted back.

Are you all right?

Where have you been?

She sent the text and waited. A couple seconds later, a response came back.

Not over phone.

Don't tell anyone. Dangerous.

She frowned. The first thing she'd planned on doing was calling Shaye. Surely she wasn't included in the "anyone." Besides, how would Ethan even know if she told Shaye?

Then she thought about the first sentence. Not over phone. Did Ethan think someone was somehow reading their texts or could listen in on phone conversations? She knew it was possible but not nearly as easy as they made it seem in movies, and someone had to have the equipment and knowledge to do it.

Please hurry. I don't have much time.

Park at the end of the lot.

She looked at the incoming texts and her heart clenched. The thought of Ethan, scared in his dorm room, waiting on her to help him, made her want to cry. It was still daylight, sort of, and she did borrow his car without asking. Ethan probably needed the car to get away and she'd delayed that already by having the keys. She only had twenty dollars on her but if Ethan told her where he was going, she could send more.

I'm on my way.

She sent the text, shoved the phone in her pocket, and grabbed the car keys from her desk. Students were returning for the night, so people were milling about the hallways and the lobby downstairs. Tara hurried to the car as quickly as she could, ignoring the angry protests from her knee. She had all night to rest, but Ethan might not have another ten minutes.

It was a short drive to Ethan's dorm. The parking lot was already filling up so finding a space close to the entry wouldn't have been possible anyway. She guided the car to the end of the lot and parked in a corner spot where the parking lot met the courtyard. Maybe Ethan planned on sneaking out the back of the dorm and coming around the side, hoping no one would see him get in the car.

She glanced around before reaching for the door handle, then hurried out as a big group of students entered the parking lot on the other side. She half walked, half limped for the dorm and followed the other students inside. Enough students milled around the hallway that Tara felt safe. Surely no one would attempt something at this time of day and with so many people around. If she screamed, she'd easily be heard.

She knocked on Ethan's dorm room and leaned close to the door, listening for any sound inside.

"Ethan," she said, her voice low. "It's Tara."

She waited a couple seconds, then knocked again, starting to worry. Had something happened? Had something forced Ethan to flee before she got there?

She reached for the doorknob and was surprised to find it unlocked. Surely if Ethan were in danger, he would have locked the door. Suddenly, a thought struck her and she sucked in a breath.

What if the killer had gotten to him? What if she opened the door and found Ethan dead?

A cold sweat formed on her forehead as she built up the courage to open the door. Finally, she said a prayer and pushed it open.

The room was empty.

She scanned the small space, taking in Brett's messy side and Ethan's neat side, but there was no sign of Ethan in the room and no indication that he'd been there. She looked up and down the hall, making sure there were people around in case things got bad, then stepped inside, leaving the door wide open. A quick review of the closets and under the beds revealed nothing. She checked Ethan's bed and desk, opening all the drawers to make sure he hadn't left a note for her somewhere.

When she was convinced there was no one and nothing to find, she blew out a breath. Something must have scared Ethan away.

She pulled out her cell and sent a text.

I'm at your room. Where are you?

She sent the text and was relieved when her phone indicated it had been read. A couple seconds later, Ethan texted her back.

Had to leave fast. Will call later.

She clenched the phone for several seconds, then sent another message.

I have the car. Let me come get you.

She watched the display as the message changed to

delivered status, waiting for the status to change to read. But as the seconds ticked by, the status remained the same. To hell with this, she thought, and dialed Ethan's number. The phone went directly to voice mail.

"Call me as soon as you get this," she said, then shoved the phone into her pocket.

Why had Ethan turned his phone off? Or had he run out of battery?

She walked out of the room and headed back down the hall. There was nothing else she could do here. Hell, there was nothing she could do anywhere if Ethan wouldn't tell her where he was. The business cards for the detectives were in her dorm room. As soon she got back there, she'd call them. They should be able to trace the cell tower the text had originated from, maybe even trace the phone if Ethan turned it back on.

The sun was just sinking over the buildings as she exited the building and hurried across the parking lot. She jumped into the car and pulled out her phone to call Shaye and let her know what had happened. As she brought up her address book, someone grabbed her from behind, covering her mouth with his hand.

Her hands flew up to grab his arm but before she could even get a good grip on him, she felt the needle puncture her neck. She jerked her head as hard as she could away from the needle and dropped her left hand to the horn and laid on it over and over again. He tightened his grip on her neck, and the courtyard began to blur. She dropped her left hand to the door handle and with every ounce of her strength, she shoved the door open and ripped herself away from her attacker.

She fell out of the car, her injured knee connecting hard with the concrete. She tried to stand but everything was swimming and her strength was evaporating. So she started screaming and crawling toward the dorm. Praying that someone would hear her.

The last thing she saw before she blacked out was a pair of blue tennis shoes. She didn't even have the strength to look up to see if it was a rescuer or the end. Then she slid into darkness.

CHAPTER SEVENTEEN

Shaye kissed her mother on the cheek, then grabbed her backpack. Given her unorthodox method of leaving the house, she couldn't carry much, but her laptop and a change of clothes were necessary. Corrine had been switching back and forth between disapproval and worry, and now her expression was a combination of both.

"I wish you wouldn't do this," Corrine said.

"There's no other way," Shaye said. "I can't hide out when that boy's life is at stake."

"But the police are handling it."

"The police aren't working for Tara. I am, and I'm going to keep my promise even if it's a little inconvenient."

"A little?"

"It's not a big deal. I'll call you when I get there."

"Be careful." Corrine teared up. "I can't handle losing anyone else."

"You're not going to lose me. Even if I wanted to do something foolish, I can't. I have to keep the police informed or I could get my license yanked and Jackson into trouble. We're all treading lightly. I promise."

Corrine nodded but still didn't look happy. Shaye

233

stepped outside into the backyard and pulled one of the outdoor dining chairs up against the wall Corrine's property shared with Mrs. Hester, an elderly widow who had lived in the house behind Corrine's her entire life. Shaye secured the backpack around her arms, stepped onto the chair, then pulled herself onto the wall. As she jumped, she kicked the chair over and the metal legs clanged onto the stone deck.

Crap. She rolled over the wall and dropped into Mrs. Hester's hedges.

And that's when the dog—that Mrs. Hester never had before—started barking.

"Come out of those bushes or I'll shoot you right where you stand." The old lady's voice sounded in front of Shaye, but the thick bush blocked her from seeing exactly who stood on the other side of the foliage. And if they were really holding a gun.

"Mrs. Hester?" Shaye called out.

After a couple of excruciating seconds of completely silence, the voice called back. "Is that you, Shaye?"

"Yes. It's Shaye Archer."

"Well for goodness' sake. I didn't even realize you were back in town. Get out of my bushes before the bugs get on you."

Shaye pushed the branches aside and stepped out. Mrs. Hester stood on her back patio holding a Chihuahua in her left arm and a .45 in her right. It was both odd and incredibly frightening. Her right arm shook from the weight of the gun and as she squinted at Shaye, she slowly lowered it. Shaye let out the breath she'd been holding.

What were the odds? Shaye's entire life Mrs. Hester had grilled fish on her back patio at 4:00 p.m. and gone straight to bed. You could have set your watch by the smell of fish that permeated the backyard. Apparently things had changed while Shaye and Corrine were away. Shaye looked at the gun that was almost as big as the dog and cringed. Maybe not for the better.

"I'm so sorry I startled you," Shaye said. "Mom and I just got back a couple days ago and now there's a bunch of reporters in front of the house. I was trying to get away without them seeing me."

Mrs. Hester scowled. "Vultures. The whole lot of them. Trying to get famous over the suffering of others."

Shaye nodded. "I'm not ready to talk to them, but I have something I've got to do, and I need to do it without a television crew around."

Mrs. Hester nodded knowingly. "You've got a man to see."

"Uh, well, sort of." She was about to see him. Just not in the way Mrs. Hester had in mind.

"That's wonderful. Every young woman should have a man worth climbing over walls for. My Frank has been gone eighteen years now, and I still miss him every day."

Shaye smiled. "I hope one day I have a marriage as happy as yours was."

"Oh, I have no doubt you will. You're a sharp one and you've already experienced so much at such a young age. You'll make a good choice and you'll be happy with it."

"Thank you." Shaye lifted her right arm to push the

strap of the backpack up, and the dog growled. "I see you have a couple of new friends," Shaye said and pointed at the dog and the gun.

"The pistol was Frank's. I never could stand the thing but with everything going on in this world, I figured it was high time I took it out of the closet and learned to shoot it. I've been taking lessons over at the gun range."

"Maybe you should consider a lighter one," Shaye suggested. If Mrs. Hester got off a stray shot, it could penetrate right through the wall of a house.

"The young man who's teaching me keeps saying that. I suppose it would make it easier to hit things the first time. Not like a burglar is going to stand still while you get it right."

"Probably not. And the dog?"

"Oh, he's a big pain. Got gas worse than Frank used to have. I've had to get up and leave the room over it. But my hearing's not what it used to be and he's got ears like a bat, which is sometimes a good thing and sometimes not. I got this new medication that gives me insomnia. Nothing like roaming the house all night with this pest yapping at every creaking floorboard."

Shaye nodded, afraid to say anything. She didn't have the time for Mrs. Hester to launch into a detailed explanation of her medication problems or the dog's gas. "Well, I best get going or I'm going to be late."

"We wouldn't want that. Do you want to use my front door? It will be a sight easier than scaling the front gate. I put locks on it a month ago. Caught kids back here swimming in my pool. Parents have completely dropped the ball."

"I'd love to use the front door," Shaye said, hoping no camera crews were parked in front of Mrs. Hester's house. It was the one element of her plan that she couldn't be sure about.

Shaye followed Mrs. Hester through her kitchen and into the formal living room to the front door.

"You take care, honey," Mrs. Hester said, "and you feel free to climb over that wall any time you need to. Maybe just call first."

"Definitely." Shaye peered out one of the side windows that framed the massive door, and her shoulders relaxed when the only vehicle in sight was Jackson's undercover car.

She opened the door and hurried outside to jump in the car. Jackson had started it up as soon as he saw her come out of Mrs. Hester's house and she ducked down low in the passenger's seat as he pulled away from the curb. She remained low and silent for several minutes, then finally crept up to a seated position.

"I was beginning to wonder if you were praying or maybe meditating," Jackson said.

"After my impromptu visit with Mrs. Hester, a little prayer might be in order."

Shaye told him about her adventure with Mrs. Hester, the .45, and the Chihuahua and he shook his head. "I don't know whether to laugh or pray myself. You're lucky she didn't accidentally fire one off."

"I know. I need to tell Mom to maybe avoid the pool until Mrs. Hester gets a lighter gun. I don't think a bullet could make it through the stone wall, but if she shot straight up…"

"Like we need more dangers to worry about. Now we have Mrs. Hester playing John Wayne."

Shaye looked over at Jackson. "I really appreciate you doing this."

"It's no big deal. I've already told you that you're welcome to borrow my car if you need to be in stealth mode. You're certainly not going to remain out of sight in your SUV. Everyone knows it and it's too easy to spot."

Jackson had acquired the older nondescript car specifically for stakeouts and had used it once when helping her follow a suspect. Shaye understood the benefit of having a vehicle that no one looked twice at, but didn't see the point of getting one herself as she had no way of keeping people from finding out she owned it. Once it was "Shaye Archer's vehicle" and not "some random car," the entire point of having it was moot. Borrowing Jackson's car was the perfect solution because no one was paying as close attention to what Jackson did.

"I knew they'd find out eventually," Shaye said, "but I was really hoping for more time."

Jackson looked over at her, one eyebrow raised.

"I know," she said. "And I realize how foolish it sounds, but somewhere out there, a killer has Ethan and I promised Tara I'd keep looking for him."

"How long are you staying at Saul's?"

"As long as I need to, unless they find me there. Then it's off to plan C, then D. Until Ethan is found, I'll keep up the disappearing woman routine."

"And when this is over?"

She blew out a breath. "I'm going to have to face the music sooner or later. Given the nature of my work, the sooner I talk enough to make them go away, the better."

Jackson looked a little surprised. "You're going to talk to them?"

She nodded. "I thought about it a long, long time, and I think the only way to get them to go away for good is to give them everything I'm ever going to. They'll hang around a while after that, hoping that I have some public breakdown, but eventually they'll move on and I can get back to my life."

Whatever that was.

Everything Shaye had ever known had been tossed upside down and sideways. With her memory returning and all the secrets of the past exposed, she had to figure out how everything fit into her life now. What mattered and what didn't. What needed to change and what needed to stay the same. It was an enormous amount of emotional baggage to be considered. She'd decided that taking it one day at a time was the best and only solution for a problem so big.

When Jackson pulled into the motel parking lot, Shaye let out a breath of relief that no camera crews were visible. She'd hoped that the media hadn't found out about her relationship with Saul, and so far, that looked to be the case. As she stepped out of the car, Hustle burst out the front door and rushed over to hug her. Then he shuffled awkwardly, looking slightly embarrassed at the obvious show of emotion.

"I swear," Shaye said. "You've gotten taller."

"Gonna eat me out of house and home, too," Saul's voice sounded behind Hustle, and he stepped up to give her a hug as well. The motel owner was an old client of Shaye's and had helped her with a recent case that ultimately ended with Saul becoming Hustle's foster parent.

"The Internet said it's a growth spurt," Hustle said, somewhat defensively.

Saul laughed. "Well, if the Internet said it, then it must be true. Let's get you all inside."

"I've got to go," Jackson said. "I've still got some things to review before I can call it a night."

"Let me give you a ride back to the station," Saul said.

"Thank you, but I've already called Uber. I'll meet him a couple blocks over, just in case." He tossed Shaye the keys. "Keep it as long as you need it and call me if you get anything."

"Thanks," Shaye said, hoping that single word conveyed how much she appreciated what Jackson was doing.

Jackson grinned and waved at them before heading off down the street. Shaye turned around and followed Hustle and Saul inside. Saul went behind the desk and grabbed a key card, which he handed to Shaye.

"I put you at the end on the corner," Saul said.

"You've got a view of the front and side of the motel. Gives you a way to check for them reporters, but Hustle and I will be keeping watch as well."

"I really appreciate it," Shaye said. "Please won't you let me pay you?"

"Your money is no good here," Saul said, then motioned to Hustle. "Show her the room and help her get set up. You've got the night off from desk duty."

Hustle perked up. "What about history?" He was taking online courses to get his GED and Saul was overseeing his studies.

"You can take the exam tomorrow afternoon," Saul said.

"Whoop!" Hustle let out a yell and Shaye laughed.

Hustle insisted on taking her backpack and they started off down the hall.

"The painting looks great," Shaye commented. One of the first tasks Saul had assigned the teen was painting the outdated hotel. Hustle, a budding artist, had picked ocean colors and the effect was not only updated but relaxing.

"Thanks," Hustle said. "I started on the murals in the lounge. If you have time, you should check them out."

"Of course!"

They stopped in front of her room and Shaye opened the door and stepped inside. Saul had given her one of the large rooms with a kitchenette and separate living area from the bedroom. Hustle placed her backpack on the tiny dining table and turned to look at her.

"What can I do?" he asked. "If you make me a list, I

can pick you up stuff at the convenience store. Saul didn't tell me why you're here, so I don't know what else to offer."

"I'm working on a case—a missing college student. All I'm really doing here is using it for my base. Reporters are staked out everywhere they expect me to be, so hopefully relocating here allows me to stay under the radar long enough to resolve this case."

"A missing student, huh?" Hustle frowned. "How old?"

"He's nineteen. A shy, smart kid with no parents but one really good friend who found me."

"Sounds kinda like someone I know." Hustle grinned.

It hadn't been that long ago when Hustle had asked Shaye to find his friend. Another street kid named Jinx. Now Jinx and Hustle were both off the streets and thriving. It made Shaye happy every time she thought about how things had changed so much for both of them.

"Except for the shy part," she said.

He laughed and a wave of happiness coursed through Shaye. This boy had been through so much, and to see him so relaxed and laughing was better than any gift she'd ever been given.

"So you're using Jackson's car to sneak around?" Hustle said.

"That's the plan."

He looked her up and down. "You going like that?"

Shaye looked down at her yoga pants, tee, and tennis shoes. "Yeah. What's wrong with this?"

"Nothing, except you don't look street. Aren't you trying to blend?"

"It's exercise clothes."

"Designer label exercise clothes. I mean, the wrinkled look is a nice touch and not your usual gig. Mostly you look like you've ironed everything."

Shaye cringed at the thought of ironing. "I sometimes run out of time to do my laundry so I take it to the cleaners." "Sometimes" meaning most all of the time.

"Uh-huh. Regular folk don't exercise in fancy, ironed clothes and their tennis shoes don't look like they just came out of the box. You need cheaper stuff."

"I have a ball cap?"

Hustle sighed.

"Well, what am I supposed to do? I can't risk a run to the mall and Amazon is good, but I don't think they can deliver to me tonight."

"Give me your sizes. I'll pick something up when I'm getting food."

"You're going to buy me clothes?"

"Someone has to. You ain't gonna get far looking like that. I'm surprised you made it as long as you did before them reporters was on you."

Shaye pulled her wallet out of her backpack and handed Hustle two hundred bucks. "Just get me a couple of microwave pizzas, some chips, and a bag of chocolate chip cookies. Oh, and some sodas." Then, feeling slightly guilty about the awful dietary choices, she threw in, "...and maybe a salad if they have it."

"And you think that's going to cost two hundred bucks?"

"You said you were buying clothes. Even non-designer clothes cost money. Tell you what, you fix me up with everything I need and if you do it for less than that, keep the change."

Hustle shook his head. "That would be robbery. Okay, I'm out. I'll be back in an hour or so. Don't leave here looking like that."

"I won't."

After Hustle left, Shaye pulled out her laptop and logged in to the motel Internet. It had taken a bit of searching, but while she was waiting for Jackson to come get her, she'd located the names of two of Brett's high school teachers and run down phone numbers for both. She grabbed her cell phone and called the first number, an English teacher named Matilda Wycliffe.

A woman answered on the second ring and Shaye identified herself as a counselor with the university and explained that she'd like to ask some questions about a former student of hers.

"Yes, of course," Matilda said. "I hope no one is in trouble."

"Nothing like that," Shaye said. "I'm just a little confused about something and was hoping you could help clear it up. It's about a student named Brett Frazier."

"Oh, yes, I remember Brett well. How can I help you?"

"All indicators seem to point to a high level of

intelligence, yet Brett seems content with being assumed a typical jock. I've tried to contact his parents, but they appear uninterested in returning my calls, so I thought I'd take a chance and see if one of his former teachers could shed some light on the duplicity."

Matilda sighed. "So he's still on that course, is he? I'd rather hoped when he went off to college, he'd see the folly, but apparently I was wrong about his strength of conviction."

"So he *is* above average intelligence?"

"Definitely. And beyond that, he's very clever, which is why he manages to fool most people."

"But why would he want to fool people? I assume he started doing it in high school?"

"His junior year. One of the senior boys, another member of the football team, lost his starting position because he didn't have the grades needed to attend practice. And no practice meant no playing. Brett was in some senior-level courses and this other boy blamed him for ruining the curve. Although there was never a formal complaint, you hear about things, and then when Brett showed up to school with a black eye and a busted lip, I figured the rumors were true."

"Then the dumbed-down Brett appeared?"

"Almost immediately. His grades slipped to solid Bs, and the only time he participated in class was when he was called on. Even then, he gave the right answer almost grudgingly."

"Did anyone talk to him or his parents?"

"Several of his teachers and the school counselor tried, but we couldn't get anywhere. Whatever that boy threatened Brett with must have been worse than what he'd already gotten, because he clammed up and refused to engage."

"And his parents?"

"I'm afraid they were as interested then as they appear to be now. All calls went unanswered, even when we left very detailed messages. Even when the counselor said Brett would lose any chance at academic scholarships if things didn't change. I understand that the family is well off, but why pay for an education if you don't have to?"

"It doesn't make much sense."

"How are his grades in college?"

"Quite good, actually, but his behavior is completely different from what his grades show. Even the way he talks makes him appear of average or quite frankly, below average, intelligence. So I got curious and decided to poke around. I thought maybe some sort of personality disorder or perhaps something simpler, like a father who was a football star and didn't want a chess champion for a son."

"I don't really know anything about his father, but it's as reasonable a theory as any."

"Well, I really appreciate you taking the time to talk with me. It's not a bad situation but the inconsistency of certain things nagged at me until I had to see if I could get to the bottom of it."

"I can appreciate that. If you're a keen observer of human nature, it's hard to ignore when things don't add up.

I hope Brett continues to do well in his studies. He wouldn't be the first successful person to act a complete fool."

Shaye laughed. "That's certainly true. Thank you for your time, Mrs. Wycliffe."

Shaye ended the call, not certain whether to be happy that the English teacher had reinforced her idea about Brett or unhappy that Ethan might have been living with his abductor. But in thinking about it, everything made more sense if Brett was the perpetrator or working with someone. It was Brett who said Ethan left for soda, but Thomas said he never made it to the store, and there certainly hadn't been any evidence to the contrary on the tapes. It was possible that Ethan had never gone for soda at all, but had been drugged by Brett and then transported out of the dorm in the middle of the night.

By the same token, George had claimed he stopped by the store that night to pick up some accounting, so he placed himself in the vicinity of Ethan's disappearance and could have accosted the student in the empty lot behind the store where there was no camera coverage.

Granted, Shaye's suspicion and Mrs. Wycliffe's confirmation weren't exactly hard science. Before she pressed Jackson to look into Brett and George, she'd see what the science teacher had to say. It would be a man's point of view and might differ or offer more insight than Mrs. Wycliffe's.

Five minutes later, she placed her cell phone on the table and began making notes. The science teacher had given her almost the same story as Mrs. Wycliffe. Two independent educators with the same opinion wasn't a consensus, but it was enough to convince Shaye that there was far more to Brett Frazier than what anyone could see.

She was just about to call Jackson when there was a knock on her door. She opened it up to let in Hustle, who was loaded down with bags.

"Good Lord," Shaye said. "It looks like you bought up the grocery store."

He sat the bags on the kitchenette counter. "Nah, but I added a couple things to your list. If you get to leave before you use it all, then take it back to your apartment. Not like your refrigerator was overflowing last time I looked."

"It's really bare now. You might find a water or a beer. Thanks for getting all of this."

Hustle grinned. "You wanna see your disguise?"

He looked so pleased with himself that Shaye couldn't help but smile. "I can't wait."

He grabbed one of the plastic bags from the counter and tossed it to her. "The whole thing was twenty dollars."

"Twenty dollars? How in the world…" She looked at the logo on the bag and saw that it came from a resale shop nearby. "There's even tennis shoes in here."

"And all of it cheap because it's so worn. But it's perfect for what you're doing. Go try them on. If they don't fit, I have time to get some more before the store closes."

Shaye headed into the bedroom with the bag of clothes and changed. She took a look in the mirror and shook her head. She hated to admit it, but Hustle had been right.

Even though her other clothes were rumpled from traveling, they still had that look of expensive quality. The basic gray sweatpants and black hoodie with the New Orleans Saints logo on it were the kind of clothes no one would think twice about. The well-worn Adidas completed the look. With her ball cap, it would be perfect.

She headed back into the living area and Hustle gave her a once-over. "Better," he said. "But if anyone knows you, there's no getting around your face."

He reached inside another bag on the counter and pulled out a wig of straight, shoulder- length auburn hair. "This should fix the face thing," he said.

"I don't know. Red hair might look weird on me."

"Like looking weird makes you stand out in New Orleans. Try it on."

Shaye stepped in front of a mirror hanging in the living room and twisted her long ponytail on top of her head before pulling the wig over it. She stared at her reflection in surprise.

"I barely recognize myself," she said. "What a difference."

Hustle gave her a critical look and nodded. "It's good. During the day, you can wear sunglasses and even a reporter would walk right by you."

"My own mother would walk right by me."

"Maybe not a bad thing if she's all parental and stuff."

"Ha." She looked at her reflection again. "I suppose at night I could use some black eyeliner and red lipstick to replace what the sunglasses accomplish during the day."

"And you can pull the hoodie up. I started to get you one of those temporary tattoos but I wasn't sure if you'd want to take things that far."

"I'll pass on anything with the words 'temporary' and 'tattoo' in them. Eleonore did one of those for some seminar she was attending and it took months before it wore off. I thought she was going to take a sander to her arm."

Hustle grinned. "If you change your mind, I could draw you something with markers. It would be there a few days, but not forever."

"I really appreciate all your help."

He blushed and looked down at the floor. "I ain't doing much."

"But you are, and you have. Without you, I'd have no access to an entire group of people that have been necessary to get answers."

Hustle looked back up at her. "I guess being poor has one advantage."

"You might not have money, but you're rich with other qualities. Would it surprise you if I said I don't worry about your future?"

He frowned and was silent for several seconds. Finally, he shook his head. "I don't guess it would, seeing what you've been through. You believe everyone who wants to be something can do it if they want it bad enough."

"Exactly."

"You set the bar pretty high, though."

"Nah. I'm just doing what we're all doing—getting

through one day at a time."

JANA DELEON

CHAPTER EIGHTEEN

Jackson tossed an employee file onto the conference room table that he and Grayson had been using to go through Malcolm St. Claire's personnel records. "That's the last one," Jackson said. "Moved to Seattle six months ago. Tomorrow, I can start checking with employers to make sure everyone who's moved away has been present during the time frames we're looking at. A lot of this happened during the workweek, and these are regular office-type jobs."

Grayson leaned back in his chair and stretched. "How many are left on the list that didn't leave town?"

"Four, but one is deceased. Suicide."

"Well, that eliminates one more. We'll start tomorrow taking a closer look at the three remaining in New Orleans. If we come up empty there, we'll branch out into the ones who moved away."

Jackson sighed. "I feel like we should be doing something more. What are we missing?"

Grayson shook his head. "I don't know. I've been over my notes a million times and I can't see any angle that we haven't followed up on. None of the Archer employees I talked to could think of anyone who might hold a specific grudge against St. Claire, although they all thought it was a possibility."

"What about the techs? Did they figure out anything about the code in the text?"

"No. They're stumped. They've been running it through encryption software for hours and haven't come up with anything."

"Maybe it's bullshit. Maybe it means nothing at all and the perp gets off on the fear and guilt he's causing before he kills the next victim."

Grayson nodded. "I'm sure that's true, but I still think the code means something. Serial killers are arrogant. They think they're smarter than everyone else. The texts are him issuing a challenge that he thinks no one will take him up on."

Jackson considered Grayson's theory. Based on the psychology books Eleonore had recommended to him, it was a good profile. Unfortunately, the problem with crazy was that it rarely fit a profile. Some aspects of behavior might while others appeared to be that of a totally different person, which made them so much harder to identify.

"I hope they find something soon. Ethan's running out of time, assuming he's still alive."

"Yeah."

Grayson looked at the folders spread out on the table and Jackson could tell he was frustrated and just a little angry. Jackson completely understood how he felt. It seemed that no matter what rabbit hole they went down, it ended at a brick wall.

Grayson's cell phone rang and he answered.

"What?" Grayson said, straightening in his chair. "You're sure? On my way."

Grayson jumped up from his chair and grabbed his jacket. "That was the hospital in LaPlace. They have Ethan."

Jackson jumped up from his chair and hurried out of the room after Grayson.

"He's alive?"

"Barely," Grayson said as they rushed to his car. "They recognized him from the BOLO. He's out of surgery and critical but I want to be there if he wakes up."

"*When* he wakes up."

"Yeah, when."

From the parking lot across the street, Shaye watched as George pulled out of the convenience store parking lot. She started up Jackson's car and headed out after him. She'd been watching for about twenty minutes, but hadn't seen anything that set off alarms. He'd spent ten minutes messing with the gas pumps and she'd seen him gesturing to the employee she saw the other day and pointing outside. A couple minutes later, the employee had gone outside to pick up trash in the parking lot. George had disappeared into his office for a bit, then exited the store carrying a bank bag, probably a deposit ready for the bank the next morning.

Now she followed a couple cars behind George's SUV, trying not to raise suspicion. If the store owner wasn't up to anything, he probably wouldn't notice her in the usual nighttime traffic, but if he was involved in Ethan's disappearance, then he'd be keeping a close watch on his surroundings. With Ethan's time running out, Shaye was hoping that if the store owner was involved, following him might provide a clue as to where Ethan was being held.

She followed George to the Marigny district of New Orleans and watched as he pulled down a street of narrow homes and parked in front of one. He got out of his SUV and headed for the front door. Shaye checked the street address and it matched the home address she'd found earlier for George. A thin woman with flour on her hands stepped onto the porch as he approached and smiled. He gave her a kiss and they both headed inside.

Shaye blew out a breath. That was that. Unless she thought George's wife was in on the kidnapping, there was no way Ethan was in that house. She drummed her fingers on the steering wheel, trying to decide on the best course of action. She could wait here and see if George left again or she could head back to the dorms and see if she could locate Brett Frazier. The student hadn't been in his dorm room when she'd checked earlier but he might be back now. The question was, which one was her best bet?

Unfortunately, she didn't have an answer.

The reality was, she didn't have any proof that George or Brett was involved in Ethan's disappearance or the murder of the other students. All she had was an older man with anger issues and a younger man faking a personality. Both had opportunity. What neither had, that she could see, was motive.

Her cell phone buzzed and she hurried to answer when she saw Jackson's name on the screen.

"Ethan's been found," Jackson said.

"What? Where?" Shaye could barely contain her excitement.

"Someone took him to the hospital in LaPlace. He's out of surgery and his condition is critical, but I don't know why or what the surgery was for, who brought him in, or quite frankly anything else than what I just told you. Grayson and I are on our way over there now but I thought you'd want to inform Tara."

Shaye clutched the phone, fear over Ethan's condition now overriding her elation at his being alive. What if Ethan didn't make it? What if they never found the man who did that to him?

"I'll call Tara and head over to her dorm right away. Please let me know more about his condition when you find out, and when Tara can see him."

"Definitely. I know 'watch your back' goes without saying, but I'm saying it anyway. This guy is still out there."

Jackson disconnected and Shaye immediately dialed Tara's number. The phone rang several times, then went to voice mail. Shaye left a message asking Tara to call her as soon as possible, then sent a text with the same message.

She started the car and turned around, directing it back

to the campus. Tara might be in the shower or hopefully, getting some much-needed sleep. If Tara hadn't returned her call by the time she got to the dorm, Shaye would find someone to let her inside. She needed to remember to ask Tara for the code for the building.

A couple minutes later, her phone rang. It was Tara.

"Tara," Shaye said when she answered.

"No, ma'am." A man's voice responded on the other end.

Shaye's pulse spiked. "Who is this?"

"This is Officer Bennett with the New Orleans Police Department. With whom am I speaking?"

Shaye's heart dropped into her stomach. "My name is Shaye Archer. I'm a private detective and Ms. Chatry is my client. Is she all right?"

"Archer you said?"

"Yes." Shaye struggled to maintain her cool since the officer had yet to tell her Tara's condition.

"I'm afraid Ms. Chatry has been attacked. She was brought to New Orleans General a couple hours ago. We're waiting on her to regain consciousness so we can question her."

"But she's going to be okay?"

"The doctors seem to think so. Would you mind answering some questions for me?"

"Not at all. I'll be there in ten minutes."

She pressed the accelerator down and moved through traffic as quickly as she could without breaking any major laws. A million questions ran through her mind. What had happened to Tara? Where had she been attacked? Had she seen her attacker? Why was she unconscious?

She wondered briefly if she should contact Jackson, but decided to wait until she had more information. Besides, Jackson needed to find out about Ethan and see if they could get information from him. If he was in critical condition, they might not have much opportunity to do so and the last thing she wanted to do was delay them, even for a minute.

When she pulled into the parking lot, her mind flashed back to the first time she'd entered those double doors—on a stretcher. It was the night Detective Harold Beaumont had found her wandering in the French Quarter with horrible injuries and no memory. She'd been there more recently for her work and personal reasons, but she always felt that tightening in her stomach when she saw the giant gray structure.

Just before she exited the car, she remembered the wig and yanked it off her head before hurrying inside. Two policemen, one older and one younger, stood in the corner of the lobby and looked up as she walked in. They both took in her appearance and frowned and she guessed the clothes didn't fit the image they were expecting. She headed straight for them.

"I'm Shaye Archer," she said.

"I'm Officer Bennett," the younger policeman said. "This is Officer Davis."

"Thank you for coming," Davis said.

"Anything I can do to help," Shaye said. "Can you tell

me more about Tara's condition?"

Bennett looked over at Davis, deferring to his senior officer as to protocol.

Davis nodded. "We're not completely sure what happened. What we know is a group of students crossing the courtyard on the campus heard Ms. Chatry screaming when they entered the parking area for the first dorm building."

Ethan's dorm, Shaye thought.

"They couldn't see anyone," Davis continued, "but they progressed in the direction of the screams and found Ms. Chatry on the ground close to a car, barely conscious."

Shaye's back tightened. "Is it her heart?"

"No," David said. "There was a needle puncture on her neck. We're waiting for identification of the substance. Why did you ask about her heart?"

"She has a heart condition. With the stress of an attack…"

"I see. The doctor didn't mention anything about heart problems, so I'm going to assume Ms. Chatry wasn't affected in that manner."

"That's a huge relief," Shaye said. "Did the other students see her attacker?"

"Two of them saw someone running across the courtyard and into the hedges along the south side, but he wore a hooded sweatshirt and it was dark, so they didn't get a good look at him. The car door was open. We found her cell phone on the floorboard and the keys in the ignition."

"Oh my God," Shaye said. "How horrible."

Davis nodded. "Can you tell me what Ms. Chatry hired you to do?"

Shaye nodded and explained her case all the way up to her reason for calling Tara earlier. When she finished, Bennett pulled Tara's cell phone from his pocket and turned the display to Shaye.

As she read the messages between Tara and the person she thought was Ethan, her stomach rolled. The killer knew exactly how to play her to get her out of the dorm. But he'd taken a huge risk attacking her in the parking lot. He was getting desperate.

Bennett looked at her. "You said Detective Lamotte informed you that Ethan Campbell is in critical condition in a hospital in LaPlace?"

"Yes. But I don't have any more information than that. I was hoping to hear something soon about his condition because I knew Tara would want to know and to see him."

Davis frowned. "Well, if Ethan Campbell is in critical condition in a hospital in LaPlace, he certainly didn't send these texts."

"Nope," Bennett said. "And he didn't attack Ms. Chatry. Given the texts and the fact that she appeared to have been driving his car, those were our first thoughts."

"They would have been mine as well," Shaye said. "Detective Grayson doesn't want the fact that they're investigating these cases as linked to get to the media. They don't know about Ethan's disappearance at all."

Davis nodded. "I can see why he'd want it kept under wraps as long as possible. Let's hope Ms. Chatry is able to speak soon and can shed some light on what happened. If the man who attacked her is responsible for three, potentially four, deaths, then I'd like to see him behind bars as soon as possible."

"We all would," Shaye said. "I hope Tara can help us out with that."

The doors to the rooms opened and a doctor stepped into the lobby. He headed over to the policemen and gave Shaye a questioning look.

"This is Shaye Archer," Officer Davis said. "Ms. Chatry is her client. We have no problem with you providing her information on Ms. Chatry's condition."

The doctor's eyes widened a bit and Shaye knew he was making the connection between her and the news reports. He stuck his hand out. "I'm Dr. Malloy. Do you know how to reach Ms. Chatry's next of kin?"

"I'm afraid not," Shaye said. "She told me her parents were missionaries currently working in South Africa. There's an aunt in another state, but no one else that I'm aware of."

Dr. Malloy nodded. "Then we'll have to wait for Ms. Chatry to regain focus to get more information."

"How is she?" Shaye asked. "Was she seriously hurt?"

"She was extremely lucky," Dr. Malloy said. "Her right knee is swollen and bruised. It was wrapped when she was brought in, so I assumed an existing injury, but some of the damage is probably from this event. There's nothing broken, and I expect her knee will return to normal after a couple weeks of rest. The more concerning part is what she was injected with."

"You've identified the substance used?" Davis asked.

Dr. Malloy nodded. "It was propofol."

"Oh my God," Shaye said. "You're sure her heart wasn't affected? She has a heart condition."

"I noticed some abnormalities," Dr. Malloy said, "but nothing appeared to be brought on by the drug. I had put it down to stress, but an underlying condition would explain the abnormalities." He shook his head. "Ms. Chatry was even luckier than I originally thought."

"Isn't propofol used for surgery?" Bennett asked.

"In some cases," Dr. Malloy said. "It's a powerful relaxant and a very dangerous one if used incorrectly."

"That's why she fell unconscious so quickly," Davis said.

"Yes," Dr. Malloy said. "She was given a pretty healthy dose. Quite frankly, I'm surprised she managed to break away, and I'm more than interested in hearing exactly how she managed it."

"How would someone get propofol?" Davis asked. "It can't be that easy to acquire."

"No," Dr. Malloy said. "It's a closely monitored drug, but there are thefts of laboratories and pharmacies. It's sold on the street for a high price."

"Do you have any idea how long it will take her to regain consciousness?" Shaye asked. "The officers need to talk to her as soon as possible. The man who attacked her is suspected of three other murders and the abduction of another student who's in critical condition now."

Dr. Malloy's eyes widened. "Good Lord. I had no idea…I'll check on Ms. Chatry again and let you know. She was starting to stir when I reviewed her vitals before speaking with you. I'll be right back."

As Dr. Malloy walked back through the double doors, Davis turned to Shaye. "Did the others have propofol in their systems?"

"No," Shaye said. "Rohypnol. Which makes more sense in the first two cases. They were both taken from parties. It would be far easier to assist someone who appears to be drunk outside and into an automobile than drag someone completely unconscious away from a large group of people. But they were all held somewhere for days before they were killed. Maybe he used propofol once they were in place to keep them immobile."

Davis nodded. "It would have worked out of their systems within twenty-four hours. They used it on my wife for surgery and I asked since I've heard bad things about it. But you said the other victim had Rohypnol in her system?"

"Yes," Shaye said, her stomach turning slightly as she realized what had probably happened to Amber. "I think he needed her to be able to walk in order to pull off the location. It was Amber Olivier."

"The girl in the coffin?" Bennett asked. "That's sick."

"Beyond," Davis agreed. "Since Ms. Chatry was already on guard and there was no party to use as a backdrop, he needed her out quickly."

"That's my guess," Shaye said. "And taking her out in the car solved the issue of transport."

The doors opened and Dr. Malloy walked back into the lobby. "Ms. Chatry is conscious, but she's still a bit scattered and is likely to remain that way for a while. She asked me to contact you, Ms. Archer. I will let the three of you speak with her, but please make it as quick as possible. She's clearly exhausted and needs to rest."

They followed Dr. Malloy down the hall and into a room where Tara was propped up in the bed. She was so pale, Shaye worried that the drugs had affected her more than the doctor realized, but then Tara hadn't been sleeping well either. Shaye went immediately to the side of the bed and put her hand on Tara's arm.

"Are you all right?" Shaye asked.

"Yeah," Tara said, her voice weak. "I mean, considering."

"I'm so sorry you had to go through this," Shaye said. "These two officers need to ask you some questions. Can you remember well enough to help?"

"I think so," Tara said.

Davis stepped up to the bed. "I'm Officer Davis. Ms. Archer has filled us in on your missing friend and we saw the texts exchanged on your cell phone. Can you please tell me what happened?"

Tara nodded. "I went to the dorm to take Ethan his car and some money, just like he asked, but he wasn't there. The door was unlocked but the room was empty. I got a bad feeling about it, you know?"

"I know that feeling well," Davis said.

"I hauled ass out of there," Tara said. "When I got in

the car, I was going to call Shaye and tell her what happened, but he was in the backseat." She frowned. "Stupid. I know better than to get into a car without checking the backseat."

"You weren't thinking clearly," Shaye said. "Don't be so hard on yourself."

Tara gave her a grateful look. "He put his arm around my head and covered my mouth so that I couldn't scream. I tried to pull his arm off but I couldn't. When I felt the needle go into my neck, I yanked away as hard as I could and opened the door. I tried to run out, but I was already getting dizzy, so I fell. I couldn't stand, so I started crawling and screaming."

Tara's eyes filled with tears. "The last thing I remember was seeing tennis shoes and wondering if the shoes of my killer was the last thing I'd ever see."

Shaye squeezed Tara's arm. "You were so brave and you acted quickly."

Tara sniffed. "Thanks."

"Can you describe the man who attacked you?" Davis asked.

Tara frowned. "No. I should have looked up and seen him in the rearview mirror, right? But I don't remember seeing him at all."

Davis nodded. "The mirror was turned all the way up and to the right when we inspected the car. We thought it might have happened during a struggle, but it appears our perpetrator thought of everything."

"He certainly fooled me," Tara said. "I was so stupid. I

should have known better."

"You're a good friend," Shaye said. "You were just trying to help Ethan. You're not to blame for this. This guy knew enough to play on your emotions."

"He knew I had Ethan's car," Tara said. "That means he's been watching me."

Shaye nodded. "I think so."

"I don't understand what he wants with me," Tara said. "I'm not part of his game. And if he wants to kill me so badly, I know Ethan is already dead."

"No. He's not," Shaye said.

"You can't know that," Tara said, beginning to cry.

"Ethan is in critical condition in a hospital in LaPlace," Shaye said.

Tara's eyes widened and she straightened. "What? Is he going to be all right? How did he get there?"

"I don't have any details," Shaye said. "Detectives Grayson and Lamotte called me on their way to the hospital. As soon as they know more, they're going to let me know."

"But he's alive?" Tara asked.

"Detective Grayson was told he was alive, but barely, and had just come out of surgery. I don't know for what. Hopefully, we'll know more soon."

Tears streamed down Tara's face. "At least there's a chance though. He got away from that psycho."

"There's definitely a chance," Shaye said. She looked over at Davis, who inclined his head toward the doctor standing in the doorway.

"You need to rest," Shaye said. "We're going to get out of here so you can do that."

"No!" Tara shook her head. "You can't leave until I know more about Ethan." Tara looked over at the doctor. "I won't be able to rest until I know."

"We'll get Ms. Archer a chair," Dr. Malloy said. "She can sit with you until you fall asleep."

"Thank you," Shaye said, relieved that she wouldn't have to leave Tara alone in the hospital.

"Would you like us to contact your parents?" Dr. Malloy asked. "Ms. Archer informed me that they're out of the country."

"Not yet," Tara said. "They'd just worry and there's nothing they can do."

"Very well," Dr. Malloy said. "Let the nurse know if you change your mind."

"Thank you for your assistance, Ms. Archer," Officer Davis said. "I'll provide Detective Grayson with all the information we have as soon as he is available."

Shaye nodded. "Thanks."

The officers left the room and a couple seconds later, a nurse came into the room, dragging a chair behind her.

"Does Clara Mandeville work tonight?" Shaye asked.

"Yes, ma'am. She comes on at eleven," the nurse said.

"Who's Clara?" Tara asked.

"A friend. Clara looked after me when I was brought into the hospital nine years ago. They won't let me stay all night, but I don't want you to worry. Clara will make sure you're all right."

Tara looked down at the blanket covering her. "How long do you think we'll have to wait to hear about Ethan?"

"I don't know, but Jackson will call as soon as he can. In the meantime, try to relax."

"I'm not sure I'll ever relax again."

"You will. I won't lie to you and say it's easy, and the reality is you'll probably never think the same way as you did before all of this. But that doesn't mean you can't have an awesome life. You just have to choose to do it and work your butt off to accomplish it."

Tara studied her in silence for a bit, then nodded. "I feel stupid thinking that way when I know what you went through—and that's just what they reported on television. I'm sure whatever they said, the reality was a million times worse."

"Don't ever feel bad for being scared or hurt or sad. There is always someone somewhere who is suffering more than another, but this is the worst thing that's ever happened to *you*."

"You always know the right thing to say."

"I had excellent teachers."

Tara smiled. "Looks like I do now, too."

Shaye's phone buzzed and she looked at the display. "It's Detective Lamotte," she said as she pressed the screen to answer.

"Do you have an update?" Shaye asked.

"Yeah," Jackson said. "He's in bad shape. The doctor said it looks like an alligator attack. His left arm was almost ripped from the socket. He was in surgery to reattach it, but the doctor can't guarantee that he'll be able to use it again."

Shaye struggled to remain calm for Tara's sake. "Is that it?"

"I wish. He had sustained so much blood loss that he was nearly dead when he got to the hospital. Between the blood loss and the trauma, there's a chance he won't make it."

"Did the doctor give odds?"

"Fifty percent."

Shaye blew out a breath. "That's better than the alternative, right?"

"At this point, we'll take what we can get. Are you at the dorm?"

"Not exactly. Tara was attacked. She's in the emergency room at New Orleans General."

"What? Is she okay?"

"She's going to be but she took a hit of propofol and they want to keep her overnight. He got away and unfortunately, she wasn't able to get a good look at him."

"Damn it. This guy keeps slipping through our fingers. Look, I want to get the details, but right now, I need you to take a look at something."

"What is it?"

"An image from the security cameras at the hospital. A guy carried Ethan into the emergency room lobby, then disappeared. He had on a hoodie but an inside camera got a shot of his face from the side. I'm hoping Tara can identify him. Give me a couple seconds to send it."

"Okay."

Shaye lowered her phone a bit to fill Tara in. The girl was so tense she looked ready to spring out of the bed.

"Oh my God!" Tara gasped when Shaye told her about the alligator attack.

"I'm not going to lie to you," Shaye said. "It's really bad. The doctor is giving him a fifty percent chance of survival and if he survives, there are no guarantees he'll have use of his arm again."

"Poor Ethan," Tara cried, tears streaming down her face. "How could that happen?"

"I don't know, but Detective Lamotte is going to send us an image. A man brought Ethan to the emergency room, then disappeared. He wants to see if you can identify the man."

"Why would he disappear?" Tara asked, clearly confused.

"I don't know," Shaye said. "Unless he was involved in some way."

"Shaye?" Jackson's voice sounded on her phone.

"Yes," Shaye said.

"I just sent you a text with the image."

Shaye's phone dinged. "Hold on," she said, and moved next to Tara as she accessed her text messages.

Both of them gasped when they saw the image.

It was Brett Frazier.

CHAPTER NINETEEN

Shaye let herself back into her motel room, locking the door right behind her. Out of habit, she made sure the rooms were clear before grabbing a soda from the refrigerator and sinking down into a chair in the living room. It was after midnight and she couldn't even remember the last time she'd had more than an hour of sleep at one time. She was running on empty.

Even though she'd wondered about him before, Tara had been distraught over seeing Brett in the image. She was convinced it was Brett who had coaxed her to the dorm and hidden in the car. No matter that she'd thought something was off with Ethan's roommate, she hadn't wanted to make the leap to Brett being the killer. Until now.

And the timing worked.

Brett had taken Ethan to the hospital hours before Tara was attacked. He would have had time to get back to the dorm and set up Tara. Or, if she went with her other theory, Brett dropped Ethan off but his partner George was the one who attacked Tara. The part Shaye couldn't answer was why Brett had taken Ethan to the emergency room, and the harder she thought about it, the less sense it made.

A knock at the door broke into her thoughts and she got up to let Jackson in. When they'd spoken earlier, they'd agreed that a face-to-face exchange would be beneficial and it needed to happen now. With Ethan in the hospital and the attempt on Tara unsuccessful, the killer might decide to cut his losses and disappear. The police needed evidence to arrest people, and they needed it quickly.

Jackson came in, looking as exhausted as she felt. She waved him to the table and he slumped into a chair, blowing out a breath as he sat.

"Soda or water?" Shaye asked, standing at the open refrigerator.

"Soda."

"You hungry?"

"Starved."

"Good, because I can't remember the last time I ate and I don't want to look like a pig in front of you." She pulled turkey lunch meat and cheese from the refrigerator and grabbed bread and chips from the counter and dumped it all on the table. Then she snagged two plates from the cabinets and took a seat across from Jackson.

"It's not gourmet," she said, "but I'm guessing you don't care."

"Looks like gourmet to me," Jackson said, and reached for the bread. "How's Tara?"

"Hurt, scared, horrified. Worried for Ethan and angry at herself for trusting the text and not listening to her instincts about Brett."

"She's being too hard on herself."

"I told her that, but I know better than most how hard that is to believe sometimes."

"But she's physically all right, considering?"

"Her knee is pretty banged up and her head was still hurting from the drugs, but the doctor said she should be okay to release tomorrow sometime. They want to make sure the drugs have moved through her system without causing any issues, especially given her heart condition. They'll retest tomorrow."

"We'll put an unmarked unit on her dorm tomorrow when she's released. Brett may have had a burst of conscience when he took Ethan to the hospital, but Tara's attack happened after that so she's definitely not in the clear."

"Any sign of Brett?" She grabbed a handful of chips and starting munching on them.

"None. Detectives questioned everyone they could find at the dorm and no one has seen him since this morning. We can't verify if he attended classes until tomorrow but my guess is no. We have a unit outside the dorm watching for him."

"And his vehicle is gone?"

Jackson nodded. "We put out a BOLO on Brett and the truck."

"Suspect armed and potentially dangerous?"

"Yeah." Jackson shook his head. "I don't get it. If Brett is the killer, why did he take Ethan to the hospital?"

"I've been wondering the same thing. I mean, he has to be involved or he wouldn't have known where to find Ethan. If Ethan had stumbled into the dorm in that condition, there would have been no reason for Brett to flee the hospital after leaving him."

"Exactly. But an alligator attack? That doesn't fit the MO of any of the previous deaths. We know all of them were held somewhere before they were killed. Assuming Ethan was held at the same place as the others, how did he come into contact with an alligator?"

"I have no earthly idea. Maybe the place the victims were held is in the swamp. Ethan might have managed to get away and then got attacked by the alligator."

"Maybe. But why rescue Ethan? He hasn't shown any mercy for the other victims. If anything, he ensured their deaths were horrifying."

"I have this theory. It's a real long shot, but I'm going to put it out there." She told Jackson about George's temper and his past arrests, then described the argument she'd witnessed between George and Brett.

Jackson frowned. "If they were working together, that would explain a lot, especially since the last two places Ethan might have been were his dorm or the store."

Shaye nodded. "That's what I was thinking."

"So do you think Brett was okay with it until Ethan was the target? Maybe he got cold feet because he had some sympathy for his roommate?"

"Who knows? The bigger problem is why. What's the motive? I can't come up with a decent motive for either one of them, much less why the two would have joined forces."

"Any connection between them?"

"Not that I could find, but I did find out something interesting about Brett. He's not nearly as dumb as he'd like people to think he is." Shaye told Jackson about the newspaper article about the chess tournament and her conversations with Brett's high school teachers.

"Jesus," Jackson said when she finished. "Yet another piece to a puzzle that has no shape or form. We're missing something."

"I know. But I have no idea where to find it."

"Me either." He rose from the chair. "And part of that is because we're both exhausted. I'm going to get out of here and let you get some sleep. We both need it."

Shaye stood up and followed him to the door. "Normally, I'd say I probably wouldn't be able to with this much on my mind, but I think my mind has officially signed off."

"Something will break. New facts will surface or we'll catch Brett and he'll talk. Something. Or maybe with some sleep one of us will be able to put it all together."

"I hope so."

"The silver lining is at least Ethan is found and safe. I know his chances aren't good but they're better than they were when he was still captive."

She nodded. "I think he'll make it. He's a fighter, clearly."

He looked at her and gave her a sad smile. "You know

all about that."

"I suppose I do."

He looked her straight in the eye for several seconds without saying a word, and more than anything, she wanted to know what was going through his mind because his expression was so intense.

"This probably isn't a good idea," he said, "but I'm too tired to talk myself out of it."

He moved toward her and as his lips lowered to hers, she felt her heart pounding in her chest as she leaned closer until their bodies touched. He brushed his lips lightly against hers, then pressed a tiny bit more before pulling his head away. His eyes searched hers, and she knew he felt he had taken a huge risk and was waiting to see if he'd blown it.

"Actually," she said, "that was the best idea you've had all day."

He smiled and Shaye knew that particular smile was only for her. "This could be complicated," he said.

"I live for complicated."

He stared at the hospital, anger coursing through him. Everything was wrong. It had started out so well, everything going according to plan. Now nothing was right. It was all falling apart and no matter what he did to get it back on track, he felt the noose tightening around him. He couldn't remain in the shadows for much longer because either the cops or that bitch Shaye Archer would eventually expose him.

He'd thought he could get Archer off the case by alerting the media to her presence, but she'd been smarter than he'd given her credit for. He'd seen her yank the wig off when she parked at the hospital, and her clothes didn't remotely resemble her usual fare. It was enough to fool reporters, who would be looking for the well-dressed brunette, not the rumpled redhead.

The nosy one was the final cog in his wheel and it frustrated him that two attempts to eliminate her had been unsuccessful. He needed to pack his things and get out of town. Start over somewhere else with a clean slate and no baggage from his past. But before he could do that, the nosy one had to die. She was ultimately responsible for ruining his carefully made plans.

He'd never manage it while she was in the hospital, but once she was released, he'd figure out a way.

Then he'd leave and become someone else.

Someone better.

Someone no one would pass over or take advantage of again.

The room was dark except for the candles on the stone shelves, flickering with the draft and causing the shadows to leap on the wall behind them. The girl on the stone altar was in horrible pain. The worst pain she'd ever felt. She was convinced her body was tearing in

two. The man and woman standing next to her wore the masks, as they always did. The woman had a tray of tools—scissors and other silver things that the girl couldn't identify.

She hoped the tools would kill her because it would mean an end to all the pain. All the suffering and fear that had gone on for so long. So long, she couldn't even remember anymore.

The woman picked up a big needle and grabbed the girl's arm that was chained to the altar. The woman jabbed the needle into her ravaged skin and the girl cried out. Seconds later, she began to feel drowsy and a wave of fear coursed through her. Had they given her something to kill her? Or was it the same as all the other times— where she awakened with more bruises and her body destroyed a bit more than the time before?

She prayed it was a lethal dose. That when she woke up, she'd be in heaven with a perfect body and no pain. With wings instead of chains on her wrists.

Free.

Shaye bolted upright, her heart pounding in her chest, and struggled not to scream. For those few seconds, she'd been catapulted right back into her horrific past, and even worse, the dream had exposed something she had yet to remember. Something she thought she'd been completely drugged during and would never remember.

But there it was, seeping out into her conscious like a toxic spill.

She knew she'd been pregnant when she was captive. Her body showed the signs of having carried and delivered a baby, but doctors had assumed it wasn't a viable birth.

Given her age and malnourishment to the point almost of starvation, doctors speculated that the baby had been premature and stillborn.

But what if they had been wrong?

The child in her dreams didn't know what forceps looked like, but an adult Shaye knew that the tools she'd seen on the tray were used to deliver a baby. Everything after they administered the drug was foggy and a lot of it blank. But somewhere, way back in the recesses of her mind, she could hear the faint cry of an infant.

Was it real? Or was her confused mind playing tricks on her?

She checked her watch. Six a.m. There was zero point in attempting to go back to sleep. After the dream, sleep was the last thing she wanted. She threw back the covers and went into the kitchen to start a pot of coffee. Hustle had apparently clued in to some of her bad habits when he'd stayed at her apartment and had bought chocolate Pop-Tarts. She popped one in the toaster and grabbed a coffee cup, hovering near the pot.

Breakfast and huge mug of coffee in hand, she sat at the table, then drank and munched in silence. Every time her mind tried to shift back to the dream, she forced herself to think of something else. The dream was something she needed to explore, but not right now. With the killer still at large, Tara and Ethan were her primary concerns. Horrors from her past could be addressed at any time. Shaye took them seriously, but they weren't life-and-death. Not anymore. Besides, she had no way of knowing how much of the dream was real versus imagined.

When her memory started to return, she'd found that certain things were exactly as she'd dreamed them, but others weren't. Some of it was probably her mind's way of protecting her from the worst of the abuse, and other instances could have been memories of news stories and movies incorporating themselves into the recall of a girl who didn't understand what was happening to her.

Shaye sat the coffee mug down and reached for her phone. Corrine had sent a text fifteen minutes before, asking her to check in when she got a chance. Clearly, it wasn't an emergency or she would have called, but Shaye knew how much her mother worried, and not just about Shaye. Corrine's heart for children had no limit. Her mother had probably been up half the night worried about Tara and Ethan, and the only thing Shaye had managed to do the night before was let Corrine know Ethan was alive but critical. She hadn't even told her about Tara's attack. It just would have upset her, and Shaye wanted her mother to get more sleep.

In a way, it was funny because the only "lies" Shaye and Corrine told each other were lies of omission. And both did it for the same reason—to protect the other person. The only person who never lied or omitted was Eleonore. No matter the situation, Shaye could always count on Eleonore to lay it out straight. It was both comforting and sometimes frustrating to have the truth spelled out.

Shaye called her mother and Corrine answered on the

first ring.

"You're awake early," Corrine said, which translated to "are you all right?"

"Lots on my mind," Shaye said. "And there's a sense of urgency with all of this. I don't want this guy to get away."

"You think he's going to cut and run?"

"I do, and Jackson agrees. Assuming he hasn't already. The main suspect hasn't been seen in a day."

"You have a suspect?"

"A whole lot more went down yesterday than what I had time to tell you about."

"Do you have time now?"

"Let me get another cup of coffee first." Shaye poured another cup, added way too much sugar given that she'd just eaten a Pop-Tart, and started filling Corrine in on everything that had happened the day before.

"Those poor children," Corrine said when she was done. "They've both been through hell and with Ethan's health questionable, I know Tara is terrified."

"She is, but she's stronger than she thinks. No matter what happens with Ethan, she'll come through this, but if we don't catch this guy, it will be so much harder."

"I know."

"Is there anything I can do? I know they're both adults in the eyes of the law, but that doesn't mean they don't need help."

"There's nothing you can do right now that I can think of but when this is all over, and assuming Ethan makes it, they could probably both use some visits to Eleonore. I'll split the cost with you."

"Deal."

"So what's going on with the media?"

Corrine sighed. "They're still staked out on the street. I counted five crews from my bedroom window, but I can't see the side street from there."

"What are you going to do about it?"

"At the moment, nothing. My attorney is coming today so that we can go over my plans to dissolve my interests in Archer Manufacturing and the other holdings. I know it's an intricate process and don't expect it to happen quickly, but I need to get things going so that I feel like I'm moving forward."

"If you're certain that's what you want to do, then I think it's an excellent idea. Let me know if you need anything from me."

"Before this is over, I'll probably need you to listen to me bitch and whine at least a thousand times."

Shaye smiled. "Will you bake before you bitch?"

"That can be arranged."

Shaye finished up the call with her mother and headed into the bathroom for a shower. Given her lack of quality sleep, she probably could have benefited from another cold one, but she couldn't make herself do it. Instead, she cranked up the heat to loosen up the muscles in her back and neck. Ten minutes later, she came out pink and feeling a million times better than she had before.

She pulled on wrinkled yoga pants and T-shirt and

headed back into the kitchen to find something more substantial to eat. The Pop-Tart was good, but sugar didn't last very long when she was hyped. An inspection of the refrigerator revealed a carton of eggs and a package of bagels, so she whipped up a real breakfast, reminding herself to thank Hustle for doing such an excellent job with the food and the clothes.

As she stirred the eggs in the skillet, she smiled, thinking about the first time she'd met the skittish street teen. It had been her first case on her own, and Hustle had come into contact with a stalker who was terrorizing Shaye's client. Hustle had been wary of Shaye but when she'd explained the situation, he'd been angry at being complicit in the stalker's game and happy to talk. Hustle's mother had been stalked and killed by an ex-boyfriend, so it was personal. It wasn't even five months prior, but when Shaye thought about how different life was for her and Hustle, and how much they'd experienced during those months, it felt like so much longer.

She plated her food and sat down at the table again, this time opening her laptop. She checked email first and then local news. The media were all reporting Corrine and Shaye's return, but with no photos and no statements, there was little else they could say beyond the usual speculation. Shaye scanned the sites for anything about Ethan or the other murders, but so far, it looked as if Grayson had been successful keeping the situation under wraps.

As she was checking the last news website, she typed in the domain name incorrectly and the address field flashed a set of numbers before shifting to a website offering her the ability to purchase the domain name. And then something occurred to her.

She pulled out her phone and looked at the string of numbers that Brenda had received. Surely it wasn't that simple. She typed the numbers into the address bar, placing periods between the numbers to create a URL address. The screen flickered and a black graphic with red lettering appeared.

You're too late.

No way this was a coincidence. She'd solved the code. But if there was any real information on how to find Ethan, it was long gone now. The killer had either changed it after Ethan was freed or the site had never contained any information in the first place. She drummed her fingers on the table. There was a way to access cached data, right?

She opened a Google search and typed the URL into the search field. When the site came up in the search list, she clicked the down arrow and then the cached link, but the only thing returned was a duplicate of the page currently posted. Did that mean nothing else was ever on the page? That Brett never intended for anyone to find the victims? Or maybe he was smart enough to somehow clear the cached file.

She blew out a breath. Her knowledge of tech stuff was decent, but she didn't have the education to delve into things like this. She kept telling herself she needed to invest some time in technology courses, but that good intention wouldn't solve the problem she had right now.

She needed someone good with computers.

And then she remembered Brittany, Amber's sorority sister. Brittany had wanted to work in forensic science. Shaye had no way of knowing if Brittany possessed the knowledge to do what she needed, but if she didn't, she'd probably know someone who could. She checked her watch. A little after 7:00 a.m. With any luck, she could catch Brittany before she left for class.

She dashed back into the bedroom and threw on her resale outfit and wig and hurried out the door. Traffic was already getting heavy, so it took about thirty minutes to reach the sorority house. Lights were on inside and a couple of girls were exiting the house and headed down the sidewalk. Shaye crossed her fingers that Brittany was still there and hurried up the sidewalk to knock on the front door.

The girl who answered the door wasn't one she'd met previously, and the look she gave Shaye after giving her a once-over wasn't overly inviting.

"I need to see Brittany," Shaye said. "Is she here?"

"I'm not sure," the girl said. "Can I say who's calling?"

"Shaye. We spoke the other day."

"Okay. Wait here." The girl closed the door and Shaye could hear her heels clicking on the hardwood floors. She expected the girl to return and tell her Brittany wasn't there, but a couple minutes later, Brittany opened the door, looked at her, and frowned. Then her expression cleared and she motioned Shaye inside.

"I didn't recognize you at first," Brittany said. "You must be hiding from the reporters. They were all talking last night about how you and your mother are back in town."

Shaye nodded. "It's hard to conduct an investigation if you're being followed by a camera crew."

"That sucks. People should just leave you alone. It's not like you haven't been through enough."

"I wish they all shared your sentiment."

"Well, I'm sure you didn't come here to chat, so what can I help you with?"

Shaye glanced around at the girls bustling through the kitchen and lobby, all casting curious glances at Shaye and Brittany. "Is there somewhere private we can talk?"

"Of course. Follow me."

Brittany headed down the hall toward the big meeting room where Shaye had talked with the sisters the day before, but instead of going all the way to the end, let them into an office-sized room with a desk and three chairs. Shaye pulled out her laptop and explained to Brittany the messages and how she'd realized it was a URL.

"Wow," Brittany said as Shaye opened her laptop and pointed to the screen. "The whole thing is so evil. I know it's real, but reading case studies is a whole lot different from being confronted with it in person."

"What I'd like to know is if that website contained different information before this. I checked the cache for the website page the easy way, but it doesn't come up with anything."

Brittany nodded. "So you want to know if there were ever instructions for finding Ethan."

"Yes," Shaye replied. She felt guilty that she couldn't tell Brittany that Ethan had been found, but she couldn't risk the information getting out. "Is there another way to find cached site information, assuming there is any to find?"

"You're in luck. We just finished covering this in one of my tech classes. Give me a few minutes to check some things. If I can't figure it out, I know a guy who can."

"That's great," Shaye said and pulled out her phone. While Brittany clicked away on her laptop, Shaye made some notes about the case that she'd been too exhausted to make the night before.

"I've got it," Brittany said, beaming.

"Really?" Shaye put her phone on the desk and leaned over for a better view of the laptop.

The site contained a time-elapse counter and two rows of numbers and letters.

"It's GPS coordinates," Shaye said, excitement coursing through her.

"Do you think they really lead to the place where Ethan is being held? Or do you think it's a trap?"

"I don't know, but either way, it could provide the lead we desperately need. Thank you for this, Brittany. If you ever decide to go the private route when you graduate, let me know. I could use someone with your skill set."

Brittany blushed. "Thank you. That's the coolest offer I've ever received and I'll be thinking hard about it." She looked down at the floor, then back at Shaye. "I really respect what you're doing. You probably have more options than almost everyone living in New Orleans, but you're doing this. This city is lucky to have you."

"Thank you," Shaye said, feeling a bit embarrassed. "Personal economics are the reason I can do this, and I'm thankful for them every day."

"Plenty of people have money. Most of them aren't doing anything to help others, especially at this level. I think it's a calling. I know I can't imagine myself doing any other kind of work."

"Then you're going to be great at it. Thanks again for your help. I'm going to get this information to the police and see what they find."

"I hope they find Ethan and that he's still alive," Brittany said. "Can you let me know?"

"As soon as the police say it's okay to release information, I promise to call you."

Shaye shoved her laptop into its case and hurried out of the sorority house, dialing Jackson's number on the way to her car. This could be the big break they'd been looking for.

Jackson answered on the first ring.

"I've got something," she said.

CHAPTER TWENTY

Jackson studied the GPS as Grayson drove down the narrow dirt road into the swamp. He'd been floored when Shaye called him to say she'd broken the code and even more surprised that it revealed GPS coordinates. They'd been looking for something to break, and this might be the thing that brought down the house of cards.

"Still no sign of Frazier?" Grayson asked.

"No. I spoke with the detectives covering his dorm and he never returned. They asked around again and no one can remember seeing him yesterday."

"What about classes?"

"One of his professors isn't due in until noon but the other two he had classes with said he was a no-show."

Grayson shook his head. "What the hell is going on here? If Frazier took Ethan, why return him? Why didn't he kill him like the others?"

"Panic. Guilt. Maybe Shaye's theory of Brett working with George Moss would explain it. Brett was okay with the others, but couldn't do it to his roommate. Honestly, I have no idea."

"That's one of the most difficult things about this job.

You know the perp has a reason, and to him, it's perfectly logical. But sometimes it's almost impossible for sane people to connect the dots."

Jackson nodded. "I've tried to connect the victims every way possible and I'm coming up blank. The only things they have in common are they're all college students and they've probably all been inside Moss's store at some point."

"Not exactly a smoking gun."

"Maybe there's not one for us to find. Maybe it's as simple as the victims resemble people Brett hates or who he feels wronged him in some way. Or George. Or neither of them, because the killer could turn out to be someone else entirely."

Grayson shook his head. "My money's on Frazier, and I'm really hoping we catch him at wherever we're going. Probably a shack somewhere."

Jackson scanned their surroundings. "I'll take a shack over a crypt."

The last time Jackson had been in a crypt—and he hoped it really was the last time—he'd found an emotionally broken Shaye, whose memory of her past had flooded back in and who'd just witnessed the death of her captor and the suicide of her grandfather. Sometimes, he had nightmares of the stone prison that Shaye had spent so many years in, and he always awakened so angry that it took him hours for the feeling to subside.

"Well, someone's been out here," Grayson said, pointing to tire tracks in the softer ground.

"And recently," Jackson agreed. "It looks like we need to veer off to the right in about fifty yards. The location is about twenty yards after the turn."

Due to the poor condition of the road, Grayson was already driving slow, but he backed off the accelerator a bit more and they both started scanning the brush, looking for any sign of a structure or another road. Fifty yards came and went and Jackson was starting to chalk the entire thing up to bullshit when Grayson slammed the brakes and pointed.

"There!"

The turnoff from the main road had large branches in front of it, leaving it almost hidden from view, which is exactly what the killer wanted. The ground in front of the turnoff showed no signs of passage by a vehicle.

"He swept the ground," Jackson said.

Grayson nodded. "I think we should go in on foot. The car offers an easy target. He could just position himself somewhere in the swamp and pick us off when we open the doors."

Jackson grabbed two sets of binoculars from a duffel bag in the backseat and handed one to Grayson, and they climbed out of the car and slipped behind the makeshift blockade and into the swamp. Jackson, who'd had the most tracking experience, took the lead. The car path was overgrown but because the forest surrounding it was so dense, it was still easy to follow. Someone had been using it recently, but the trampled foliage wasn't completely brown, so it hadn't been in use for too long.

They crept down the path until they could see a clearing. Jackson pointed to the swamp and stepped off the path and into the brush. The path offered their opponent too much line of sight, and they would be harder to spot moving through the dense forest. At the edge of the clearing, Jackson stopped and lifted his binoculars, peering through a thick hedge.

"There," Jackson said. "Twenty yards in and to the right."

Grayson nodded. "I see it."

"There's a padlock on the door. It looks new."

"Sounds like the right place. No car there, though."

"No. But there's water nearby. He could also be accessing it by boat."

"Can we get any closer?"

"Yeah. If we skirt the edge of the forest around to the side, it will put us half the distance we are now."

"Maybe we'll luck out and there won't be any windows."

Jackson headed off to the right, leading them around the clearing and near the side of the shed. As the side came into their field of vision, Jackson was relieved to see there were no windows. They inched up to the edge of the forest and Jackson pointed to the ground on the side of the shed.

"Looks like someone dug a hole," Jackson said.

"Maybe it was Ethan."

Jackson sat the binoculars on the ground and pulled out his nine-millimeter. "Let's go see if we can figure it out."

They crept out of the woods and inched toward the shed, listening for any sound inside. When they reached the side, Jackson knelt down and looked through the hole. He rose back up and pointed to his legs, then the shed, hoping Grayson would get that he could see legs inside.

Grayson nodded and pressed his ear against the side of the structure. Jackson did the same, but nothing moved inside. Grayson pointed to the front of the shed and they moved around the side. Grayson took position several feet away from the shed at the corner and Jackson stood a couple of feet away right in front of the door. He looked over at Grayson and nodded.

Grayson lifted his pistol and fired a single shot into the lock, breaking it off the door. The instant he fired the shot, Jackson kicked open the door and burst in, gun in firing position. It took only a second for Jackson to recognize the figure attached to the legs. The body slumped in the corner belonged to Brett Frazier.

Jackson lowered his gun and rushed over to check the student's pulse. "He's got a pulse."

Grayson scanned him up and down. "No sign of injury. No blood."

Jackson looked at both sides of Brett's neck and pointed to the needle puncture. "Drugged."

Grayson nodded and pulled out his cell phone. "I'll get a forensics team out here, but I'm betting this is where Ethan Campbell was held. We need to get him to the hospital."

As soon as Grayson finished speaking, Brett started to

stir. He blinked several times, then looked up at Jackson and bolted upright, a frightened expression on his face.

Jackson pulled out his badge. "I'm Detective Lamotte with the New Orleans Police Department. Are you all right to stand?"

Brett's expression shifted from frightened to relieved. "Oh my God. When I saw the guns, I thought you were him."

"Who is him?" Grayson asked.

"The guy that stabbed me in the neck with something." He reached up and rubbed the side of his neck where the puncture wound was.

"You can identify him?" Jackson asked, getting excited.

Brett shook his head. "He ambushed me."

"What were you doing here in the first place?" Jackson asked.

"Looking for Ethan," Brett answered.

Grayson frowned. "You found Ethan. You dropped him off at the hospital, then fled. Now we find you here, in the location Ethan was probably held captive. So we'll ask you again, why are you here and how did you know about this place?"

Brett looked back and forth between the two of them and then his eyes widened. "Am I a suspect?"

"What do you think?" Jackson asked.

"No!" Brett struggled to rise from the ground. He was a bit shaky, but finally stood, looking at them. "I didn't do anything. I swear. I looked on Ethan's computer and found the code in that journal of his that he thinks no one knows about. I figured out what it was and got the GPS coordinates off that website."

"Why didn't you call the police?" Grayson asked. "Two uniforms interviewed you, so you knew we were looking for Ethan. A private detective spoke with you as well."

"I thought if I found Ethan, it would look good on my résumé."

"Your résumé?" Jackson asked.

"I've been thinking I want to be an FBI agent or maybe CIA. Some cool James Bond shit. So I thought if I could find Ethan and catch the kidnapper then that would give me some leverage over other candidates."

Jackson stared at the student as if he'd lost his mind. "You thought you were qualified to chase down a killer? This guy has murdered three people and attempted to murder two more."

Brett paled a bit. "Murdered. For real?"

"Yes." Grayson looked over at Jackson, and Jackson knew his partner was wondering the same thing he was— was Brett telling the truth, or was this simply more of his elaborate acting?

"The coordinates in Ethan's journal were from the text he received about Amber Olivier," Jackson said. "Why would you think Ethan would be in the same place?"

"I don't know," Brett said. "Ethan thought the text was about Amber and she wasn't found until days after she disappeared. I figure the kidnapper had to keep them somewhere, right? Amber couldn't have been in that coffin the whole time or the funeral home would have noticed. And what are the odds that he stashed them in two different places?"

Jackson clenched his jaw. Brett's logic was correct, of course, but he still couldn't wrap his head around the student's actions.

"Did you find Ethan in this shed?" Grayson asked.

"No. I missed the turnoff the first time. It was hidden pretty good. I drove past it on the road and heard gunshots. I went through the woods in the direction of the gunfire but never saw anyone. Then on the way back to my truck, I saw Ethan on the bank of the bayou. He was messed up bad. So I carried him back to my truck and hauled ass to the hospital."

"You'd found Ethan," Grayson said, "so why did you go back to the shed?"

"I didn't know who the kidnapper was," Brett said.

"You were planning on apprehending a murderer by yourself?" Jackson asked, still finding the entire story hard to believe.

"I wasn't going to arrest him or anything. At least, I don't think I was going to do that. I guess I just wanted to see who it was, then I figured I'd tell you guys." He frowned. "Now that I think about it, I don't guess I had a plan. It probably sounds kinda stupid."

You have no idea how stupid, Jackson thought. "And you never saw anyone either time? Or a vehicle?"

Brett shook his head. "There was an old silver sedan parked at the empty lot where you turn off the highway when I came back the second time. I was thinking it was an odd place to park because there's nothing around, but then maybe it was someone hunting off season."

"Make and model?" Jackson asked. "License plate?"

"Toyota Camry. My grandma had one like it for fifteen years. I didn't even look at the license plate." Brett shook his head. "I guess I'm not as good at this as I thought I was."

Jackson held in a sigh. You could throw a rock in New Orleans and hit an old silver Camry. Not to mention that since Brett was still a suspect, nothing he said could be taken as fact.

"Let's get you to the hospital," Grayson said. "Then we can revisit this entire thing."

Jackson could practically feel his partner's frustration and he completely understood. The hospital would be able to verify if Brett had any drugs in his system, but the puncture wound was located in a place where Brett could have administered the drug to himself. Maybe when Jackson and Grayson arrived, Brett staged the scene to look like he was attacked. Administer a tiny dose of the drug so that it was in his system, then claim it had happened earlier.

There was also Shaye's theory to consider. If Brett was working with someone else, maybe his partner was the one who'd drugged him and locked him up in the shed. But if Brett told the truth, then he'd be implicating himself in three murders and two attempted murders. The student had appeared genuinely surprised when Jackson had mentioned the three deaths, but then he'd managed to look like an idiot the entire time he was attending college, so his acting skills were top-notch.

Maybe once they got him cleared at the hospital and sitting in an interrogation room, Brett would realize just how serious things were. If that didn't do it, then showing him some pictures of the other victims might be in order. Even if all that failed, they still had DNA, and Jackson was betting on a match to the other victims.

One way or another, Jackson was going to expose the killer.

Shaye's cell phone rang as she pulled into the hospital parking lot. It was Jackson. She'd spent a couple of hours on pins and needles, waiting to hear if they'd caught the killer or at least found a clue as to his identity. Jackson had texted her when they were on their way back to New Orleans and told her they had Brett Frazier and he'd call her as soon as he could. He'd managed that call while Brett was at the hospital and Shaye had been surprised and confused by the story he told.

The hospital had confirmed a low dose of propofol in Brett's system, but there was no way to know if it was a large dose that had dissipated over time, which would align with Brett's claims, or Jackson's theory that he could have administered a low dose to himself when he heard the car coming. The fact that Brett had been locked inside the shed might indicate another person, but he might have been able to squeeze through the hole. If he'd heard Grayson's car, he could have injected himself with a tiny bit of the drug, thrown the needle into the swamp, and crawled into the locked shed before Grayson and Jackson got there.

It was risky, but not impossible.

A simpler explanation was that Brett had a partner and he'd decided Brett had outlived his usefulness or knew about Brett's taking Ethan to the hospital and had decided to make him pay for the betrayal. Based on Shaye's account of Brett's run-in with George Moss, Jackson had asked Brett about the argument between the two, but Jackson said Brett appeared confused by the question and said the old coot had accused him of stealing before even though he hadn't and told him to stay out of his store. Brett had told him to call the police over it.

Unfortunately, everything looked suspicious, but they had no proof that Brett wasn't telling the truth. Attempting to get brownie points for future law enforcement employment wasn't the smartest thing to do, especially with no training and regarding a murder investigation, but it also wasn't the dumbest thing Shaye had seen someone do. So what was the truth? And how could they prove it?

She entered the hospital and headed to Tara's room. The nurse didn't even look up at her as she walked by and Shaye relaxed a bit. So far, no one had paid attention to the redhead in rumpled, worn clothes. When she walked into Tara's room, the girl stared at her and frowned, then her eyes widened.

"Oh my God," Tara said. "It's you. I didn't recognize

you."

"That's the idea."

"Well, it's a good one." Tara was silent for a couple seconds, then asked, "Is there any update on Ethan?"

Shaye nodded. "Jackson spoke with the hospital this morning. Ethan did well overnight and the doctor is more optimistic. He said the more time that passes with no additional issues, the more likely Ethan is to recover. Of course, he still can't make any predictions about the arm, but the rest of the news was positive."

Tara sniffed and Shaye could see tears in her eyes. "I can't believe all of this is happening. They gave me something to sleep last night and I crashed, but when I woke up this morning, I was so confused for a minute. It felt like I'd dreamed it all and then I realized I hadn't, even though it's outrageous."

Shaye nodded. "I've done the same thing many times."

"How do you get past it?"

"Time. No one wants to hear that, because time is something they can't control. But your mind can't let go until we find the killer. Not completely."

"Did the police find Brett yet?"

"Yes. But I'm afraid it's made things more confusing, not less." Shaye told Tara about her discovery of the code and everything surrounding the police's detainment and questioning of Brett.

"He's got to be lying, right?" The tone of Tara's voice and her expression broadcast her fear. "He's got to be the one. No one else makes sense."

"I honestly don't know. Things seem to point to Brett being involved but there's nothing concrete. Jackson is hoping that putting Brett into a room at police headquarters will make him rethink his story."

"Will they have to let him go?"

"If they don't charge him, they will have to eventually, but they've got some time."

Tara bit her lower lip. "I hope it's enough time."

"Me too. So, are you ready to get out of here?"

"I think so."

"You don't sound certain. If you're not feeling well, I can talk to the doctor and see about your staying another day."

"It's not that. I don't really like it here, but then I suppose most people don't. I'm sorta scared to go back to my dorm."

"I understand, but you don't have to be. Your room is secure and Jackson has arranged for an unmarked unit to be placed in the parking lot of your dorm. You'll have two armed policemen only yards away."

Tara's shoulders relaxed a bit. "And you'll let me know if they have to let Brett go?"

"Of course, and the police will put a tail on him if they release him. Trust me, Brett can't even get near you without someone seeing him."

"That makes me feel a lot better. And it will be nice to sleep in my own bed."

"And not have someone interrupt you every hour to take your temperature and blood pressure?"

Tara gave her a small smile. "That too."

"Then let me get the nurse and we'll get you checked out of here."

Shaye arranged everything with the nurse, Tara signed some paperwork, and she was free to leave. She was limping because of her knee, but refused a wheelchair.

"I've been trying to walk a little bit all morning," Tara said. "It stiffens up something awful the longer I don't move it."

Shaye opened the car door so that Tara could work her way into the front seat without twisting her legs. "It's good to move it some," Shaye said. "Just don't overdo or you'll end up in worse shape. When you get to your dorm, you can start icing and heating it again. That will help a lot."

Tara was silent the entire ride to the dorm and Shaye knew a million things were running through the young woman's mind. She was alternating between fear and anger and sadness, and all of those emotions drained you, especially when you had no idea how to stop them. Shaye knew that finding the killer was key to Tara's letting go of what was happening. It would take some time, but the girl was a fighter. Shaye had every confidence that she'd move on from this and do well. It would change her, but it didn't have to restrict her.

It was lunchtime when they arrived and the dorm was quiet. A couple of students said hello as they walked past, but no one asked questions or seemed to notice anything out of the norm. Apparently, word hadn't circulated everywhere on campus about Tara's attack. Either that, or people weren't sure who the victim was. Either way, it brought Tara some peace.

Shaye checked Tara's room before allowing her inside and drew the dead bolt as soon as she closed the door behind them.

"Once people hear about what happened to you," Shaye said as Tara took a seat on her bed, "some are probably going to want to talk. I think it's best if you don't answer the door for anyone but me or the police. At least for now."

Tara frowned. "You still think Brett could be working with someone."

"Yes. And that could easily be a woman, so don't think you're safe with one sex versus the other. I don't want to scare you, and I think the risk is small, but we need to do everything we can to mitigate the ability for the wrong person to get to you."

"I understand. If someone knocks, I just won't answer."

"If it's me, I'll tell you through the door. When I leave, I'll talk to the officers and ask them to do the same."

"They're here? I didn't even notice them."

Shaye smiled. "Good. That's the idea. They're in the parking lot in a white work van with a plumbing logo on the side. They can easily see out of the side panels, and there are cameras facing all directions, but no one will be able to see them inside. It's the kind of thing they use for a stakeout."

"That's cool. I really appreciate all the trouble everyone

is going to for me."

"We're all just doing our job. You're going to get through this. I'll make sure of it."

Shaye opened the refrigerator and took out the ice pack and a bottle of water and handed them both to Tara. "If that knee starts hurting, take something for it before it gets too bad. If your head hurts or you start to get dizzy or just feel funny, call me. I'll get you back to the hospital. If you need anything else, call me. Even if you just need to talk."

Tara let out a breath. "Thank you so much, for everything. I don't know how I'm ever going to repay you."

"Move forward. Have the great life you always intended to have. Maybe with someone you thought was just a friend."

Tara's eyes widened and Shaye could tell it wasn't the first time the girl had rethought her relationship with Ethan. Maybe that was the silver lining in all this horror.

"Is it okay if I grab a water?" Shaye asked.

"Of course."

Shaye snagged a bottle from the fridge and headed for the door. "I hate to make you get up, but you need to come lock this after me."

Tara pushed herself off the bed. "Trust me, I'm happy to get up for this."

"Call me if you need anything," Shaye said. "Anything. And don't leave unless you have to."

Tara nodded and Shaye stepped into the hall and closed the door behind her. She heard the dead bolt slide into place a second later.

Shaye stopped to speak to the cops, then headed to Jackson's car. She climbed inside and sat for a bit, trying to decide what to concentrate on next. The police might have the killer in custody and no one could argue about opportunity where Brett was concerned, but they were still missing the most critical piece of the equation. Motive. The reality was, tens of thousands of people probably had opportunity, but only one person had a reason for it.

During the entire investigation, Shaye had felt that the killings had a personal element to them because of the suffocation. She was certain it meant something beyond just method. Maybe it was symbolic. But why those particular victims? Were they the actual people the killer held a grudge against or were they representative of someone else?

Shaye had known Ross St. Claire through social events. He was the typical spoiled son of a rich man. Shaye knew Malcolm had a lot of enemies in business. Was Ross paying for his father's actions? Then there was Amber, the next victim. Nothing Shaye had learned about the student caused her to believe that she had intentionally caused someone else harm, but then that boiled down to perspective, and sometimes the person you saw now wasn't the same person that you would have seen a year ago. Then there was location. The other victims had been found in convenient locations—a hiking trail, an abandoned house—but the killer had risked breaking into a funeral home to seal her in a coffin. Amber, who was claustrophobic.

Shaye frowned. That couldn't be a coincidence. All of the killings probably had a personal element, but Amber's death seemed more personal than the others. It was almost as if someone knew about the claustrophobia, which meant someone who knew Amber well. Brittany had mentioned a boyfriend in high school. Maybe Shaye would have another conversation with the sorority sister and see if she knew more about the boyfriend or if there were any other guys who'd sought Amber's attention and been shot down.

Starting with Brett Frazier.

CHAPTER TWENTY-ONE

Jackson looked through the window of the interrogation room and shook his head. "This is going nowhere."

"Yeah," Grayson agreed. "I thought for sure he'd break from that story once we got him in a room but he's holding firm."

Brett was drinking a soda and looking a bit nervous, but not nearly as nervous as Jackson thought he should be. He'd stuck, unwavering, to his original story of trying to solve the crime to boost his résumé, and nothing Jackson or Grayson had said could shake him out of his stance.

"I'm at a loss," Grayson said. "If he's the killer, he should be more scared than that because we've got him. If he isn't the killer, he should be more scared than that because we think he is."

Jackson frowned. "Most serial killers think they're smarter than the cops. Maybe he thinks he's going to get away with it. After all, we can't disprove his story and him taking Ethan to the hospital gives our side a credibility issue. Why not just kill him?"

"If he's not the killer, then why isn't he shitting kittens

in there?"

"Because he's a teen with an ego and thinks he can't go down for something he didn't do. He voluntarily gave us DNA. Clearly he doesn't think it's going to link him to the other cases."

"Yeah, well, I'm about tired of all the egos."

"Me too. So what do you want to do? The lab is rushing the tests. We might be able to hold him until the results are in."

Grayson stared at Brett a while longer, then blew out a breath. "Cut him loose and put a unit on him. If he steps on a crack in the sidewalk, I want to know about it."

"You think he'll give himself away?"

"Maybe. If Brett's our guy, then he saved Ethan and that doesn't make much sense unless he did it to throw a kink in our theory. But Tara was attacked after Brett brought Ethan in."

"So he spared Ethan but for whatever reason, isn't extending the same courtesy to Tara."

Grayson shrugged. "Someone wants her dead. If it was Brett, then maybe that ego will send him her direction again. The only difference is we'll be ready."

"I'll call the unit at the dorm and let them know."

"Good. And call Shaye and ask her to fill Tara in. I think this news will be better coming from her."

Jackson pulled out his cell phone as he watched Brett lean back in his chair and stretch. What was going on in the student's mind? They knew he was smart, but how smart? Was he a smart guy who'd made a stupid decision?

Or was he a smart killer who might walk away smiling?

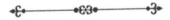

Shaye put her phone on the passenger seat and blew out a breath. The phone call she'd just had with Tara, explaining that Brett had been released, was as hard as she'd thought it would be. Tara hadn't taken it well. She'd tried to be brave, but Shaye could hear the overwhelming fear in her voice and prayed the girl would work on relaxing before she worried herself into a heart attack. Considering her medical condition, Tara had been extremely fortunate so far that her heart had shown no signs of damage given what she'd gone through, but Shaye had hoped Tara could avoid any more strain than she'd already experienced.

Grayson's decision to turn Brett loose made total sense. Shaye would have done the same thing in his position. It just put added strain on Tara, but there was nothing that could be done about it. Tara had protection. Brett would be followed. Maybe they'd get lucky and he'd screw up and give them the evidence they needed to pin the murders on him.

Or maybe he'd been telling the truth and the killer was still roaming scot-free.

Shaye climbed out of the car and started up the sidewalk to the sorority house, hoping Brittany would be there but not counting on it given how empty the parking lot was. Most of the girls were probably in class, at work, or off for some fun with friends. She knocked on the door and was surprised when it swung open almost immediately and Brittany looked out at her.

"I was in the kitchen and saw you coming up the walk," Brittany said and waved her inside.

"Are you on your way to class?" Shaye asked as she stepped inside.

"No. I have a night class, but this is my light day. I usually use it to catch up on reading and papers."

"I don't want to get you behind."

Brittany waved a hand in dismissal. "I'm always ahead. The other students hate me. Honestly, I don't even know why I'm in the sorority. I almost never do social things, but my mom was a legacy, and you know how mothers can be."

"I definitely do."

"We can talk in the room we used before," Brittany said as she headed down the hall. "I met your mother at an art opening my mother dragged me to last year. She's really pretty and super nice. I bet she's a champion hoverer."

Shaye laughed. "World champion hoverer."

Brittany walked into the room and closed the door behind them. "It's annoying, but I get it. And with your situation, things had to be a million more times intense, especially since you didn't know who'd abused you. I think that's the thing I admire about you the most. That you walked out of your house every day and went on with life, even though you knew the person who'd held you could be the guy who just sold you coffee or drove you in a taxi. What you did took serious balls." She grinned. "Figuratively."

"Thank you. It was definitely something I thought about all the time, but now it's over."

Brittany cocked her head to the side. "Is it? I mean is it ever really over?"

"In some ways it's not. But in the most important ways, it is."

"Good. Because I'd like to believe that the people I help in the future can move on to a great life, even after something horrible happens."

"I believe they can."

"Look at me babbling again. I know you wouldn't come here again unless it was important. Did the police find something at the location? Can you tell me?"

"They found a shed and someone drugged inside it."

"Another victim?"

"Maybe, or maybe a very clever killer."

Brittany's eyes widened. "And they don't have the evidence to prove one or the other."

"I'm afraid not."

"Wow. That's got to be frustrating. What can I do to help?"

"Earlier, I was thinking about the victims. The one thing I've been unable to come up with is a motive. I can't find a connection between all of the victims, but there has to be a reason they were selected, even if it makes no sense to us. But the one that stands out the most to me is Amber. The killer took a big risk with the way he killed her. The others were left in easily accessible places with a much lower risk of visibility."

Brittany nodded. "But he broke into a funeral home for Amber."

"I think Amber might have been more personal than the others. You're pretty sure she didn't know Ethan Campbell, right?"

"Not that I'm aware of."

"What about his roommate, Brett Frazier?"

Brittany frowned. "Jock dude? Sorta dumb?"

"That's him."

"I've seen him at parties, but Amber never mentioned him and I never saw him approach her. It doesn't mean he didn't. A lot of guys tried to talk to Amber. She was really pretty."

Shaye nodded. She'd figured as much, but had been hoping one suitor stood out over the others. "When I first came here, you mentioned a high school boyfriend that her father didn't approve of," Shaye said. "I don't think you knew his name, though."

"No. She never told me."

"Did any of the sisters go to the same high school as Amber?"

Brittany shook her head. "I don't think so, but Amber's things are still in her room."

"The police didn't restrict access?"

"No. Her roommate, Katey, is still using the room. If Amber really liked the guy, she might still have a picture or something. Let's go see." She paused. "I mean, if it's okay that I help."

"Of course. You have no idea how much I appreciate

the help you've already given me. When this is all over, I owe you a steak dinner."

"Deal."

They headed out of the room and upstairs, where Brittany opened a door to a bedroom, showing two twin beds, one with a pink comforter with tropical flowers and the other a Star Wars comforter.

"Amber was the pink side," Brittany said. "Her desk is the one with all the fingernail polish on it."

"Great," Shaye said, and went over to the desk. "I'll start here. Why don't you take a look in her closet and see if she has any boxes of old stuff, like maybe pictures or a high school yearbook."

Brittany nodded and opened the closet. Shaye turned her attention to the desk and started going through the drawers. She found a bag of makeup and several containers of jewelry on one side. The other contained scarves and hair items and a small photo album. Shaye pulled out the album and started flipping through the photos, but all of them were of Amber in the French Quarter with other girls, some of whom Shaye recognized as her sorority sisters. The one framed picture she had on her desk was Amber with an older woman who looked a lot like her. Shaye assumed it was her mother.

"Nothing?" Brittany asked.

Shaye turned around and shook her head. "What about you?"

"Only clothes and shoes. Her parents could tell you his name."

"Perhaps, but I'd hate to disrupt their grieving over something that might not be anything. Not to mention, cast suspicion on someone who probably isn't guilty of anything but getting dumped. I can look at a copy of her high school yearbook at her high school. They usually have a copy of every year on file."

"You're hoping there's a picture of Amber with her boyfriend?"

Shaye nodded and rose from the desk, slightly disappointed that her idea hadn't yielded anything. It had been a long shot, at best, but long shots had become her trademark.

Brittany followed her to the front door looking as disappointed as Shaye felt. "If there's anything else I can do," Brittany said. "Please let me know."

"I will."

Shaye headed to her car and climbed inside. She opened the bottled water she'd snagged from Tara and took a big swig. She had time to go to the high school and request a look at the yearbook before the library closed for the day, and that was probably what she should do. It would be easier to simply call Amber's parents and ask, but with Amber's father threatening a lawsuit against the sorority, Shaye was going to guess he wouldn't have any interest in telling her about an old boyfriend he didn't approve of. And the last thing Shaye wanted to do was send Amber's father chasing after someone else. The ex-boyfriend might be some perfectly nice guy who didn't need the aggravation and Shaye certainly didn't want to be the source of ignition.

She took another drink of water and started the car, then pulled out of the parking lot onto the street. First, she'd stop by and check on Tara, then she'd head to the high school and see if she could find a clue in the yearbooks. She was a couple blocks away from the sorority house when her phone signaled an incoming text. She glanced down and saw it was from Brittany.

Shaye pulled over to the curb and checked the message.

I found a picture of Amber and a guy! It was hidden behind that framed picture of her and her mother.

No name on it though.

Shaye shook her head. She should have thought to check behind the other picture. She texted back.

That's great. Can you take a pic of it and text it to me?

Shaye reached for the air conditioning control and turned it on. It was a balmy day but not overly hot. Still, she felt a bit flushed and wondered briefly if the lack of decent sleep was catching up with her.

She took another drink of water and rubbed the cold bottle against her forehead. The text from Brittany came through and she looked at the picture and frowned. Amber's hair was in a ponytail and she wore a cheerleading uniform. The boy beside her was wearing a football jersey and had his arm around her and a big grin on his face.

The photo provided a good shot of him and Shaye figured a teacher at the high school would easily recognize him. But instead of putting the car in gear and heading for the high school, she stared at his face a bit longer. There was something about him that was familiar. So familiar that she was certain she'd seen him somewhere before. Older maybe? Or maybe just in passing and that's why she couldn't zero in on where it was or when.

It hit her like a bolt of lightning and she gasped. It was Thomas.

Geeky, shy Thomas who wore glasses and rode a bicycle. A Thomas who looked nothing now as he did in this picture.

Playing the role.

She'd thought from the beginning that someone wasn't whom they pretended to be, and when she'd discovered Brett's past, she'd been certain he was the one. She'd never considered Thomas. She switched to her phone list but as she stared at the numbers, her vision started to blur. Her head bobbed a bit and she felt a wave of nausea pass over her.

Thomas. Whose mother had cancer.

Propofol was sometimes given to chemo patients.

Her gaze locked on the bottled water and she let out a cry. The water she'd taken from Tara's refrigerator. She put the cap back on the bottle and turned it upside down. A tiny trickle of water came out of the almost invisible puncture near the top. It was drugged! She'd taken one of the front bottles out for herself and given the other to Tara. She forced herself to focus on the phone and dialed Jackson's number.

"It's Thomas," she said as soon as Jackson answered.

"From the convenience store. He drugged Tara's water and I drank some. You have to go there. He's probably already inside."

Shaye knew Jackson was probably surprised and more than a little confused but he didn't even hesitate.

"On my way!" he said. "Call 911 for yourself now."

Shaye dropped the phone on the passenger seat and put the car in gear. She had no idea how far away Jackson was but she was only two blocks away. She might not be sound enough to fight, but the two cops in the parking lot certainly were.

She wasn't going anywhere until she knew Tara was safe.

Tara looked down at her iPad and blinked as the graphics began to blur. She closed her eyes but the room still felt as if it were moving. Maybe the doctor had missed something. Maybe she'd hit her head when she fell. What if she had a concussion? You could die from that, right?

Calm down.

The tiny sliver of sanity that she had left chimed into her scattered thoughts, and she took a deep breath and slowly blew it out. If she'd hit her head, the doctors would have seen bruising on her scalp. She was just exhausted and the pain med she'd taken earlier for her knee was probably making her a little dizzy. She hadn't felt like eating much, so that was adding to the effect of the medicine.

What she needed to do was sleep, but she'd been forcing herself to surf the Internet, struggling to stay awake in case something happened. It was foolish because now was the best time to rest—while it was daylight and the cops outside could easily spot Brett if he came anywhere near the dorm. At night, he might be able to sneak in with a group of students.

She shook her head, still unable to believe they'd just turned Brett loose. Shaye had explained why Detective Grayson had made the decision and she got it, but knowing that she had sorta been dangled as bait didn't exactly make her want to sing with joy. She knew it would be suicide for Brett to attempt to get to her, but if he was crazy, he might not care. He might figure he was already going to go to prison so he might as well finish the job. Whatever the hell job it was he imagined he was doing.

Her throat grew dry again and she reached for the bottle of water and knocked it off the desk and onto the rug next to her bed. The top popped off and the water began to pour onto the rug. She struggled to shift her legs around enough so that she could lean over the side of the bed for the bottle, but by the time she lifted it, there was only one swig left. Sighing, she downed the last of it and put the empty bottle on the desk. What a waste. Two whole drinks out of the entire bottle and now she'd have to get up to get another one.

To hell with it. She put her iPad on her desk and lowered herself into her bed. She'd already thought everything to death and the facts weren't going to change no matter how many times she ran them through her mind. Nor was she going to come up with a good reason for what Brett had done because for a sane person, there was no good reason for what Brett had done. She needed to go to sleep and give the headache time to go away and her knee a chance to heal. Sitting here fretting over everything was only making it worse.

It took only seconds for her to drift away.

Thomas lifted the ceiling tile and peered down into Tara's room. She was lying in the bed facing him and her eyes were closed. He spotted the empty water bottle on her desk and smiled. Things might have gotten off a bit, but he was about to get them back on track. Everyone who'd contributed to the ruination of his life had paid. The nosy one hadn't been on his original list, but she'd caused all the problems he had now by bringing Shaye Archer in.

This was the last one. Then he'd disappear. A new identity. A new place. A new future.

He'd heard the nosy one on the phone earlier and knew that the police had questioned Brett Frazier. Thomas had no idea how he'd gotten out of the shed, but he didn't care. If the police had put a tail on him, then he was a suspect, and as long as the police were focused on someone else, it gave Thomas even more room to operate. But that might not last forever.

Still, even if the police ever figured out it was Thomas,

he'd be long gone. And they'd never find him where he was going. One of the huge advantages to being so smart was the ability to create a new identity and become fluent at other languages. With five languages under his belt, Thomas had a lot of options. Maybe when he got where he was going, he'd send Brett a keg of beer as a thank-you, assuming Brett wasn't rotting somewhere in prison for a crime he didn't commit.

He pushed the tile completely to the side and turned around, lowering himself down the side of the dorm wall, legs first. When his arms were fully extended, he let go and dropped onto the roommate's bed. It creaked some but otherwise, his entry into the room had been silent. He reached into the pocket of his hoodie and pulled out the plastic bag and duct tape.

This one was going to be easy and his best feat yet. He'd tape the nosy one up, let himself out of her room, and simply walk out of the dorm. Right past the officers parked out front in the plumbing van. Did they really think that would fool him?

He was so much smarter than them and he almost hoped they would eventually figure out who the real killer was. Then his cunning could be recognized, maybe even recorded as a case study for how to let the bad guy get away. The thought amused him.

But now was not the time to bask in his own cleverness. It was time to finish the job.

He placed the tape on the desk and grabbed the plastic bag with both hands.

CHAPTER TWENTY-TWO

In her dream, Tara heard someone moving around her room, then her mind sharpened and she realized it wasn't a dream. She opened her eyes and saw the clerk from the convenience store standing over her with a plastic bag, moving it down toward her head. For a split second, she was so stunned that she didn't do anything at all. What was his name? Thomas? Thomas was the killer? They barely knew him.

Then she snapped back into reality and screamed as she bolted up from the bed, shoving Thomas's arms away from her as she sprang. Thomas rocked back a step, but quickly regained his balance and launched for her, his hands reaching for her neck. She grabbed the can of Mace from her desk and swung around, spraying him directly in the face.

He let out a cry and stumbled backward into the door, completely blocking her exit. Tara looked for something to hit him with, but the room began to spin again and she felt her knees weaken. Even if she had a baseball bat, she wouldn't have the strength to take him out. She looked at the bedroom window and at Thomas, who was blinking wildly, trying to lock in on her.

Seeing no other option, she pushed open the window and lowered herself over the edge. Thomas grabbed her arms and tried to pull her back inside. She screamed again but he held fast and she felt her body scraping against the bricks as it inched back upward. She jerked her head over to the side and clamped her teeth down on his arm.

Thomas yelled and let go of her. She grabbed at the ledge, hoping to lower herself before dropping, but she was too weak. Her arms slipped from the window and she plummeted to the ground. Her legs buckled as she hit, and she fell over and rolled down the slight incline behind the dorm. She looked up and saw Thomas looking out the window, trying to focus his damaged eyes on her. A second later, he flung a leg over the ledge.

He was coming after her.

She forced herself up, gasping in agony over her knee. Her chest constricted so hard it sucked the breath right out of her. This couldn't be happening. After everything she'd been through, her heart could not give out on her now. Everything was slightly blurry, she could barely breathe, and her knee felt all but destroyed, but she didn't care. She half limped, half ran as fast as she could for the corner of the building. If she could get around the building to the parking lot, she would have help.

The nightmare would be over.

Shaye flew into the parking lot and squealed to a stop right in front of the entry to the dorm, not even remotely concerned that it wasn't meant for parking. The detectives staking out the parking lot were already entering the dorm so she yanked off her wig and ran after them. Her legs were a little wobbly and everything was still a bit blurry, but none of that mattered.

She ran up the stairs after the detectives, yelling Tara's dorm number at them and telling them to turn left off the staircase. By the time she caught up with them, they were banging on the door. Shaye yelled at Tara to open the door, but no one stirred inside. She pulled her cell phone out and called. A cell phone sounded inside the room but no one answered.

"Break it down," she told them.

One of the detectives took a step back and launched at the door, but the dead bolt Shaye had installed held. He backed up and launched again, and this time, the cheap wooden door splintered in half and the detective fell inside. The second detective rushed in behind him, gun drawn, and Shaye hurried behind, but the room was empty.

"The window," the second detective said and they ran over to peer outside.

"There!" Shaye pointed to Tara, who was running for the end of the building, Thomas not far behind.

"Go out the back exit," the detective said, "and I'll go out the front."

They ran out of the room, Shaye hot on their heels,

praying with every step that the detectives got to Tara before Thomas did. The drop from the window with her bad knee left her at a huge disadvantage, and that wasn't even considering her heart. Shaye's legs started to buckle as she ran down the stairs but she forced herself to steady them without slowing. She had to get to Tara. She'd promised the girl she'd be safe, and damned if Thomas was going to make a liar out of her.

Tara stumbled on a tree root and barely managed to stay upright. Adrenaline alone had kept her moving long after her knee wanted to give out. Her chest hurt so much it felt as if it were slowly tearing apart. She opened her mouth to try to yell again, but all that came out was a weak gasp. She simply didn't have anything left in her lungs to give. Every part of her body was working beyond its limit just to keep her moving.

She knew Thomas was somewhere behind her. Hopefully, his vision was bad enough that it slowed him down, but she couldn't count on it. The thick shrubs scattered throughout the green space provided some coverage but not enough to disappear in. She had to get to the front of the dorm before he caught up with her. She didn't have the strength to fight him. If he caught her, it was all over.

A burst of hope rushed through her when she saw the end of the building and she rounded the corner, certain that help wasn't far away.

And ran into a backhoe.

Her head slammed against the bucket of the machinery and she fell. The ground rushed up at her face and she thrust her arms out, trying to break her fall. She felt her wrist pop and her arm buckled, causing her to face-plant into the turf. The dizziness came back and everything started to spin. She forced herself onto her knees, her eyes filling with tears as rocks pressed into the tender skin of her injured knee.

When she'd run, she'd opted for the shortest path around the dorm, completely forgetting the construction and the temporary fencing that stretched a good thirty yards from the corner of the dorm. She looked behind her, afraid that Thomas would be standing there, grinning down at her as he had been in her room, but she couldn't see him anywhere.

Knowing he couldn't be far behind, she forced herself up from the ground, pain shooting through her wrist and knee as she shoved herself up. Her stomach rolled and she barely managed to keep from retching, but that was one more thing she didn't have time for. She leaned forward, forcing her legs into action as she tried to focus on the fence. With every step she managed, the spinning increased in speed until her surroundings were a whirling blur. She reached out until she found the edge of the fence and increased her pace, keeping her fingertips in contact with the fence as she went.

She counted every step, trying to keep her brain from

shutting down. With every movement, her body screamed at her to stop. Just give up. But she kept pushing. She had to be close to the end of the fence. It couldn't be far.

When the first bullet whizzed by her head, it took her a second to realize what it was. She struggled to draw in a breath and could barely get enough air in to keep from passing out. Every intake felt like someone had taken an ax to her chest and each breath seemed quicker and more shallow than the one before. She stumbled to the side and lost contact with the fence, and flung her arm back out, desperate to find the metal again.

Her foot connected with something big and hard and she pitched to the side, right into the fence she'd been searching for. Her head connected with a metal post and everything went momentarily dark. She managed to bring herself back to consciousness, but it might have been better if she hadn't.

Her vision cleared for just a moment and she saw Thomas walking toward her, a pistol leveled right at her head. He was smiling.

She pulled her one good leg up and circled her arms around it, ducking her head to her knee. She said a prayer for Ethan and her parents and prepared to die.

When the shot came, her entire body gave out, nothing left to give.

Pain rushed through her and she closed her eyes, waiting for it to end. She was barely conscious when she felt someone shake her shoulder.

"Tara? Can you hear me?"

The voice sounded so far away and at first, she thought she was in heaven and her grandfather was calling for her, but then a burst of pain shot through her head and when her eyes jerked open, she saw Detective Lamotte kneeling next to her.

"Can you hear me?" he asked again.

"Yes," she barely managed to get the word out.

"Good. Don't try to talk anymore and don't move. An ambulance is on the way."

"Shot?" she asked.

"You're going to be all right," he said, not answering her question. "Just hold my hand and keep breathing. Try to relax."

"Thomas," she whispered and clutched her chest. She had to let them know who the killer was. He couldn't get away.

"He's dead."

The tension left her shoulders and she started to cry.

It was over.

CHAPTER TWENTY-THREE

Jackson rushed into the hospital and paused at the reception desk just long enough to ask for Shaye before dashing off down the hall. He burst into the room without even knocking and hurried to the side of the bed and leaned over to cup Shaye's face and kiss her. When he finished, he heard a whistle behind him and Shaye laughed.

He held in a groan as he turned and saw a grinning Eleonore and a pensive Corrine.

"Praise the Lord and get a room," Eleonore said. "Oh, wait. Technically, this is Shaye's room." She stood and grabbed Corrine's arm. "Let's give them a moment."

Corrine grabbed her purse and started to leave, but when she reached Jackson she stopped and stared at him for several long, uncomfortable seconds. He was just about to say something when she stepped forward and hugged him.

"Thank you for always looking out for her," she whispered. Then she released him and hurried out with Eleonore.

Jackson turned to Shaye, feeling slightly overwhelmed. "That was surprising."

"Well, it *was* quite an entrance," she said.

Instantly, he felt contrite. "I'm sorry. You probably wanted to tell Corrine in your own time and I totally blew it."

"Are you kidding me? You totally saved me that awkward conversation. I'll just get a million questions. That I can handle. I've been doing it for years."

Relieved, he scanned her up and down. "How are you? What did the doctor say?"

"I only ingested a little of the drug and it won't take long to process out of my system. I may have a headache or feel queasy for a bit, but there's no damage. I get to leave tonight."

"And Tara?"

"She's in a lot worse shape than me, but she's tough. I don't think she knew just how tough and neither did I. When I realized she'd jumped out of that window to get away, I couldn't believe it. Most people would have frozen."

Jackson nodded. "She was really brave."

"Her wrist is broken and they've put a brace on it. The doctor said tests showed some swelling from the head injury and her vision is still blurry, but he thinks that will go away as the swelling goes down."

"And her heart?"

"Remarkably, it's good. When I saw you kneeling next to her and how she was clutching her chest, I just knew she'd had a heart attack."

"I was afraid of that myself. What about her knee?"

"It's banged up pretty bad. She won't be doing much walking for a while, at least not without crutches." Shaye shook her head. "I still can't believe it was Thomas. If Brittany hadn't found that picture or I hadn't taken the water…"

"How did you know just seeing the picture? I still haven't put that together."

"I don't know. I'd felt all along that someone was pretending to be something they weren't and when Brett proved to be a fraud, I thought we'd found our guy even though I couldn't reconcile him taking Ethan to the hospital. But when I saw that picture of Thomas, with no glasses and wearing a football jersey, something clicked. It all fit. He had access. He had opportunity. And finally, we had someone with motive, at least for Amber."

"I told you that you had great instincts. Even if you'd been wrong about it being Thomas, you were dead-on about the water being drugged. I hate that you drank some, but if you hadn't, Tara wouldn't have made it."

Shaye frowned. "I get that Thomas was holding a grudge against Amber. I thought that murder was more personal than the others, but I still don't have a reason for the rest. I guess it doesn't matter since he's dead and there won't be a trial, but I can't help but wonder."

"We're not closing the investigation. Families will want answers and Grayson and I are going to try to give them some."

Shaye reached over and took his hand in hers. "Jackson?"

"Yes?"

"Thank you for being a good shot."

CHAPTER TWENTY-FOUR

One week later.

Shaye pushed open the door to Ethan's hospital room and stood back so that Tara could maneuver herself inside using the crutches she'd formed a love/hate relationship with. Ethan was pale and thin but the smile he had for Tara told Shaye everything she needed to know. Ethan Campbell was going to be all right and was slowly regaining use of his arm. It might never be perfect again, but the prognosis was so much better now than it was even days before.

Tara hurried to the side of the bed as quickly as the crutches allowed and leaned over to kiss Ethan firmly on the lips. He looked a bit startled at first but there was no mistaking his expression of pleasure immediately following.

Shaye couldn't help but smile. Going forward, things were going to be a lot different for Tara and Ethan.

She slipped out of the room and headed back to the parking lot. She had a date with Jackson to discuss what they'd uncovered about Thomas. Chief Rhinehart was preparing to release a statement to the press but Jackson thought she deserved to know what they'd found before the rest of the population did.

A couple of reporters were waiting in the hospital parking lot, but she gave them the usual silent treatment and headed to her car. She'd held a press conference two days before and told the media everything she ever intended on sharing. And she'd made that clear. She would never answer another question about her past. Some die-hards would hang on for a while, hoping to best the others out of some additional tidbit, but eventually, they'd be forced to move on.

Jackson opened the door to his apartment holding a barbecue fork. He leaned over to kiss her, then backed up to let her in. "Sorry," he said. "My hands are dirty. I just opened a bottle of wine and put some chicken on the grill."

Shaye followed him out to the patio and took a big whiff of the amazing aroma coming from the grill. "Have I told you yet today how awesome you are?"

"You're just hungry."

She laughed. "I *am* hungry, but you're also awesome."

Jackson checked the chicken while Shaye poured them wine from the bottle on the patio table. They both sat down and Jackson looked over at her.

"We figured it out," he said. "All of it."

"Seriously? I mean, I hoped, but I was afraid you wouldn't find enough to piece it all together."

"So was I, and we're guessing on one thing, but I think the rest of it is solid."

"Tell me."

Jackson took a drink of wine and said, "I guess I'll start

at the beginning—when Thomas's life began to fall apart. His dad worked for Malcolm St. Claire as an outside salesman. He made great money and the family had a nice life spending every dime of it. Then he got fired. The personnel reports that we got from St. Claire said that they caught him taking kickbacks from customers. He denied it, but they let him go anyway."

"So the great money went away."

"Yep. Thomas's father was the only support. So along with the salary went the big house, nice cars, two vacations a year—"

"And the girlfriend whose father didn't approve of his daughter dating the son of a man who'd been fired over ethics."

"Even worse. Thomas's father committed suicide, and Thomas and his mother moved to public housing in Bywater."

Shaye shook her head. "So Ross St. Claire was payback for Malcolm firing his father. It probably killed Thomas to see Ross living the high life that he'd once had."

"I'm sure. And by killing Ross, Malcolm suffers more."

"Amber was the most personal, because he loved her. I knew there was something different about her. What about Ethan?"

"Ethan and Brenda both took a lot of ingenuity and a crap-ton of digging but I think we figured it out. Ethan and Thomas were both in contention for the same scholarship—a full ride."

"And Ethan got it. That makes so much sense. I mean,

as much as any of this does."

"Thomas got another scholarship, but it didn't pay for everything. He told people he was in school full time, but in reality, he was only taking two courses."

"It would have taken him a long time to finish that way."

Jackson nodded. "Brenda was a bit tougher to figure out, but when we interviewed her mother again, we asked specific questions about Thomas and she remembered that he applied for a position with the university library. It would have covered part of his tuition and paid a decent hourly rate."

"But he didn't get it."

"She gave the position to the daughter of a friend of hers."

"So Thomas had to get a job working nights at the convenience store, with no school aid and probably a lower wage. What about Tara?"

"That's where we're totally guessing, but neither Grayson nor I think Tara was originally a target. We think Thomas ended up targeting her because she brought you in to investigate, which led to us tying all the cases together. Basically, she messed up his perfectly made plans."

Shaye took a drink of her wine, everything Jackson had told her rolling through her mind. It was all fantastic, but it all fit. They might not be able to prove any of it, and with Thomas dead, they didn't need to, but Shaye would bet anything that Grayson and Jackson were right on every point.

"The only thing that's still a bit of a question," Jackson said, "is why now. Thomas's dad committed suicide over a year ago and Amber broke up with him right after that. Maybe it just kept building until he snapped."

"I think Thomas broke from sanity a little bit at a time, starting with his father's death, but my guess is the catalyst for all of this was his mother's death."

One of the first thoughts that had crossed Shaye's mind when she was in the hospital was how Thomas's mother was going to react. The woman had been through enough with the cancer, but finding out her son was a serial killer was going to be a lot worse. They'd all been surprised to learn that his mother had died six weeks before.

Thomas had told Shaye his mother was "fine now." She supposed given Thomas's damaged mind, that was true enough.

Jackson nodded. "I bet you're right. The timing makes sense. We found DNA evidence in her car. Thomas had been using it to transport the victims and his bicycle. I think he wanted to keep up the act of the poor, geeky college student."

"It was a good act. I fell for it."

"So did George Moss. I've never seen a man more perturbed. When he learned that he'd been employing a serial killer, he called his attorney right then and told him to list the store for sale."

"Good. He needed to retire. How did things go with Brett?"

Jackson laughed. "The new and improved Brett didn't

have a single stupid thing to say. I think he finally grasped just how close he came to dying or being arrested for murder. I think that whole FBI idea might be off the table."

"Maybe he'll stop pretending as well."

Shaye stared out over the patio and into the pretty courtyard. She was happy for George and for his wife, who needed him at home with her and not angry all the time, but that wasn't the thing that was at the forefront of her thoughts. The thing that had been plaguing her for days was front and center, daring her to address it.

"Is everything all right?" Jackson asked.

It was now or never.

"No," she said. "There's something I've been wanting to tell you, but you have to promise not to tell anyone else."

Jackson frowned. "Of course."

Shaye looked directly at him. "You read my medical reports, so you know everything that was done to me."

"I do."

"You know I was pregnant and the doctors assumed the baby was stillborn because of my condition."

Jackson nodded and she could see his jaw flex. He cared for her so much, she couldn't imagine how hard it was for him to know what had been done to her. The man who'd tortured her was dead but she wasn't sure that was enough for Jackson. Wasn't sure it ever would be.

"I've been having dreams about the past. Sometimes the dreams are the truth and sometimes they're not. When they're the truth, I start remembering more and the things from the dreams eventually take focus. I've been dreaming about the birth."

Jackson's eyes widened as if he knew what was coming.

She took a deep breath. "My baby was born alive."

The End

To receive notice when a new book is available, please sign up for my newsletter at janadeleon.com.